PORCELAIN

THE SOUL THAT
NEVER BROKE

MIRANDA DODGE

Copyright © 2022 Miranda Dodge

ISBN 979-8-9861918-0-5 (Ebook)

ISBN 979-8-9861918-1-2 (Paperback)

ISBN 979-8-9861918-2-9 (Hardcover)

First paperback edition August 2022

First hardcover edition August 2022

First ebook edition August 2022

Proofread by Leighton Wingate

Cover art by Baby Steps Design on 99designs.com

Audio narration by Joshua Macrae

Miranda Dodge

www.reunitingtherealms.com

FOR THOSE WHO NEED HELP

FACING THEIR PAST.

YOU DON'T NEED TO FACE IT ALONE.

YOU ARE STRONGER THAN YOU REALIZE

PROLOGUE

Footsteps sounded in the stone dungeon before a creak was heard. "Unchain her, Sangchul," the man said. The blindfold that created constant darkness was removed, and the heavy weight around her ankles, wrists, and neck were gone. Her knees buckled from her freedom, and hands brushed against her breasts to get to her waist before she collapsed. "Get your hands off her," the man said with a snarl.

She looked toward the voice, and a muscular black-haired man stalked toward her. *Franko.* He grabbed Sangchul and threw him, causing her to fall onto the stone floor. Sangchul's slim body lay back against the stone, his usual slicked brown hair now disheveled from the blow. "Time for breakfast, baby doll," Franko said.

He led her to the kitchen. "What would you like for breakfast today, Franko?" she asked.

"What did I tell you to call me?"

"Master, what would you like for breakfast today?" Her body shook at her mistake.

"That's better." He sat in the chair. "Eggs, sausage, toast, and coffee," he said.

"Of course, Master." She began preparing the meal as the coffee machine went off. She poured a cup, taking it over to him. He stood up, pushing her onto the table, and unzipped his pants. "I was going to wait till later, but Sangchul pissed me off when he touched you. You're mine," he said.

Her back pressed against the wooden table, he took her pants off her, and positioned her. His cock was large, and he didn't use any lube to help ease the pain of his insertion. He went fast and hard, slamming her farther into the table as Sangchul stopped in the kitchen doorway. Blood formed on the inside of her mouth as she bit down from the pain on her neck. Franko's teeth caught her skin as he stared at Sangchul. Sangchul walked away, thinking, *She's only thirteen, and he's putting her through this torture?*

Hot liquid spread in her body as he cummed. He sat back down, and she finished breakfast. "You'll be training today, and then tomorrow you'll be going on an assignment. I have someone I want you to kill for me," he said.

"Okay, Master," she said.

I

DOCTOR

The lecture hall bustled with noise as the once-empty chairs became occupied with interns, residents, nurses, and doctors. A small stage separated the audience from the speaker, and a line of four proud people sat in chairs facing the audience. A man flicked the lights off and made his way to the stage.

A tall, large Black man picked up the microphone as he addressed the audience. "Hello, everyone. My name is William Cooney, and I'm the chief of surgery here at New York Medical Center. For those of you who don't know, we are a training hospital, and we are here to welcome our four newest members who have graduated and taken up full-time jobs here. I'll be speaking about each new attending, the position they hold, and a few of their memorable moments with us during their intern and residency years."

Chief William Cooney walked over to the podium as he addressed the new attendings. "Attendings, when I call your name, please join me over here at the podium for your new lab coats, and to tell us why you became a doctor. First up, we have Dr. Thomas Bradley."

I didn't know we would have to explain why we became a doctor! What do I even say? she thought.

"Dr. Jennifer Hudson," Chief Cooney said.

I mean, I know why. I was forced to kill a lot of people, and now I'm trying to do the opposite. But I don't want to share that with them.

"Dr. Jonathan Keller," Chief Cooney said.

Maybe I can just get away with telling them that I want to save lives, or maybe that I've always been fascinated with brains? Maybe that will work . . .

"Dr. Ashton Lure," Chief Cooney said.

Oh, that's me. I better get going!

She stood up, her long dress hugging her ankles, making it hard to walk as she made her way to the podium. A pounding resonated in her chest, her palms sweaty, and an unnatural smile plastered on her face.

The white folded fabric of her new doctor's coat was held between her and the chief, and she took it. Unfolding it, she saw her name written in the upper corner in gold lettering. She slid her arms through and tugged it on.

"Dr. Ashton Lure is an extraordinary doctor. She is one of the youngest to complete our neurosurgeon program, and with top honors. At first, I thought she wasn't going to make it, but she showed me that she has what it takes. When she first got here, she was shy and timid, keeping to herself. She had quite a few days in which she was lost, but in the end, she always made her way around the puzzle, so to speak. Throughout her intern and residency years, she has endured countless difficult surgeries, the scorn of several of her classmates, and roadblocks of the clinical trial she is helping with. She has collaborated with several of the doctors here to produce writing in some of the most prominent medical journals. We expect great things from her! And now, Dr. Ashton Lure, would you please tell us why you became a doctor," he said.

She let out a shaky breath as she took the microphone. "It would be a delight, Chief William Cooney." She took a step toward the audience. "I know it is standard for doctors to tell you they had lost loved ones from tumors or some type of illness, but I can't say that. Instead, my reason for becoming a neurosurgeon is simple: I'm fascinated with the brain. How it works to create our cognitive behaviors and how certain damages can be undone by pulling out that foreign object. There were a lot of times where I watched others die, and now, I can do something to save them. Thank you for accepting me as an attending."

She gave the microphone back to the chief, her heels clacking on the stage as she took her seat beside the other attendings. "Thank you, Dr. Ashton Lure. I would like to invite the new attendings to take a seat in the front row. I, along with a team of others, have put together a video of some of the growing points and finest moments of each of the new attendings. Let us enjoy those moments."

The new attendings made their way to the front-row seats as the chief pressed play and the projector screen flashed to their first day and progressed through their intern and residency years.

A loud bang caused everyone to jump as a man's voice boomed through the lecture room: "We need Ashton Lure, now. We have incoming neuro patient who has suffered a knife wound to the head."

"Dr. Lure, go ahead," Chief Cooney said.

She stood up and made her way through the door, following the man down the hall. The emergency room was busy with patients of all types of injuries. As she moved to trauma room two, she saw a man with a splint on his arm, a female with an obvious broken leg, a child with cat marks. She walked through the door to the trauma case and stopped— the knife's handle protruded from the man's head as he fought against restraints.

"Have we got any scans yet?" she asked.

"Not yet, he just got here from the prison," a nurse replied.

Ashton moved to the man as she examined the wound. Blood matted his hair, and the knife went through the skull. "Let's get some scans on this. You're going to have to have surgery, there isn't any way around it. But we will know how to better remove the knife once we have an image of what's going on inside," she said. "You, what's your name?" Ashton asked as she looked around and pointed to a female.

"Me? I-I'm Melody Sandings, one of the new interns," she said.

"Good, you oversee taking him down to get his scans. I'll stay around this area, and I expect you to let me know when he's back," Ashton said.

"O-Okay," Melody stumbled, taking the brake off the gurney and heading for the scans.

Ashton exited the room, walking toward the nurses station, when someone bumped into her arm. "Sorry about that," the man said as he closed a patient's chart before looking up.

"Oh, it's all right," she replied, seeing the renowned cardiovascular surgeon standing in front of her.

"Hey, Ashton. How did the inauguration go?"

"It's actually still going on. Turns out the chief put together a video of all of us. But I was pulled out to work on a trauma case. How's your day going, Collin?" she asked as she leaned against the nurses desk.

I can see why he's the playboy of the hospital—I mean, look at that toned body, the muscles, his brown hair and eyes. I haven't had sex with anyone but my master, but maybe he would be the one to try with. Maybe I'll work up the courage today to ask if we can have dinner at some point. Even if I can't do the sex part, maybe I can at least make a friend? Being trapped in the chamber without human interaction made it hard for me to be social when I broke free. But it's been ten years. I must start trying, and the people here at the hospital are nice. At least, that's what I've gathered.

"It's going well. I've had a few surgeries, all of which have gone smoothly, and I've got another one coming up soon," he said, flashing her his pearly white smile.

"That's good. You always do your best. I'm expecting a surgery, just waiting for the scans." She smiled back.

"D-Dr. Lure," Melody said with a stutter.

"Ah, here they are. Yes, Melody?"

"The patient is back, here are the scans."

"Maybe we'll run into each other after our surgeries," Collin said, winking.

"See ya later," she said. "Melody, come with me."

They went down the hall to the right, finding the image room. She placed the scans on the panel and turned on the light. The blade had gone right through his frontal lobe.

"Melody, are you interested in neuro at all?" Ashton asked as she continued to look over the scans.

"I-I'm not sure yet, I haven't really had a chance to find out what field I want to specialize in," Melody replied.

"What do you see in the images?" Ashton asked as she watched Melody's changing expression.

"Umm, well, if you look here, you can see that the knife has gone through the frontal lobe. And that it missed a major artery," Melody said.

Ashton noticed Melody's nervous behavior as she pointed to different spots on the images and explained what they were.

"And what are the damages that could be done with and without surgery?"

"It could result in loss of m-movement, partial or complete paralysis, and speech problems."

"Very good. Go prep the patient for surgery. You'll be scrubbing in to watch."

2

COLLIN'S SECRET

The operating room was bright, and it took Ashton's eyes a moment to adjust. The surgery was successful, and the nurses took the patient back to his room. Hallways were clean and sterile—a faint smell of antiseptic was in the air as she made her way to the nurses station. "Ashton, how did your surgery go? You look exhausted," Collin said, slamming a chart folder onto the desk.

"I could say the same for you, Collin. You look just as tired as I do. And yes, the surgery went well. He will make a full recovery, thankfully. How about yours?" She placed the charts on the desk waiting for his reply.

"He will make it to see another day. He's strong and has a good fight in him," the doctor said as he leaned against the nurses station. "Well, I'll let you go. I'm sure you want to get home."

"Yes." She turned to walk away. *What am I doing? This is the time to ask, even if it's just to get dinner!* She turned back, a smile on her lips. "How would you like to grab dinner?"

Her hazel eyes mesmerized him—fierce, powerful, and delicate. Heat flooded his body, his groin rising. "Sure, let's head over to the locker rooms and change out of our scrubs," Collin said.

They walked down the busy hallways, a few nurses interrupting Collin before they got to the locker rooms. "I'll meet you back out here when I'm done changing." He smiled at her.

"Okay," she said as she opened the door to the women's locker room. The carpeted flooring was refreshing compared with the white tiles in the hospital hallways and rooms. She went to her locker and grabbed her change of clothes.

Her dirty scrubs landed in the laundry hamper, replaced with a long-sleeved purple shirt. She took the brush she kept in her locker over to the mirror and stared at herself. She was five foot seven with olive skin that matched the long, wavy blonde hair that fell in tangles onto her back. Her jawline was narrow and angled, while her nose was slightly crooked from being broken multiple times. She wasn't overweight, but she wasn't so skinny that she looked starved, either. Her lips curled in a smile even with the tiredness her body felt, and the shine of the successful surgery still gleamed in her hazel eyes. She brushed the tangles out of her hair before making her way to the locker. She placed the brush back in, grabbed her bag, and found the cold metal doorknob.

"Are you ready? I was thinking we could order some pizza and take it back to my place. Maybe watch a movie?" Collin asked as she exited the locker room.

"Yeah, that sounds like a great plan. How about that place on the corner of Fifty-Second? It's always good," she said as they made their way through the hallways to the elevators.

"I've been there, they do have good food! Why don't you follow me, and we can choose what we want before we head back to my place? Since you don't know where I live . . ." he asked as he pressed the ground-floor button.

"Okay," she said nervously as she looked at the ground.

The hospital doors slid open as Ashton and Collin made their way to the parking lot. A breeze floated across the grounds, creating a melody as it fanned the leaves that decorated the lawn. Car doors slammed in the distance, interrupting the song nature created.

"I'll meet you there, the one on the corner, right?" Collin asked.

"Yes, that's the one. I'll see you in a few minutes."

Ashton parked her car, getting out while Collin stood waiting by the entrance. She moved toward the pizza joint, and a shiver ran through her body. In the distance was a man in the shadows—his gray eyes bore into her. She halted in the middle of the sidewalk, and her heart rate picked up as her mind took her back to when she was four years old:

"Mom, Mom, what's wrong? Why are you screaming?" Little steps pattered through the hallway at her mom's fearful cry.

"Stop, don't come out here," her dad's voice cried.

The hallway that once held her blanket forts closed in on her as the BANG resonated through them. A man's intense gray eyes met hers, and the second BANG rendered her parentless.

"Come with me, Ashton," he said.

"I don't know you." Fear gripped inside her.

"It's okay, I'm taking you somewhere safe." He led her to the underground, a dark and cold chamber that became her home.

"Ashton! Ashton!" A hand shook her arm, causing her to flinch.

"Hmm?" Chocolate eyes searched her expression and followed her gaze.

"Are you all right?" Collin asked, concerned.

"Yeah, yes, I'm okay. I just thought I recognized someone. Let's go decide on a pizza," she said, placing her go-to smile on her lips.

They entered the pizza joint and decided on a simple pepperoni pizza, talking about their surgeries as they waited. Collin paid for the pizza, and they left the building, Ashton following him in her car to his apartment a few blocks away.

"Well, this is my home," he said, unlocking the door.

"It's nice, I like it. Very modern," she said.

Collin placed the pizza on the marbled countertop before he grabbed two plates. "How many slices would you like?" he asked.

"Just one for now," she said, eyeing the apartment. A marble countertop separated the kitchen and living room. An area rug covered most of the walnut flooring, and a leather sectional was placed in the center of the room. The fifty-inch TV was mounted on the wall, and a walnut coffee table ran parallel to the sectional.

"I don't have any DVDs, but I do have some streaming services," Collin said as he made his way to the living room with the plates of pizza. He picked up the remote, turning on the TV, and handed it to her, suggesting that she decide.

"Oh, um. Do you have any preference? Maybe a comedy?" she asked as she flipped through the movie titles.

"There are the Three Stooges, have you ever seen them? They're hilarious and usually help me unwind," he said as he sat on the sectional.

"Sure." She searched for the TV show and pressed play, taking her seat a few feet away from him.

They ate in silence, laughing when Moe poked Curly in the eye. Her nervousness faded with each laugh they shared.

See, this isn't so bad, she thought. *If only I could bring myself to scoot closer to him. It's only a few feet, so why is my heart pounding so much? Just move the distance; I can do this.* She placed the plate on the coffee table and fiddled with her hands.

Collin set down his plate and looked over at Ashton. Her teeth caught her bottom lip, sexualizing her beauty further. His cock twitched beneath his pants, creating tightness. He closed the distance between them, putting his arm around her shoulder. She brushed her hair out of her face and looked over at him.

His lips crashed against hers as his tongue protruded into her mouth. Her lips matched his movement, allowing his tongue to intertwine with hers. A moan escaped his lips as his hands roamed her body, memorizing her curves and landing on her breasts.

I can do this. I can do this! His hand fiddled with her breasts, squeezing and probing as he kissed her more roughly. She leaned farther into the couch, trying to match his pace as her hands rested on his shoulders. His hand slid down her side and landed on the hem of her shirt, sliding it up.

Her hand flew to the shirt and pushed it down. Panic set in, and she began to shake. "I-I can't. I can't do this!" she said as she tried to slide away from him. One hand gripped her shoulder, and the other pulled her against him. He went to kiss her again, but she pulled her head back. "I said I can't," she told him.

"Come on, I'm all worked up. What am I supposed to do without you?" he asked as he went to kiss her again.

"I thought I could, but I really can't. I tried, I really did," she said as she put her hands on his chest, pushing him away.

"Well, I don't take no for an answer. You made me hard, and now you are going to fix it," he said as he grabbed her hands.

"I said no! Now get your hands off me," she said with as much fierceness as she could muster.

His hands tightened on her, and she flung her knee up, hitting his stomach. He released her, and she ran for the door. She slammed the door shut and locked the doors of her car. As she began to pull out of the driveway, she saw the man again, across the street. *Franko!* Her foot slammed on the pedal as she flew down the street trying to get away from Collin. Trying to get away from Franko. Memories of her past flooded back to her:

"Please, please Franko, please! I was good today." Her pleas *reverberated in the damp, stone-walled chamber.*

"Shut up. I don't care if you were good today, you still hesitated to shoot him. That means you get punished!" the gray-eyed man named Franko screamed.

The whoosh came as his belt flew, landing on her back. "AAHH." Another and another. Tears stained her cheeks.

"Stop crying, it's a sign of weakness. I didn't choose you to be weak. I chose you to be my successor! Now, start learning!"

HONK! Ashton jumped and swerved, realizing she almost hit a car. "I'm almost home, I must make it home."

She landed in her driveway, hands quivering as she caught her breath. The moon and waves danced as she entered the pass code to the house. Keys found the hole, unlocking the door.

She placed the keys on the hanger, entering the house she had meticulously designed. A glass case in the kitchen held homemade chocolate chip muffins—sweet bliss that helped ease her tension—and she poured milk to chase it down.

Her elbows were propped on the counter as she nibbled the muffin, eyes sweeping the room. Three empty guest rooms lined the wall, a dining table for eight collected dust, and the living room held no laughter.

Muffin gone, she ran upstairs to the library, placing her mail on the desk for a later date. Back in the living room, she paused, looking at the basement door. It remained locked, housing the training room. It served as a reminder of the past; training was what she knew.

A trail of clothes was left on the floor as the water came on in the shower. Her body shivered from the fresh coolness on naked skin as the reflection in the mirror held a hollow soul. Hazel eyes were not present, only desolation.

Welcoming warmth engulfed her body, nerves edged on the brink of calmness. Dirt, grime, and day washed off the skin, leaving it clean. She sat on the floor of the shower, water moving over her body as it pleased. She felt a soothing sensation of gentle pinpricks tapping on her skin as the pitter-patter of water hit the fiberglass of the shower with rhythmic tranquility.

Her dainty fingers traced raised white bumps on her arm—old markings left from the beatings. Eyes closed, she inhaled sharply before releasing it. She stepped out of the shower, wrapping the towel around her. Changing into her nightwear, she crawled into bed.

She tossed and turned, body flailing before bolting upright, heaving for air. Her back against the backrest, she calmed her breathing from her nightmare.

3

TRAINING

Ashton pulled the last batch of cupcakes out of the oven and placed them on the cooling rack. She turned off the oven, cleaning up before heading down to do some training. "Kaname, unlock secure location." She heard a click and opened the door, heading down the stairs.

The porcelain tea sets she bought each year lined the wall by the stairs, leading to the medical bay. Opposite was emptiness with three walls. She walked over to one of the walls and pressed in a code. The wall opened to display a variety of weapons, and she took a gun. She walked over to the platform that was in the center of the walled room. "Kaname, turn on simulation five for guns."

"Yes, Ashton," a voice said.

Several computer polygonal men came after her, and she aimed the gun at each of their hearts. The noise resonated through the basement walls as the bullets sped through the air, landing at her precise destination. The polygonal men dissipated.

She put the safety back on and reloaded the gun before replacing it in the proper spot. She sat on the floor and stretched, making sure her body was loose enough for combat training. Sighing, she stood up. "Kaname, turn on simulation two for combat training."

"Yes, Ashton," the voice said.

She rolled her neck and kicked the polygonal man in the chest. He flew back and ran toward her, almost punching her, but she dodged in time. Her hand fisted and landed on his nose. "Enough warm-up. Kaname, turn on simulation five for combat training."

The polygonal man in front of her threw punches one after another, and she flung her arms in blocking motions. The man picked up speed and went to kick her side, but her knee blocked the attack. The opening was clear, and she slammed her elbow into his face. He backed up, and she spun around kicking him. He grabbed her ankle and threw her a few feet. The ground was hard, and she rolled before hitting the wall.

She stood back up, running at him, and sent punches flying at high speeds. He blocked the best he could, but her fist was brutal when it landed on his stomach. He dissipated, and she sat with her back against the wall.

"What do I do?" She said aloud to herself, "I have the day off from work today and tomorrow, but then I have to go back. Even though the hospital is large, I know I'll run into Collin again. Was I the only one he did that to, or has he done the same to others? I told him no, but he continued. If he saw my scars, what would he have done? People would think I'm hideous if they saw them."

She brought her knees to her chest and hugged herself. "And how do I escape Franko? The agreement was that he wouldn't have any contact with me, even from afar, and yet, the day after we signed the contract, I saw him in the distance, stalking me. I've turned a blind eye, but I know that he's just waiting for his chance to come after me."

I'm twenty-five now; I'll go and ask for my freedom. He can't do anything worse than he's already been doing to me, she thought. She walked up to Franko when training was over and confronted him. "Master, I want out. To be away from the underground," she said with as much courage as she could muster.

"You want out? What the hell is wrong with you? You have it made here, everything is provided for you—food, water, shelter, and I even allowed you to do that school thing that kids need when you were younger," he said, laughing at her.

"Master, I'm grateful for all that you have provided, but I don't want to be in the underground anymore," she said.

"Fine, if you want out, then I'll give you an impossible task. If you complete the task, then we can sign a contract, and you'll be free."

"What is the task, Master?"

"There is a large get-together for Jackson Mall's six-year-old child. There will be parents and other children there, and I want you to kill them. He owes me a lot of money and hasn't paid up. It's only fitting that he should repay me with his life."

"Very well, Master."

Ashton stared out the window of the vacant apartment building across from the party hall. The detonator to the bomb she had planted was in her hand. "No emotion, no hesitation, and no mercy." She pressed the first button, and the building across from her boomed and filled with black smoke. The second and third button were pressed, detonating the other two bombs. Screams could be heard, and she looked through the scope of her sniper rifle, firing on the few that managed to escape.

She packed up and headed for the door. She flew as something went off on the opposite side of the room by the window. Her head swayed, eyes half-closed, and her limp body lay in a heap of rubble.

Her eyes opened and closed several times before staying open. Her body screamed in agony as she stood up, making her way down the stairs of the vacant apartment. Police were focused on the building across from her and didn't notice as she moved farther away from the scene.

She walked back into the large building and marched up to Franko. Shock was written on his face, eyes wide and his jaw dropped. "I want that contract now! You'll never see me again, not even from a distance, and in return, I'll relinquish all rights to kill you," she demanded as she came to a halt in front of him.

He opened the desk drawer and handed her the contract to sign. She read every bit of it carefully, not wanting him to have added something without her knowledge. When she finished, she took the pen and signed it, giving it back so he could sign. She turned and stalked out of there.

Her hands racked her hair at the flashback of their agreement. "Ten years. I've spent ten years making something of myself, and yet, somehow, I still can't get away from my past. When I go to work, I see him. When I leave work, I see him. At night, I have nightmares about what he did to me. And now, Collin tried to force me into sex when I told him I couldn't."

She wiped her nose with the back of her hand as tears slid down her cheeks. She screamed, "Why do bad things always happen to me? Why can't I find someone who will love me and be patient with me? All I need is someone who can help me overcome my post-traumatic stress disorder. Why can't I have something good happen to me?!"

She let out a shaky breath and checked her watch. "Well, I guess I should go and frost the cupcakes. The homeless shelter will be expecting them for the dinner rush." Getting up, she headed for the stairs and told Kaname to lock the door behind her.

Stepping out of the shower, she went to the kitchen and frosted the cupcakes before placing them in the carriers. She took them to the car and headed for Liberty Light Shelter—a local, safe place for the homeless to eat and sleep.

After parallel parking in front of the brick building, she stepped out and stacked the carriers. Three at a time, she took them in through the already-propped-open door. The volunteers stopped and smiled at her as she walked up to them. "Here they are," she smiled and set the carriers by the other desserts. "I'll see you next week," she said as she picked up the other containers she had left the week earlier.

Back at her house, she changed into her fuzzy pajama pants decorated with snowflakes and her fuzzy white sweater that read "believe" in gold lettering. Pouring a bowl of cereal, she made her way to the sectional and turned on the DVD that was in the player. She watched *Pay It Forward* and then crashed in bed for the night.

4

WHERE AM I?

Her head shook, blinking. The room shifted, or at least, she thought it did.

Blink . . . Blink . . . Blink . . . *Whoa! What happened? I was somewhere else.*

Blink . . . Blink . . . *Where am I? This isn't my room.*

The magnificent ceiling was so high that a giant could fit in the room. Windows lined the walls with a view of a dark-red moonlit sky. Royal-green drapes hung from the windows, and the design that connected the windows and the ceilings consisted of mandala shapes. Intricate and delicate, almost commanding respect to be viewed with beauty. In the middle, a chandelier was hanging from the ceiling. The room itself was like that of a dance hall for an elegant ball in which a prince and princess would take the first dance of a fading evening.

Her mouth gaped in amazement before realizing that others were in the room. Her nerves shook and her eyes went wide as she took in the people in front of her. Instinctively, her fists formed into balls, ready to fight if needed.

The fanciest-clothed person with beaming gold eyes bellowed, "Welcome! You must be Ashton Lure." Her eyes shifted from a muscular, orange-haired person to his. "This must be a shock to you, let me explain. This is the Demon Realm, and I'm the prince, Lord Diavolo." His hand swept to the right, modeling black nails; the bronzed tint in his hair reflected the moonlight. "To the right of me, you'll find the seven demon brothers: Lucifer, Mammon, Leviathan, Satan, Asmodeus, Beelzebub, and Belphegor."

The first demon, called Lucifer, straightened more as if proud to be called first. His red eyes were like lasers, and his skin was paler than the rest. Mammon, the second demon, had snow-white hair with gold tips. His eyes matched his hair, and his demeanor was like that of a gangster—hunched shoulders and a jacket hanging off the shoulders. The third demon, Leviathan, was nervous. His fingers fiddled with one another, and his head was lowered. Yellow eyes contrasted with his blue-purple hair.

The fourth demon, if she remembered correctly, was Satan. A scowl was present on his expression, and his green eyes seemed annoyed. The olive color of his skin went with his beach-blond hair and lean body. Asmodeus, the fifth demon, beamed with glee as he bounced on his legs from what seemed like excitement. His wavy blond hair danced with each bounce, and his orange-yellow eyes glowed. His paler olive skin looked as if it were as smooth as a silk feather.

The sixth brother, Beelzebub, was the orange-haired demon she had seen earlier. His skin was pale like Lucifer's, but he didn't hold himself proudly. His muscles were prominent, and he held his stomach as if he were hungry or had a stomachache. Next to him was the seventh demon brother, Belphegor, who looked half-asleep. Dark-purple eyes seemed heavy-laden, and his hair was a navy blue with gray tips. His skin tone was olive, but a darker shade from the others.

Lord Diavolo then caught her attention. "To the left of me, you'll find those who are currently in the exchange program: Adrian, who is also from the Human Realm, Simeon and then Seth, who are from the Celestial Realm. They're the angels that were chosen."

The one called Adrian, a silver-haired man, pale in color, wore black and was smiling. His stance showed ease, no weariness of being near demons that could kill him. He tilted his head and said, "You're staring! Am I that gorgeous?" He laughed and watched as her forehead creased.

"You aren't scared to be around demons?" Ashton asked.

"Not at all! They're some of my closest friends," he told her.

"Hmm," she replied as her eyes darted to the smaller angel.

Seth's smile was alive; it was like moonlight giving light to the darkened walkway. His dirty blond hair and bright blue eyes would make any female fall for him when he got older. He fisted his hand as if trying to ground his excitement; like Asmodeus, he was practically bouncing up and down. The other angel, Simeon, made her heart stop when she looked at him. His toned body held just enough muscles, his black hair went perfectly with his darker skin tone, and his sapphire-blue eyes mesmerized her. He smiled, and like hers, his heart stopped at the sight of her.

Lord Diavolo continued, saying, "Behind you is Barbatos—he is my loyal butler." She turned at his gesture, meeting green-tinted eyes mixed with yellow. A green-haired man smiled at her, bowing. He wasn't muscular, but he wasn't superskinny, either—he could do damage if he had to. Lord Diavolo's sweet, dripping voice filled her ears.

"The exchange program is something I've put together to try to reunite the three realms: Celestial, Human, and Demon. The goal is to give you the experience to see what the culture is like down here for a year. Like an exchange student in the Human World, when one student swaps with another of a different country to attend each other's school, and in this case, you've been chosen. While you're here, you'll be taking a few classes to help you better understand demons and angels. You'll be living with the seven demons and be fully enriched by the experience here. Is this something that you would be interested in?" he asked.

She looked at the floor, mulling over what she heard. She spoke before she could stop herself, saying, "So, I'm in a different realm? I'm no longer in the Human World?"

"Yes, that's correct." A smile grew on his lips as he answered, bright excitement in his eyes.

This isn't the Human Realm. It's far away from Franko; he wouldn't be able to get me here. That would mean the stalking would stop, and maybe even the nightmares. But what about my job, the surgeries? Can I just willingly give that up? I worked hard for the past ten years to get that job. I know it's important to me, but so is being somewhere that Franko can't get me. Yesterday in the training room, I screamed, "Why can't something good ever happen to me?" Maybe this is that something good? Yes, this is a change that I need. I need this to get away from Franko, she thought as a bright flower bouquet came into sight, sitting on a stand in the corner. The off-green door with fancy design complemented the room.

"I know this might seem scary, but please keep in mind that you have my word that you will not be injured by any demons while you're here," Lord Diavolo said.

She whipped around, facing him, eyes locked. "I'm not scared of a demon. I've looked death in the eyes my entire life. It's just, wow!" Her hand rubbed her forehead, and her breath huffed out. "I never thought that demons and angels existed. I thought that they were mythological. So, you can understand how this can be bizarre." She flung her hands out. "I mean, what is your purpose in reuniting the realms? Why were they separated, anyway, and why choose me as an ambassador?"

"Those are exceptionally good questions, and I can certainly understand your disbelief. Let me explain," he started saying. "It is perfectly acceptable for you to believe demons and angels don't exist. My father a long, long time ago was part of a war that created a wedge among the three realms. The demons separated themselves from the other worlds and were forbidden to go to them." Lord Diavolo looked at Simeon and said, "Simeon, correct me if I'm wrong, but the archangels did the same as well—they forbade the angels to go to any of the other realms." Simeon nodded in confirmation.

"I, however, thought that it was too much—to continue to separate ourselves from the other realms. So, I put together this exchange program to reunite the Celestial Realm, the Human Realm, and the Demon Realm," Lord Diavolo said.

"What created the war?" she asked as she listened.

"A soul. When humans pass, they're sent to either a version of the Celestial Realm or a version of the Demon Realm. There was a particular soul that was meant to go to the Demon Realm but was sent to the Celestial Realm. My father didn't take kindly to this, and he confronted the archangels," Lord Diavolo said. "The human representative became involved, and the three realms fought. Each side used its own unique weapons to take revenge, and many were killed in the crossfire. I never agreed with my father on this matter, and I believe it unfit to allow this separation to continue. So, I'm trying to fix what my father started." He spoke the truth of their history.

"What happened to the soul?" she questioned further as she fidgeted with the hem of her sleeve.

"Everyone agreed that the soul would be reincarnated as an animal in the Human Realm. The soul, I believe, became a blue jay, and the three realms shut their portals. No one was allowed to move among the realms freely anymore. Do you have any more questions?" He was proud that she had many questions; it showed how interested she was.

"Why me?"

"Lucifer and I spent hours searching through the paperwork for the perfect candidate, until we found yours: Ashton Lure, thirty-five-year-old neurosurgeon. It was the fact that you were a doctor that caught our attention. We figured that you must be someone who loved to learn and help people. That perhaps you could show us some of your knowledge of the human brain and take up some courses on the demon and angel physiologies. If you would like to learn about those, that is," he added.

"Um, I would get to compare the three and see how they are different and similar? And what about Adrian? Is one human not enough?" she questioned him more, intrigued now that she would get to further her doctorate to include demons and angels.

"Adrian is an exceptional exchange student and has been in the program for a few months now. He is a sorcerer who focused on spells and potions, which helped him in his path of learning here. However, I feel the program would work out better if there were two humans. Preferably a male and female, since they hold different perspectives. What do you think? Will you join the program?" he asked as he watched her continue to fiddle with her sleeve and look around nervously.

Her eyes swept over the demons and angels and landed on Adrian. *He's a human, and he's been here awhile. It must not be bad, considering he said they were some of his closest friends. That must mean that they aren't cruel and malicious creatures, since he doesn't even look scared at all. And the prince said I can study demons and angels, so I can still use my medical skills. Plus, the most important part—Franko won't be able to stalk me anymore!*

She looked into the honeydew eyes of the demon prince, and said, "Okay, I'll do it." Her eyes were narrowed and held confidence. "I'll become a human ambassador and help you reunite the three realms."

The whole castle went silent; defiance filled the air with an icy chill, sending shivers down their spines. Going against all odds, she would help them fight for peace, to bring the three distinct realms back together. The realms were already aligning from her spoken words. A smile crept on the demon prince's lips as her eyes remained on his, fierce with no fear, and she radiated like nothing they had ever seen before. There was something about her that was different from the other humans they had met—perhaps it was her powerful demeanor and how she presented herself. Nervous, yet strong.

Everyone always shows slight fear of me being the demon prince, never treating me as an equal. Yet, here stands a female human, the weaker of the species, treating me like a counterpart. It excites me and ignites a fire within my body, Lord Diavolo thought as he stood frozen.

"When can I change into proper attire? I'm still in my sleepwear," she asked.

"Ahem, the demon brothers will show you to your room. You'll be staying at their Victorian house at 69 Devil's Way. When you've been shown your room, Lucifer will go with you back to the Human Realm to get your belongings." He smiled and addressed everyone in the room, saying, "there'll be a celebration dinner tonight at seven in the castle to welcome Ashton Lure—"

"Doctor," she said, continuing at his confusion. "It's Dr. Ashton Lure. I have a doctorate in neurosurgery. I'm accustomed to being called Doctor Ashton Lure in formal settings such as this," she said in a matter-of-fact tone, demanding respect. Shocked expressions and gasps were noticeable. "As you're Lord Diavolo and prefer others to call you by your title, my title is Dr." She shrugged her shoulders and looked down at the ground, stretching her neck.

"My apologies, *Doctor*," he continued. "We'll have a celebration dinner at seven in the castle to welcome *Dr.* Ashton Lure. This meeting is dismissed, you may carry on your way."

Lord Diavolo's coat flared out behind him as he stepped off the small platform. He walked toward the door, exiting, Barbatos following closely behind him.

5

NEW SURROUNDINGS

The demon brothers and Ashton arrived at 69 Devil's Way. It was immaculate. The walls were cream-colored with elegant designs and hanging portraits, strategically placed. Dark mahogany trim framed the doorways and railings, while the polished wooden floor peeked out from under the edges of the red and gold rugs. A grand staircase in the center led to the bedrooms.

Eyes wide, she stopped, awestruck at the sight. It was as if she had stepped into a different era; smiling, she took it all in. Demons ran up the stairs at the look Lucifer gave them. "Your room is right this way," he said, his arm held out for her.

"You certainly know how to make them scatter," she said. She gulped, looking at his arm, and took a step away. Mistrust and doubt formed in her eyes as she investigated his red lasers. She trembled.

"You don't have to be afraid, although I personally like that you are. It means you'll have the sense to stay away from bad situations with the other demons who are not as keen on Lord Diavolo's program." He crossed his arms, and a smug smile formed his lips. He took a step toward the stairs, and his frame was bigger than any human she had ever seen, even a wrestler. He was smaller than his demon brothers, yet he could easily intimidate the strongest humans with his stance alone.

She followed behind him as he led her up the stairs to a bedroom. He opened the door, stepping aside so she could walk in. She stared into his eyes as she stepped inside. Neutral walls accompanied the white-and-gold dresser and vanity wonderfully. The wooden floor creaked with each step, and the four-poster bed had feather-like silk curtains. A window in the corner opened to a garden.

A creak filled the room as she opened the window; cool air whipped into the room, shivers going down her spine. Tapping of steps sounded as Lucifer made his way to the window, the scent of flowers meeting Ashton's and Lucifer's senses. A sweet aroma.

"Ah yes, I love the smell of flowers." His eyes went wide, realizing he spoke the words aloud.

She let out a nervous laugh. "A demon who likes flowers, what are the odds of that? Well, I also love the different scents they give off."

"I thought you would. That's why I suggested this room because it overlooks the garden."

"There are flowers that resemble roses, they're my favorite. I'm surprised to see a lot of similarities between the two realms. At least in the flowers. Roses, tulips, marigolds, lilies, and I think that one is a forget-me-not." She pointed a shaky finger out the window at a blue flower.

His eyes followed where she pointed. "You're correct. All of those are exactly what you said. You'll see there are similarities, like the food. Some can vary, but we do have human food as well. Our school systems are similar—the appearance is darker, though. It's always night, and the moon is always present unless it hides behind clouds. Ashton, is that a problem?"

I'm not exactly afraid of the nighttime, but I'm not fond of it. Even though I was home safe when the sun went down, it always felt like Franko's eyes were creeping up on me.

"Is that a problem?" he asked again, leaning forward and shaking her arm to gain her attention.

She jolted at the physical contact and brushed her hair behind her ear. "Hmm? What did you say?"

"Is that a problem that it's always night? You got pale when I mentioned that."

"Oh, ha, I-I'm just not fond of the nighttime, that's all." Her eyes darted between each of the flowers, avoiding his eyes at all costs.

"You don't have to worry, all seven of us are here to help—with anything, even if it's to be in the room with you. It's scary being around demons, especially when you are a human female."

"I'll keep that in mind, but I-I should be good. Thank you."

A breeze brushed her hair, the sweet aroma of the flowers clearer now. He watched before turning to the garden. "There are rules in the house, such as taking turns making dinner. Dinner is at seven for whoever is attending, though we do like all of us to be there. Lord Diavolo doesn't want you going out unattended, so make sure you always have someone with you if you leave the premises. And there will also be meetings to talk about how the exchange program is going and how you are settling in," Lucifer said, finishing.

"Thank you for giving me this opportunity." She leaned against the window frame, her arms crossed, admiring the garden. "I'll follow all the rules."

"We'll get you on the schedule to start your rotation on dinners once you get more settled in. But for now, if you're ready, we can go pack some of your belongings."

"You like escorting me around, don't you? It brings you pride because your lord put you in charge of something important." She gave him a knowing, curious, yet compassionate look with an eyebrow raised.

"Let's get to the transportation device." He turned and stalked out of the room with his head high.

She walked beside the black-haired demon, taking in her surroundings. Volkswagen-style cars lined each side of the street; every fifty meters, streetlamps illuminated the cobblestones. Brick buildings held a variety of shops below while up above were homes and light shone through curtained windows at random. The murmur of demons conversing filled the sidewalks, and some stopped to stare at her.

Most demons were in human forms, larger built, but still human, while others were twice the size in demon form. Horns of all shapes and sizes protruded from their heads— some were small stubs while others were long and curled, and yet, others had the style of antlers or tree branches. The wings came in all sizes and colors, except white, large birdlike ones forming from the back, while others were daintier and bat-like. There were even some that had tails instead of wings. The tails came out from their rears and were long, like a cow's tail or a lion's, while some were thicker around the base like a dragon's.

Light pressure touched her back, and she startled. "It's just me," Lucifer said, a warning growl following his threatening glare. He transformed into his demon form, growing larger in size as black bull horns sprouted from his head and beautiful black raven wings from his back. She looked between Lucifer and the demon, which was larger than Lucifer. Her heart rate picked up, and she swallowed hard as she became rigid with fear. *Okay, so between the two, I would much rather be closer to Lucifer. At least he's under orders not to kill me.* She scooted closer to Lucifer, and his arm tightened around her waist as he continued to growl at the demon.

The demon huffed out smoke and walked away. Her breathing evened out as Ashton and Lucifer walked the last few blocks to the transportation device. He opened the device's door, and she stepped in. "Thank you," she said, grimacing.

"You're welcome."

"For a demon, you have polite manners. I wasn't expecting that," she managed to say through her fear.

"Well, I've been around for a long time. I know to be a gentleman and how to treat a lady. Every single one that I meet. Now, this may be a bit rough, so just hang in there. Take my arm, it'll help keep you steady."

Her hand shook as she took his elbow, and he started the transportation device. Her stomach flipped; it was like being on a roller coaster. The device stopped, but she didn't move, continuing to hold his arm. She glared at him as he chuckled. "I don't mean to laugh." The back of his fingers caressed her pale face. She leaned her forehead on his shoulder, trying to gain control of herself.

She straightened, letting go of his arm as she held her stomach. "I don't think I'll ever get used to that!"

He laughed. "You find that funny?" She glared at him and crossed her arms.

"N-no. It's just maybe I misjudged you and gave you less credit than you deserved . . . You seem to be quite *different*, something I never expected."

"How am I different?" she questioned.

"Even though you're scared and nervous, you still have this attitude about you. I mean you have to be different if you disregarded and interrupted Lord Diavolo so easily."

"That's a good thing, right?"

"That you are different, yes. That you disregarded and interrupted Lord Diavolo, no."

"Well, it's not like I meant to. I don't know anything about being around royalty. And you aren't what I expected as well."

"I'm not? And what were you expecting?" His eyebrow raised, intrigued.

"In the mythology books, demons are always mean creatures. But you and that prince don't seem so bad." She shrugged her shoulders while rubbing her arm. "And your laughter is actually enlightening. I've only ever known anger and hatred, so hearing a demon laugh is different," she mumbled.

"What do you mean anger and hatred are all you've known?"

"Nothing, I don't talk about it! I'm going to pack now."

The transportation device had placed them in her room, and she went to grab a bag. Clothes, books, toiletries, and electronics were spread across the bed.

"Would you like me to help you with anything?" he asked.

"No, I've got it. I'm almost done," she replied. Her eyes met his before she turned back to neatly pack everything. She zipped the suitcase and folded her favorite blanket on top. "I think I'm all set . . . Wait! How could I forget?" She reached over the bed picking up a stuffed animal.

A warm sensation coursed through Lucifer's body as he watched Ashton stroke the stuffed animal's ear, pulling it into a hug. He looked away, annoyed, when she turned to him. "Are you ready?" he said with a scoff, hiding that his pride shrank from the slight variation of happiness at what he saw.

"Yes, there's just one more thing I have to do." She placed the stuffed animal on the suitcase and spoke to the air, saying, "Kaname."

"Yes, Ashton?" a man's voice replied.

Ashton looked at Lucifer. His eyes darted everywhere for the sound. "I'm leaving for a while. You're now in charge of the house until I return. Keep it safe and locked away. Don't let intruders in, and let me know by our secure method if anything should arise."

"I'll do my best, Ashton."

She grabbed the stuffed animal, blanket, and suitcase, turning to Lucifer. "I'm ready now."

"What was that?" Lucifer asked.

"A strong demon like you is on edge about a voice that I talk to? That's funny. I'll explain on the way to the house. Also, is there any way I'll be able to send my letter of resignation to the hospital this week? It'll be hard to leave that job, but I'm actually excited to learn about the brains of demons and angels."

"Yes, we do have mail that goes to the Human Realm. Satan may be a good demon to help you with that, he's good at studying."

Lucifer took the blanket, tucking it under his arm, and then grabbed the suitcase. He held his free arm out for her, her sweaty hand enclosed around his biceps. Within minutes, they were inside the dark room, eyes blinking and becoming accustomed to the dark.

Lucifer opened the door, gesturing for her to exit. A soft pressure was on her back, and she spun around, whamming Lucifer on the chest with her hand as she landed with a thud on the pavement. She looked up and saw Lucifer looking down at her, not fazed in the least about her hand hitting him.

She rubbed her hand and grimaced before reaching for Lucifer's hand. "If you're done falling, then we should get going. I have work to get done before the feast," he said. She nodded, and they began walking.

"Kaname is a computer-generated program that I designed myself. I wanted something that had never been made before and that I knew could keep me safe. So, ten years ago, I created him. I can talk to him, and he'll respond according to my commands, but he'll only follow my orders." She jumped out of the way as a demon in his demon form came at her. With his eyes, Lucifer sent daggers at the demon and stepped between the demon and her, warning him to keep walking.

Her voice quivered as she continued talking. "He alerts me to anyone who isn't supposed to be on the premises and tells me if someone tries to break in while I'm not there. Overall, he is a security system."

Lucifer looked at her, a stern expression on her face, and nodded, his questions unasked. When the house came into view, he dropped her off at her room and went to his study. Ashton unpacked, finding homes for all her belongings before she plopped on the bed.

"I should get changed, I'm still in my pajamas. I can't believe I've been around demons all day, and all I've had on was pajamas. That's embarrassing!" she said, getting up to change. She sat in the vanity chair, looking at herself. "Wow, my hair is a mess. Urgh!"

There was a knock and the door burst open, and a demon with wavy blond hair and orange-yellow eyes skipped into the room, perching on her bed.

"I'm Asmodeus, but of course, you can call me Asmo—everyone does." He used his hands to talk and emphasized each word with enthusiasm. She jumped back in her chair, almost tipping it over.

"Um, I-I'm Ashton, it's a pleasure to meet you, Asmo," she said, forcing a smile.

"I wanted to introduce myself earlier, but Lucifer made sure that everyone stayed away until you had some time to yourself," Asmo said with a chirp. "I'm going on a shopping trip tomorrow at one of the malls—why don't you come with me? I can show you all the fabulous stores, and we can buy you some new clothes. What do you say?"

"Umm . . . sure."

"I can help you pick out the perfect creams that'll complement your skin. Just leave everything to me."

"I'm partial to the cherry-blossom scents, though."

"Then they can be cherry-blossom scented, but we can test out some new scents and see which ones you like."

"That sounds like it is going to be a lot of fun."

"Oooh, I'm loving this more and more. And your hair is a mess! We need to take care of that."

"I haven't had time to brush it all day. After all, I arrived in a different realm without being prepared."

"Leave everything to me!" He skipped over and grabbed her hand. She pulled her hand away, and took a step back. "Oh, right, I forgot you aren't used to this! It's all right, we're just going to my room, since I have the perfect dress for you to wear tonight. Let's go," he said.

"Ah, okay," she said and timidly walked behind him.

Asmo stopped, and Ashton stumbled. Tender hands wrapped around her waist, her head landing on a firm chest. Her eyes were met with hazel that could match hers; he had magnificent blond hair and a to-die-for smile. "Um, w-who are you?" she asked, swallowing hard.

"I'm Satan," he winked.

"Could you let go of me now? I have my balance," Ashton asked. She placed her hands on his chest and pulled away from him, shaking.

"Where are you taking her?" Satan looked at his brother as he released her waist.

"I'm going to go and get her ready for tonight," Asmo said.

A hand tugged Ashton's, pulling her to a room. Her wide eyes darted between Asmo and Satan. Satan followed them into Asmo's room. "You two sit on the bed, and I'll go pick a dress that will look stunning on Ashton," Asmo said.

The air was heavy with nerves as Ashton sat on the edge of the bed. It dipped as Satan followed. "Did you enjoy your trip back to the Human Realm to get your stuff?" Satan asked.

"Y-yeah, I did. Lucifer was exceedingly kind." She fiddled with her fingernails and avoided making eye contact with him.

"That's a first, he's always uptight and stiff."

"I can see that, but he was still a gentleman, which is much appreciated. Especially since I'm in a new place." She rubbed the back of her neck with her hand.

"Of course, his pride would allow him to be nothing but that." Satan paused before adding, "Don't tell him I said that . . . it would go right to his head if he knew one of us gave him a compliment."

The demons so far were all pleasant to be around. Not that she was scared, but she was used to being alone and not having others around—it was all new. But the more they all talked, the more at ease she started to feel.

"Go put this dress on," Asmo said as he reappeared.

She took the pale-yellow dress and went to change. Satan's mouth dropped open, his heart quickening at what he saw. She twirled her blonde hair soaring around her; her bright hazel eyes sparkled with beauty. The dress bellowed out—a floral sleeveless design that accentuated the waist area with a simple bow. Black tights and thin sweater covered her bare skin, matching the dress perfectly. She was like a dazzling sunflower, sending blood pumping right to his manhood.

"You look stunning," Satan said, breathlessly.

"T-Thank you," she replied, blushing.

"Ah, look at how gorgeous you look! I knew it would be the perfect dress for you," Asmo said.

"I'll excuse myself, start getting ready myself," Satan said.

He exited the room, leaning against the wall with his eyes closed. *This is going to be a long year. Her beauty is astounding— no one has gotten that reaction from me before. I need to get a grip on this; my cock is throbbing just by looking at her. I must control this,* he thought as his hand came to the bulge in his pants. *Mmm, she was so hot!* His hand rubbed faster, and he made his way to his room.

Asmo finished her hair and makeup, getting ready himself. "Ready?" he asked.

"I guess," she said.

Asmo led her to the stairs, and she stopped halfway down. The six brothers were staring at her with gaping mouths and wide eyes. *I hope those mouths aren't gaped open to eat me! What do I do? What do I do? I don't know what to do!* She bit the inside of her cheek, tasting copper as she tried to keep her nerves from rattling. Unwillingly, her cheeks dusted red, and her eyes landed on the one demon she felt a tiny bit comfortable with—Lucifer. A smile crossed his lips, encouraging her.

"Come on, no need to be shy." Asmo flashed her a perfect white smile. "We won't bite," he said and swished his hand all girlie-like while rolling his eyes. Lucifer closed his eyes and face-palmed.

"R-right of course, what was I thinking." She raised her eyebrows and forced a smile.

Compliments flooded her at the bottom of the stairs, and the coolness of the air chilled her flushed cheeks. Lucifer walked beside her. "Since we are higher-up demons than most, the house is closer to the castle. Only a few blocks." He smiled at her and drew back behind everyone.

He admired the way the moonlight glowed on her hair. *Hmm . . . she keeps flinching when my brothers touch her; she did earlier as well. I wonder why? I know that she is new here and has mistrust in us, but at the same time, most people don't flinch that much.*

"STOP!" She flung her hands in the air and halted. The seven demons and others stopped to stare at the outburst. She looked at each of the demons with petrified eyes. "I know I'm the new toy, but could you please stop touching me?"

"Sorry, are you okay?" Beelzebub muttered, lowering his head and hunching his shoulders in submission. She nodded. "Yeah. I-it's just overwhelming."

Lucifer came to her side. "Let's get moving. We're going to be late."

They made their way up the curved driveway of the castle, Lucifer using the door knocker to signal their arrival. "Welcome, glad you could join us." Barbatos placed a gloved hand on his torso and bowed as he opened the door.

"Thank you, Barbatos," Lucifer said.

Barbatos led them to the dining area, where Lord Diavolo, Adrian, Seth, and Simeon were already seated. They turned and watched as Ashton made her entrance. An amused grin spread across Lord Diavolo's face as he took in her dress, adoring how it made her radiate even more than she already did.

Simeon closed his eyes, taking in a sharp breath; his heart skipped several beats. His body flooded with a sensation he wasn't aware of. Always the perfect angel, never going against the laws, yet here, his body reacted to her. He saw countless perfection in angels and even humans, but he had never had this reaction. *You're here to experience the culture, not be smitten with a human,* he thought as he let out the breath he held.

Seth bounced in his seat, excited to talk with someone who wasn't a demon, oblivious to the sexual tension in the room. Adrian blushed and his eyes grew; his outer demeanor was poised, but inside, his breath caught. *I can't wait to get to know her. Maybe we could be study partners? I'm sure she would appreciate the help.*

Ashton rubbed her arm while biting her lip and walked in, meeting Simeon, who was seated there. A buzz filled her body as she walked to her seat, admiring the black-haired angel with an ever-present tan.

She was almost to her seat when surprise took over as Lord Diavolo stood up, pulling her chair out for her. He kept his eyes on hers, not letting them stray over her body, wanting to stay a perfect gentleman. She sat down, and the chair lightly pressed against her legs. "Thank you." She nodded as Lord Diavolo took his own seat. He smiled back at her.

"How are you settling in? I know that my first week here was difficult, and it took some adjusting," Simeon asked as he fidgeted with his hands.

"I'm settling in well—everyone is very accommodating." Ashton looked at Simeon, her face still flushed, and their eyes met. Butterflies took flight in her stomach, and she wasn't sure what to make of the feeling. She wasn't supposed to start her girl thing for another two weeks, yet her stomach felt weird. *What could this feeling be?*

"Yes, everyone was helpful when Seth and I came here, although I'm sure they are more helpful since you're living with them," Simeon said. Pins and needles tapped under his skin as he tried to keep a calm composure. *What could this feeling be?*

"That would make it easier for them to help me. Where are you and the others staying?"

"We're in a different building, not too far from the place you are staying. If I remember correctly, it is about two blocks away. A ten-minute walk, I think." He touched his cheek and tilted his head, smiling.

"Oh, that's not extremely far. It would make it easy to be able to go to each other's houses to spend time together." She blushed and quickly added, "Getting to know each other as exchange students, you know?"

"I know exactly what you mean. I like that idea, and I think Seth would like it as well," Simeon said with a chuckle.

Seth popped his head around Simeon's side, trying to glimpse Ashton. She leaned forward, looking at the child—he couldn't be more than thirteen. "Hi," she said to him.

"Hey! I'm Seth. It's so nice to meet someone else who isn't a demon. I'm not fond of them at all," he said matter-of-factly.

"Is that so?"

"Seth is having a challenging time adjusting. We haven't been here exceptionally long, either. About a month before you. He's not fond of demons, but it's a good chance for him to learn more about them on a firsthand basis," Simeon said, answering her questioning look.

"Thank you for elaborating." She winked at him.

"Of course," he replied. His smile stiffened, and his breath hitched.

Lord Diavolo sat back smugly in his chair as he watched the exchange between his students. He wanted her attention, but how could he mess up this moment? This was what the program was set in place for. His hand brushed Lucifer's leg under the table, and lust filled his eyes as they met Lucifer's, glad when Lucifer's hand covered his. "It seems like she's doing well. How's she settling in with you and the others?" Lord Diavolo asked.

"She seems to be getting along very well. Everyone seems to be quite fond of her already. Asmo, of course, helped her get ready for tonight, and if I heard correctly, they're going shopping. I'll give her some demon dollars so she can buy things she wants and needs," Lucifer replied, a blush on his cheeks.

"Good, I'm glad she's settling in."

Lord Diavolo thought to himself, watching everyone converse: *She's like the small, timid David who stood up to the giant Goliath. It was obvious she was nervous, but she stood her ground. Adrian was already aware of demons and angels, since he's a sorcerer, but she didn't have any clue. My father was wrong all those centuries ago, and because he couldn't let one soul go, a war created a wedge between all of us.*

I hope this program works. That demons, angels, and humans can begin to learn how to interact with one another again. Not just kill like our instincts are, but actually accept them for them. If I'm wrong about this program, then I'll lose the support of many demons, which could be my downfall as prince. But it's a chance I'm willing to take, and I believe that she is the person who can help it succeed—that each species can learn about one another, respect one another.

She's a brain surgeon, so perhaps she can lend us her knowledge of medical skills. Maybe the knowledge that our doctors have can be enhanced by something we didn't even realize when she did? The possibilities are endless, and who knows, maybe this program will flourish to the point at which more humans and angels can come to the Demon Realm at a time instead of just two. He admired her before turning to grin at Lucifer while his thumb continued to caress Lucifer's.

6

FEATHERED NECKLACE

The sign read "Devilicious Pastriest," and the door chimed as Ashton and Asmodeus entered. She tried listening to Asmo, but his talking was like a bee speeding past—she could make out only part of what he was saying. What she gathered was "Devilicious Pastriest" was the place to go for breakfast in the Demon Realm.

Glass cases displayed several pastries in all shapes and sizes. Some were chocolate, vanilla, strawberry, and others; she wasn't sure, but the insects killed her appetite. They sported scorpions, spiders, and other insects baked right into them. She ordered the least insect-infested pastry she could find, and relief filled her when she found that tea was a choice.

They took their food to go, eating on the way to the mall. "Ouija Streaks is the hottest clothing store. They sell only the latest and newest trends," Asmo said, squealing and raised his shoulders.

"That sounds interesting," she said.

They entered the mall, which was a majestic three-story structure with escalators inside. A circular fountain was in the center and it sprouted multicolored water in the air. Medium-sized plants gave privacy to the benches around the fountain, hiding conversations. Lining both sides was a variety of shops offering tattoos, piercings, jewelry, clothes, shoes, books, furniture, and more.

"Let's go, we have to go straight to Ouija Streaks," Asmo said, taking her hand.

When they got to the store, he held up clothes, piling them into her arms for her to try on later. *Who knew clothes could be so heavy?* She looked out the storefront window into the interior of the mall and spotted a green-haired demon. *I know him; which one was he again? Urgh, come on, stupid brain, think! Oh, Barbatos the butler.*

"Looks like you have quite the handful there," Barbatos said with a chuckle as he walked up to them.

"Um, yeah. Asmo picked them out for me." She rolled her eyes. "What brings you here?"

"Lord Diavolo has given me the day off, and I decided I would use it to shop," Barbatos said.

"Shopping is a must on days off—it's the best thing to do," Asmodeus said.

"W-why don't you join us today?" Ashton mumbled.

"That's an excellent idea! I was just about to have her go try on these clothes!" Asmo clapped his hands together and gave her a mischievous grin. "Although, I wouldn't mind having her go naked." He licked his bottom lip. She shriveled and took a step away from Asmo, looking at Barbatos.

"It would be my pleasure to shop with you," Barbatos said, bowing.

She tried each item on, getting Asmo's opinion and taking the items of choice to the register. Asmo paid, and they exited the shop. They walked down the pathways, viewing items, and talking about the upcoming year.

She stopped as the glint of sapphire and hazel pulled her to the jewelry-store window. A necklace sported two feathers, a hazel that matched her eyes, and a blue sapphire held together with a gold chain. She couldn't take her eyes off it. "Do you like it?" Barbatos asked, approaching her side.

"Ah," she said, jumping.

"Sorry, my lady. I didn't mean to startle you," Barbatos said as he held his gloved hand to his torso, standing straight.

"N-no, it's all right. Yeah, I do like it, it's really pretty," she said, her eyes still on the necklace.

Barbatos watched as a gleam became present in her eyes and she placed her fingertips gingerly on the glass. Her fingers moved to her jeans pocket, showing two hundred demon dollars. He could tell she was contemplating it, but she took one last look between the money and the necklace before stepping away.

"My lady, would you be opposed to me buying you the necklace?" Barbatos asked her as Asmo grinned.

"Ooo, you must let him buy it for you. That is just so sweet," Asmo said, bringing a dainty hand to his chest.

"It's five hundred demon dollars. I wouldn't feel right if I let someone spend that much money on me," she started saying, but they were already heading for the door.

"Is there anything I can help you with?" the succuba behind the counter asked.

"I'd like to get the necklace in the window, the one with the two feathers," Barbatos said.

"You really shouldn't feel bad, Barbatos wants to. Actually, I think he wants this exchange program to work out for Lord Diavolo's sake. And that would make him happy to make you happy to help the cause." Asmo paused before continuing: "But, that's not the only reason. Because I'm the avatar of lust, I have the ability to see auras. From my experience, humans tend to have dull or weak auras. But not you. Your aura is very bright and vibrant, kind of like the northern star in the Human Realm." Asmodeus tried to explain how her aura, which teetered between bright green and yellow, pulsated off her.

"You're partly correct, Asmodeus. I do want the exchange program to work out for Lord Diavolo's sake, but that isn't the reason I bought this for her," Barbatos told Asmodeus while turning to face Ashton.

He took the necklace out of the box, gesturing for her to turn around. Barbatos whispered in her ear, "I got this because it complements you wonderfully." Her face flushed as she turned, stumbling over her feet but catching herself. "Just as I thought—it truly does complement you," he said, his eyes on her.

"That looks fabulous on you." Asmodeus placed a fake smile on his face and rolled his eyes. His foot tapped the floor, impatient and jealous of the attention she was receiving.

Ashton brushed her hair behind her ear. "Thank you. Here." She reached into her pocket for the demon dollars.

"No, it's a gift," he said as he rejected the money. *Her flustered cheeks were too cute and hard to resist, worth every demon dollar spent to see it. But I must remain composed; it's my duty as a butler of the royal family,* Barbatos thought.

They exited the store, and a heavy weight came upon her shoulders. Her body lurched forward, hitting something hard, and she crashed to the ground. Her eyes went wide as the demon in front of her hovered, turning into its demon form. He grew twice the size; large, curled horns sprouted from his head, and hefty wings sprouted from his back. A growl echoed through the mall. All eyes turned to the scene.

"What do we have here? A human, this should be good," he said, snarling and sniffing the air.

Fear shook her body, breathing heavily, her legs and hands backing her away as the demon came close. "I-I'm sorry, I d-didn't mean to," she said with a stutter.

Crying is a sign of weakness, crying is a sign of weakness, crying is a sign of weakness. Her mind remembered the words Franko programmed into her as a child.

"That's right, tremble in fear," the demon said as it licked its lips.

Barbatos changed into his demon form—antler horns grew from his head, and a double-tipped tail grew from his rear. He jumped over Ashton and blocked the demon's way, shielding her as the demon lunged for her. His grip caught the demon as his tail wrapped around the ankle, throwing it to the ground.

The demon rushed toward Barbatos, landing a punch to his shoulder while his tail wrapped around the demon's torso. He spun around several times before releasing the demon, which went soaring through the air a few hundred feet away. The demon slammed into the fountain, water soaking the floor. Barbatos stood ready, a growl emanating from deep in his throat, but the demon glared and huffed off.

Asmo looked at his nails, making sure they were still perfect before kneeling on the floor beside Ashton. "It's all right, Barbatos took care of him. He's not going to hurt you, and besides, you'll get wrinkles and ruin that beautiful skin of yours."

The lump in her throat refused to be swallowed as she stared ahead of her. Barbatos eased back to his human form and met her eyes, wide and filled with fear. Her lip and hands quivered as her fingertips brushed Barbatos's. His gloved hands enclosed hers. "You're okay." He helped her stand. "Why don't we go to the food court? Sit down for a bit," Barbatos suggested.

"That would be a good idea," Asmo said.

Barbatos released her hand, and she snapped her head toward him. He smiled. "I'm sorry, I didn't mean to upset you. Here, is this better?" He interlocked his fingers with hers, and she nodded.

They made their way to the escalators, and stepping off at the top, she saw a busty brunette grip Asmo's shoulder. She twirled her hair with a well-manicured finger and batted her long, unnatural eyelashes at him.

Ashton watched the succuba lean into his ear, whispering as he burst out giggling. Asmo reached his hand around the succuba's waist, gripping it, and brought her closer to his slim body, whispering back. "They know each other," Barbatos pointed out.

"Oh," Ashton said, uncomfortably.

"My friend here will be joining us for some food. What do we all want?" Asmo asked.

Ashton watched as the succuba whispered into Asmo's ear before reading the signs. "We are going to go to the sandwich booth, meet up with you later," Asmo said as he was dragged away.

"How do you feel about Chinese food?" Ashton asked Barbatos as she brushed her hair behind her ear.

"Sounds delicious."

They got their food, finding a spot to eat. "I hope you enjoyed the welcome feast," he said.

"I did, it was a good chance to meet the others and have a great meal."

"I'm glad you enjoyed it. You seem to be having a good time so far."

"Well . . ."

"Besides the incident earlier, I mean."

"Yes, besides that, I think I'll like it here. Everyone seems nice." She paused, taking a bite and swallowing. "What do you usually like to do in your spare time, besides shopping?"

"I like to bake. I'm teaching Seth how to make delicacies of the Demon Realm."

"Really! Baking is a lot of fun. I enjoy it myself when I have the time."

"What's your favorite dessert?"

"Hmm . . . I'd have to say brownies, which doesn't sound remarkably interesting, but they're my favorite." She chuckled, taking another bite of her meal.

A ding sounded from Barbatos's phone, and he looked at it:

Tell Ashton I'm really sorry, but I won't be able to take her home.

Could you make sure she gets home safely? Asmo ♡

How could he abandon her when he's the one who wanted to go shopping? Leaving her in the mall, a place she doesn't even know? Irresponsible idiot, he thought as his jaw clenched.

"Brownies are quite tasty, and they can be interesting depending on what you put in them. How would you like to join Seth and me for baking today?" Barbatos asked, keeping his composure—he was a well-rounded butler, after all.

"What about Asmodeus? And are you sure Seth would be okay with that? I don't want to interrupt anything and get in the way."

"It won't be a problem, and that was Asmodeus who messaged me. He says to tell you he is sorry, but he won't be able to take you back to the house." He watched her expression fall. "I'm sure Seth would be thrilled if you joined us." He gave her a heartwarming smile, melting her nerves.

"Okay," Ashton said, smiling back at him.

They were making their way to the main entrance when a small hallway appeared to the left. She almost missed it, but movement caught her sight. A succuba was bouncing up and down against the wall, legs wrapped around a waist, and skirt hiked up. Wavy blond hair tickled her neck as lips left marks, a demon's hips thrusting into her.

The succuba looked at Ashton before yellow-orange orbs turned, and Ashton realized it was Asmo. The succuba smirked and brought Asmo's lips to hers. The succuba moaned and gripped Asmo's hair as he thrust faster into her, biting her neck again. Ashton's mind took her back to fifteen:

Cold metal chains enclosed her wrists and ankles; her back lay against soft fabric. Rough movements of Franko's cock made its way into her dry pussy, causing sharp pains to resonate through her body. "Ah, you're so tight!" Franko said.

His cock slammed into her. "This is your punishment, Sangchul. You're going to stand there and watch while I fuck her, knowing you want to. And if I ever catch you talking with her again, I'll kill you."

Her head turned to the side, and Sangchul stood in the corner, watching as their boss defiled her body.

"Ashton?" Barbatos tried to gain her attention, his skin boiling with rage underneath as he followed her gaze. *I'd love to send him to the torture chambers that lie under the castle.* He took a breath. "Ashton?" He placed a hand on her back; she jumped.

"Hmm?"

"Don't pay any attention to them. He's the avatar of lust, although he should have more control over himself. Let's head back to the castle."

She ran her fingers through her hair. "Right, yeah."

Back at the castle, Barbatos and Ashton talked, waiting for Seth to arrive. The door knocker rang through the castle and signaled his arrival. Barbatos opened the door, bowing. Seth's expression lit up. "Ashton! I didn't know you'd be here?"

"If you'll let me, I'd love to join," she said.

"I suppose that'd be okay." He averted his eyes, and his cheeks flushed.

Ashton looked up at Simeon, winking before turning back to Seth. "Thank you."

Barbatos led Seth and Ashton to the kitchen, pointing out that brownies were Ashton's favorite. Seth decided they would make brownies. Barbatos collected the ingredients, Ashton preheated the oven and got the pan ready, and Seth assembled the ingredients. They sat in the common room, sipping tea and talking, waiting for the brownies.

RING RING

They checked on the brownies, placing them on a small tray. They ate, enjoying the sugary taste of sweetness while sipping their tea. "Do you think Lord Diavolo would like one?" Ashton asked.

"I believe he would. Let me prepare a tray, and you can take it to him." Barbatos smiled at her caring behavior, glad that she thought of his master in such a time.

She knocked on Lord Diavolo's office door. "Come in," he said. She opened the door and closed it behind her.

"Hey, we, um, we made brownies and thought you would like some," she said.

"They smell delicious," he said, gesturing for her to sit.

She placed the tray on his desk and took her seat across from him. He picked up a brownie, taking a bite. "So, ah, what d-do you do as a prince? I mean, I-I'm sorry, it's just I've never, never been around ro—" She rubbed the back of her neck, her eyes opening wide.

"It's perfectly okay, ask any question that you would like." He held his hand up. "As a prince, I'm running different parts of the kingdom, learning how to become the future king. There are three classes of demons—the lower demons, the higher demons, and the royals. The difference is their poverty levels, and it's one of my jobs to make sure the needs of all the demons in each class are taken care of." He paused, taking a sip of milk and leaning back in his mahogany chair.

"I have frequent meetings, lunch, and dinners with them, and I host grand balls a few times a year for their entertainment. That way, they can come to me, and I can greet them and send them my blessings, so to speak. There are also dedicated days when I sit on the throne listening to their problems and solve them. And the least favorite part of the job is a lot of paperwork, which is what I have Lucifer help me with."

"Wow, you sound really busy," she said.

"It is a lot of work, and I would lose my head if Barbatos didn't keep track of my schedule for me." He took a bite of the brownie, chasing it down with the cold milk.

"And you still found time to put the exchange program together. It must really mean a lot to you."

"It does mean a lot to me, and I want nothing less than to have the three realms reunited."

There was an energy about him as he spoke the words, such passion and hope for success. *Hmm . . . He must be the strongest demon since he's the prince, yet he's like a teddy bear.* "Well, I-I should get back. I just wanted to bring you a treat," she said, stuttering.

"Of course, thank you for thinking of me." He beamed at her thoughtfulness.

She exited and headed to the common room. Simeon stood talking with Seth and Barbatos as she entered. "How'd he like it, Ashton?" Seth said.

"He loved it and said you did an amazing job," she said.

"I like your necklace, Ashton." Simeon pointed to the spot on his chest where the necklace was on her.

"Oh, thank you, it was a gift from Barbatos," she said as her leg twitched.

"Oh, it's a very lovely choice, and it complements you perfectly," Simeon replied, voice strained, his smile becoming forced. *Calm down, we aren't dating, there is no reason to be jealous. Angel-human relations are strictly off-limits,* he thought.

"That was my thought exactly. Although, she did pick it out herself. It caught her eye as we were walking through the mall today," Barbatos spoke proudly.

"It's lovely," Simeon said. "Shall we get going, Seth? I made dinner while I was waiting."

"Um, Seth, don't forget the brownies we saved specifically for Simeon. I'm sure he would enjoy them very much," she said, catching him as he was leaving.

"I almost forgot!" Seth gave her big puppy-dog eyes.

Ashton watched as Barbatos led Seth back to the kitchen to retrieve the brownies. "I'm glad I got the chance to bake with them today—it was a lot of fun and helped me feel a bit more confident about this place."

"It seems like they both enjoyed having you around," Simeon replied as he looked at her, his stomach now doing that tingly butterfly thing again.

"It wasn't originally planned. Asmo and I were shopping, and we ran into Barbatos. We were headed to the food court when Asmo disappeared with a succuba. That's when he invited me to join in today. He didn't think Seth would mind. But before Asmo ran off, I had an encounter with a demon that wanted to attack me. Turns out they aren't so forgiving when you bump into them," she said as she shrugged her shoulders.

"Are you all right?" His hand reached out without permission and rubbed her arm. She flinched, and he withdrew his hand. "I'm sorry. I-I didn't mean anything by it. I just wanted to make sure you were all right."

"It's okay, I'm just not used to so much positive physical contact. I've only ever been around negative physical contact .

. . I'm all right, though. He didn't hurt me. Barbatos turned into his demon form and fought it."

Why bring that up? Flinching at everything, he probably doesn't like me, anyway. I'm a human, he's an angel, and besides, we only just met! So stupid, but he did seem jealous about the necklace.

"I also don't think Barbatos would have bought the necklace if I'd been able to take my eyes off it," she added. Butterflies scurried in her stomach as Simeon blushed.

"I would've done the same thing if I'd seen you looking at it," he said. A dark shade of red tinted his cheeks, his sapphire eyes connecting to her hazel ones. Blue-and-green energy coursed around them; magnetic forces attracted them to each other. Their lips parted as heavy, hot breaths swirled together, creating an intoxicating aroma.

"Simeon, Simeon, we made brownies today from the Human World since they're Ashton's favorite." Seth rushed into the common room as Simeon and Ashton jolted several feet apart.

"They look delicious. I can't wait to have one after dinner, and I'm sure Adrian would enjoy one as well," Simeon said.

"Simeon, would it be all right if I caught a ride home with you two? That way, Barbatos wouldn't need to make a special trip out," she asked.

"We don't mind giving you a ride," Simeon replied after getting a nod from Seth.

"That's quite kind of you to think of me like that, Ashton. That'd be helpful, as I should see if Lord Diavolo needs anything for the evening," Barbatos replied as he bowed.

A small hum came from the Volkswagen and was intensified by Seth's nonstop talking. Her arm rested between her and Simeon, mere inches apart. Electricity flickered through their bodies, jolting them as bumps in the road brushed their arms together. He looked at her from the corner of his eyes, his core sprinted like a rabbit, and his mind rebuked his body for betraying his oath to the archangels.

Simeon parked the car in front of the house, everyone exiting. Seth gave her a hug and she returned it, surprised. "Thanks for baking with us," Seth said.

"I should be thanking you for letting me join," she replied.

Simeon escorted her to the door.

"Thank you for the ride home," she said.

"Just let me know if you need anything. I'm more than happy to help," he replied.

They lingered on the porch, anxious of what might happen, the earlier energy flooding the air. *Don't become attached to a demon and certainly not a human*—archangel Michael's voice echoed in his mind. *Put up a wall, put up a wall,* he repeated to himself. He took a step to leave, and she lunged, tightly embracing his neck.

He closed his eyes, hugging her tightly; a smell drifted, and he sniffed. "Cherry blossoms."

"It's my shampoo," she said.

"It smells nice," he said. Her shampoo and scent went right to his groin, and he struggled to keep his serenity.

"Thanks."

She released him and made her way inside. He let out a pained breath before heading to the car. He drove home, not hearing anything Seth said. *What was that back at the castle? That pull was intense, not able to break free from it. And her scent, cherry blossoms, I've never been this drawn to anyone. Michael said not to get attached to anyone, but that pull made it hard. The best way would be to avoid her,* he thought.

Ashton flopped onto the bed. *That was strange; I've never felt anything like that pull. What does it mean? Simeon is kind, sweet, and wow. Attracted to him . . . That can't be right, can it?*

7

REDWING DEVILS' ACADEMY

Ashton eyed the knee-length black skirt and burgundy dress-shirt with a maroon button-up cardigan. She tugged the school uniform on and put her hair in Pippi Longstocking braids before heading downstairs to the dining room. The seven brothers stared at her as she entered, and Lucifer gestured to the seat beside him.

"Redwing Devils' Academy is the top school for higher-class demons," he explained as she took her seat. "Lord Diavolo has entered you in the classes you'll be taking. You have demon history with Beelzebub, angel studies with Simeon, and then you'll be in the last two classes on your own for demon physiology and angel physiology. Your books are in my office. I'll bring them down before you leave."

"Okay," she said as she grabbed what looked like toast.

She packed her books in the bag Lucifer gave her, and Beelzebub waited by the door. She walked behind the orange-haired demon and tried to stay out of the other demons' ways as they passed her. A growl sounded, and Beelzebub brought his hands to his stomach. "I hope they still have food in the cafeteria. I'm hungry."

"But y-you just ate," she said.

"I know, but I'm hungry again. I want food."

They walked through the double doors of the school and came upon a stone staircase leading to countless classrooms and hallways. "Our class is over here," Beelzebub said. He led her down three corridors and into a classroom with four long wooden tables, two on each side. The rows in the back were raised, and light flittered through windows on the side. "You can sit next to me, and we are using this book." He went to his seat and showed her the textbook.

Class ran an hour and a half, and when it was finished, a bell rang through the room. She followed Beelzebub out of the room to where Seth, Adrian, and Simeon stood talking. "Ashton! You have angel studies with Simeon next, and that's right next to my classroom. I have to take a child version, which I don't think is fair," Seth said, pouting and wrinkling his forehead.

"I'm Adrian," he said, holding his hand out for hers. "It's nice to meet you up close and not from across a table."

"You, too," she said, reaching out and shaking his warm hand with her clammy one. Her eyes moved to Simeon, and he gave her a weak smile that didn't reach his eyes.

"We should all get to class," Simeon said as he began moving down the corridor. She grimaced and followed a few steps behind him. She waved to Seth and Adrian as they continued down the corridor.

The room held two rows of stone walls in a semicircle for seats and pillows. Vines with flowers grew on the walls, and she took the seat closest to her while Simeon sat on the far side. She took out her textbook and tried to pay attention, but her eyes kept darting to Simeon. His forehead creased, and a frown was present.

Just focus on the teacher and not on Ashton's braids. James 1:14-15 says, "But each person is tempted, when he is lured and enticed by his own desire. Then desire when it has conceived gives birth to sin, and sin when it is fully grown brings forth death." Just ignore her. Simeon struggled as he listened to the teacher.

The bell echoed through the room, and he walked right past her to his next class. "What's wrong?" Adrian asked as he waited for her outside the room.

"N-nothing, do you know where these rooms are?" Ashton asked, pointing to the piece of paper.

"I'm taking classes beside them. You can walk with me."

They walked down the corridor and up a flight of stairs, paintings of old principals hung on the walls. "What did you do in the Human Realm, before you came here?" she asked as they rushed to class.

"I was an apothecary who sold potions, spells, and other ingredients. It allowed me to be able to practice my potions and magic," he said. "Well, that's a shame the walk was too short. Your classroom is right here, but maybe we could get together and work on some homework soon?"

"Yeah, that sounds like a lot of fun," she said, nodding. "And thanks for showing me where my classes are."

The last two classes went smoothly, and Lucifer met her outside of angel physiology. They walked home, and Lucifer asked her about her day. She explained her timidness in the new environment and was glad he asked. *Is he asking because he cares, or because it is his duty to Lord Diavolo?* When they reached the grand Victorian house, Lucifer went to his study, and she walked to her room to start her homework.

A week passed, and Lucifer had her on the dinner rotation after Belphegor, who usually bought dinner since he was too tired to cook. She wasn't used to cooking for so many people but was thankful she had to cook only three times a month.

At school, the other demons stayed away from her, since she was accompanied by either one or more of the brothers, Seth or Adrian, at all times. Redwing Devils' Academy wasn't that bad, except when she saw Simeon. She saw him in the corridors at school and tried to talk with him, but he'd disappear before she got the chance. When she left her demon history course, Simeon no longer joined Seth and Adrian while waiting. *Did I do something wrong?* she thought as the excited, jumpy angel and the mellow sorcerer walked her to class each day. When she walked into her angel study classes, he'd be sitting, smiling. Their eyes would meet, and he would look away, closing his legs tightly.

The days began to merge, and she stood outside the principal's office, where her meeting with Lord Diavolo and Lucifer was. Her hand found the doorknob, and when she went to open it, she saw blue eyes looking at her. The eyes fell to the cobblestone flooring, fists clenched at Simeon's sides.

"Was there something wrong, my lady? Lord Diavolo is waiting for you," Barbatos said as he bowed.

"No, nothing's wrong. Sorry about that." She went through the door and walked to the desk.

"Ah, Ashton, are you ready for your monthly checkup?" Lord Diavolo asked, his sweet voice sounding from behind the desk.

"Yes." She took the seat opposite him.

"Good, now Lucifer tells me that you've been doing a lot of studying to keep up with your homework. How's that going?"

"It's a bit difficult at times, but nothing that I can't manage," she replied.

"Have you considered asking Satan for help? He's one of the better brothers for studying," Lord Diavolo pointed out.

"I haven't asked yet, but I've gone to Adrian's a few times to study. He was pretty helpful," she said.

"So, your academics are going well, but what about your social life? That's important as an exchange student," Lord Diavolo asked as he looked over at Lucifer.

Her leg shook with nerves as she answered: "Oh, um. I guess I could be a bit more open to a social life, but the brothers keep me busy and want me to do a lot of things with them."

"And you said that you've been spending time with Adrian. What about Seth and Simeon?" Lord Diavolo asked.

"Seth and I go on walks sometimes when our homework is done. He actually showed me a lot of pretty places around here," she said.

"And how do you feel the exchange program is going? Is there anything that should be changed?" Lord Diavolo asked with his eyebrow raised.

"Well, there is one thing. Maybe not have so much insect-infested foods," she said as she averted her eyes, embarrassed. "It's just, in the Human Realm, we aren't used to eating things with insects, that's all."

Lord Diavolo boomed with laughter. "Duly noted. I think that we can handle that!" It took him several moments to settle down. "I think you're fitting in nicely, and that concludes the meeting. Barbatos, would you mind taking Ashton back home? Lucifer and I have some business to attend to."

"It would be my pleasure, my lord." Barbatos placed his gloved hand on his torso and bowed. "Whenever you're ready, my lady."

8

TO SIN OR NOT TO SIN

Simeon spent months avoiding Ashton. He saw her in the halls at school, turning around, not making eye contact. Somehow, he always had others around to distract him from her. In the one class they had together, he sat far away, leaving as soon as the bell rang. The house he stayed in was his sanctuary—a safe zone, where he could collect himself.

"It's right this way, Ashton," Adrian said.

"Okay, are we doing spells or potions today?" she asked.

"I was thinking potions, there's a new one I wanted to try," he said.

"Which one is that?"

"It's a color-changing potion. It's supposed to turn things distinct colors, depending on the pigmentations one puts in it."

"Oh, hey, Ashton. I didn't know you were coming over today," Seth said as he popped his head out of his room.

"Well, I couldn't say no when Adrian asked," she said, chuckling.

"I'm sure Simeon will be thrilled to see you—let me go get him," Seth said.

"I don't know, Seth. He doesn't seem to want to talk to me lately," she said.

"I don't think that's the issue," Adrian said.

"What do you mean?" she asked.

Simeon quickly opened the door to his room, meeting Ashton, Adrian, and Seth as he heard Adrian draw closer to his true feelings—what he'd been fighting against since he met Ashton for the first time. "Hi, hey," he said.

"H-hey," she said.

"Well, I'll meet you in my room. I'm going to go set up the potions. Which color did you want to try?" Adrian asked.

"Hmm, how about blue?" she asked.

"Perfect, I'll get it set up." Adrian left, tugging Seth along with him.

Simeon and Ashton watched as Adrian and Seth disappeared, and a heavy anxiety filled the air. "So . . ." Ashton said, rubbing the back of her neck, her back pressed against the wall as she looked at the wooden flooring.

"H-how have you been?" he asked.

"I've been all right." Her hand reached for her feather necklace, twirling it.

"That's the one Barbatos got you, the necklace," Simeon said, jealousy lacing his tone. *It's for the better; she's better off with him. How can that be? Better with a demon than an angel?* he thought.

"Yes, it's the one that Barbatos got me. I wear it a lot," she said.

"That's good. He's good for you," Simeon said.

"I guess. He's becoming a close friend, which I've never had. He often invites me over for tea." She bit her bottom lip. "I should go, Adrian's probably done setting up."

"Oh, okay."

He watched her walk down the hall to Adrian's room, disappearing. His head pressed against the door frame as he tried to get hold of himself. He closed the door, pacing the room. His chest fell in heavy beats, hair disheveled from his sweeping hands, and her laughter vibrating through the walls.

What are these feelings? Jealousy toward Barbatos for giving her that necklace, anger toward Adrian for bringing her over, and confusion? Love, anger, jealousy, fear, sin—all which surge through the body, leaving it trembling. It's the first time I've ever wanted to go against the angel laws. First time I've recognized love. First time for wanting to kiss someone, more than just kiss. What are these thoughts? Lust? No, not lust. Love, he concluded within his thoughts.

Fight against the feeling, fight against the sensation. Don't give in, he thought. "Ah, I spilled some!" Ashton's voice came through the walls. Simeon raced for the wall closest to Adrian's within his room. His palm and forehead rested on cold, unyielding wood. His soul yearned to be near her, for him to stop resisting.

"It worked!" she said, squealing.

"I'm sorry, archangel Michael, but I can't fight this anymore. I need to know her, to be near her!" he said, speaking aloud his defeat.

He stepped out of his room and waited in the living room for her. Adrian and Ashton walked out of the room, laughing at their success. Simeon looked toward them, swallowing the lump in his throat. "Well, it was great having you over, Ashton, but I think I'm going to go clean up now," Adrian said.

"But I—," she started to say, but he was already gone.

"I can drive you home," Simeon said.

"O-okay." She walked toward the door, and he followed.

"Ashton," Simeon started to say.

"Hmm."

He reached out and brushed her arm. She stopped and pulled her arm away. "Ashton, I'm sorry. I-I didn't mean to shut you out, I just had to work through some stuff. A-and I was c-curious if y-you would like to go on a date, with me," he said with a stutter.

"You spent months avoiding me. Now you want to go on a date?" she asked incredulously. "What exactly did you have to figure out that took months, when right from the beginning there was electricity?"

"It's a sin, and I'm an angel. I struggled with not sinning by being attracted to you. Angel-human relations aren't allowed, and Michael will strip me of my wings for this. That's why I denied it, but I-I can't anymore." He let out a shaky breath and raked his fingers through his hair. "I've never had feelings for anyone else before." He lowered his head and swallowed the lump in his throat as he spoke.

"I won't be the reason you lose your wings. I'll find a new way home, thanks." She turned and ran down the steps. He ran after her, grabbing her wrist. "Please, I don't care about my wings, let me love you," he said.

"I've never been close to anyone, so I don't know how to do that."

His hand caressed her cheek. "Then let me show you how I can care for you, cherish you, and love you." His eyes moved between hers as he waited with anticipation.

Her heart skipped a beat. "One date. We'll go from there," she said.

"Okay, I can do that, and I'm so sorry for hurting you." He let out the breath he held while his fingers caught a strand of silky-smooth blue hair. "The blue, it's lovely." He smiled. "Let me take you home," he said.

CR♥ઠ

Simeon paced his room, racking his brain about what to do for their date. It was coming up quickly, and he didn't have any idea of what to do yet. *Think, think.* A light bulb flashed above his head, and he ran from his room. He knocked on Adrian's door. "Adrian, can I get your help on something?"

"Sure, what is it?" Adrian replied, opening the door.

"You've been talking about a device that can transform a room or something?"

"Yeah, you set it on the floor, and it projects a scene around you. It puts you into a whole new place. It can even allow someone to act out plays as if they were real."

"What if there were a boat, would you be able to use the boat to move down a small stream?"

"In theory, yes. What were you thinking?"

Simeon told Adrian what his thoughts were, and Adrian accepted the challenge. A few days passed, and Simeon anxiously awaited the device. The day before the date, Adrian knocked on Simeon's door, handing him the device and showing him how to use it. His body shook as he paced the room. *It's my first-ever date. She said one date, and then she would see from there. I better not mess this up.*

Ashton used the curling iron, creating long, soft waves in her hair, and put on the final additions of eye shadow and lip gloss when a knock sounded. Her nerves shook as she made her way to the common room. Lucifer sat, talking with Simeon, and they looked over when she came in.

Simeon's mouth dropped open, his mind blown by her beauty. "Wow." Blue shoes, black tights, a gorgeous blue dress that went to her calves, and a thin sweater that covered her arms. He sat frozen, unable to take his eyes off her.

Lucifer looked at Simeon's expression, chuckled to himself, and walked over to Ashton. "You look splendid," he said as he placed a kiss on the top of her head. "Don't keep her out too late, and if you hurt her, you'll have me to answer to." He disappeared into his study as Simeon stood up, shaking on his way to her. She bit her bottom lip, looking at the rug.

"Y-you look amazing," Simeon said.

"Thank you."

He held the door open for her, opening her car door as well. They drove down the highway, light music playing in the background. Trees lined both sides of the road, a clearing opened ahead, and Simeon pulled into it.

He opened her car door, reaching in the back seat to grab a picnic basket and the device. She eyed him curiously as he led her farther into the clearing. He placed the device on the ground, pressing the button Adrian told him to.

She spun around, mouth wide open, mesmerized by the bright atmosphere. Clear blue skies peeked out from bright, plush pink flowers. Petals floated through the air to be swept away by the slow-moving river. A gondola swayed in the faint waves, awaiting departure. Cherry-blossom trees bordered the river, and plush pink shimmered a pathway through the water.

"H-how is this possible? And how'd you know that cherry blossoms are my favorite?" she asked.

"Adrian spent the week building it, and your scent smells like cherry blossoms. So, I guessed. D-do you like it?"

"Yes, yes I love it."

"Shall we?" He held out his hand to her and helped her onto the gondola, unable to take his eyes off her.

They drifted along the river as she watched the petals fall. He smiled, watching her, the shimmer from the blossoms reflected in her eyes. His hand reached over, brushing the flowing hair out of her face. A gentle breeze sent a shiver down her spine. He shrugged out of his jacket; scooting closer, he draped it over her shoulders. "Here, take this, it'll keep you warm."

She turned, their lips inches from each other. "Thank you."

"You're welcome." His eyes darted from her lips to her eyes and back to her lips. Their breath intertwined, enticing them, causing the boat to rock, and she fell into his lap. "Are you all right?" he asked.

Her hand rested on the side of the gondola, helping her readjust, the sleeve of her sweater bunched up. His hands went around her waist, helping her reclaim her seat as white marks came into view. "What's that?" His fingers went to her arm when she was settled.

She went pale and rigid. "It's nothing," she said as she quickly pulled her sleeve down.

His forehead creased as concern coursed through him. "Did you—"

"NO!"

Her fingers curled, tightening around the wooden seat, breathing heavily as she watched the pink trees. Noticing her reaction, his fingers brushed against hers, and hers tightened around the wood even more.

"Are you hungry? I packed a picnic," he whispered.

She nodded, taking in a few deep breaths before turning to him. "Yeah."

He began setting up the picnic when her hand clasped his; her face was fallen, and he knelt in front of her.

"I didn't, I didn't hurt myself. I promise," she whispered.

Her eyes hold so much pain, and I long to understand her. "It's okay. I believe you." His arms engulfed her, one on her lower back, the other on her head. "I believe you."

"I just don't talk about what he did to me." She snuggled into his chest, and her arms snaked around his waist.

"We don't have to talk about it, but if you want to, I'm here to listen."

"Okay. We should eat now."

"Let me finish setting it up."

"I can help."

She knelt beside him in the gondola, helping to set up an arrangement of items. The cloth covered the wooden bench in front of them—sandwiches, grapes, cheese, crackers, coconut macarons, and a bottle of sparkling cider placed on the bench.

"We should play a game while we eat," she suggested.

"What game?"

"I think it's called Would You Rather."

"Hmm, sounds interesting. How do you play?"

"Let's see if I can get this right. Asmo tried to teach it to me awhile ago. So, we go back and forth asking each other questions. Like, I'd ask, would you rather eat spicy food or sweet food? And then you'd answer." She plopped a grape in her mouth and watched him as he answered.

"I like both, but if I had to pick, it'd have to be sweet."

"Good choice. Now it's your turn to ask me."

"Would you rather receive a necklace or a bracelet?" *Does she really like the necklace Barbatos got her so much? She's wearing it again today, and it's making me jealous.*

"I like necklaces more, but I'd rather receive a bracelet."

"Why is that?" he asked.

"I have a challenging time picking out bracelets for myself. Okay, would you rather hold hands with someone or cuddle with someone?" She looked away, nervous.

"I wouldn't mind both, but I like cuddling more. Would you rather stay over there alone, or have me hold you?" He rubbed the back of his neck, holding his breath.

Her hands shook as she shifted, moving closer to him, her forehead connecting to his chest. She twirled, her back landing on his chest and her head on his shoulder. "I'd rather have you hold me."

His arms wrapped around her waist. "You're shaking. Are you okay?" he asked.

"Do you remember when I first arrived, you went to pick Seth up from the castle?"

"Yes."

"I mentioned that I wasn't used to the positive physical contact—well, that's still true. I-I get nervous with physical contact. But I want this . . . us."

"We can stop at any time, whatever you're comfortable with."

"We could just stay like this and let the water drift us for a while."

"I like that idea," he said while smiling.

"Oh, and yes, we can go on more dates," she said.

"I want us, too," he whispered in her ear while she watched the trees sway in the soft wind. *I don't care if I'm stripped of my wings. If it means I get to spend my life with her, then I'll gladly give them up. I'm sorry, archangel Michael, for I have sinned.*

9

INVITE

Ashton's knuckles rapped on Lucifer's study door. A faint "Come in" sounded, and she opened the door. "Ashton, is everything all right? It's late, you should be in bed by now." Lucifer looked up from the mountain of paperwork in front of him. "Please, have a seat."

The room was partially dark, light coming from only a lamp near the desk. The armchair gave slightly as she sat across from Lucifer. "Hey, you seem busy as always," she said.

"Yes, it never ends. But you didn't come in here to talk about paperwork, did you?"

"No, I just wanted to get your permission to invite Seth, Adrian, and Simeon over for dinner tomorrow night. It's my turn to cook, and I thought they might like to join."

"If you'd like to invite them, then go for it. But why ask so late at night?"

"I thought a little stroll would help me sleep better."

"Have you not been sleeping well?" He folded his hands over his chest, leaning back.

"Eah, it's nothing. It happens from time to time. Well, I should go and try to sleep. Thank you for letting me invite them over."

10

NIGHTMARE

The blankets were thrown off her, legs kicking the air, arms flailing as she bolted up, a bloodcurdling scream escaping her throat. Lucifer jolted awake, racing for her room; he saw the other brothers do the same. A growl sounded from him, halting his brothers, and he cracked the door open. Ashton's arms were wrapped around her knees. She was staring ahead, rocking and shaking.

Lucifer walked over, kneeling on the floor, and he heard his brothers file in, keeping a distance. His fingertips brushed against her arm. "Please, please, Franko, please. I've been good. N-no, no don't whip me," she muttered. Her hands flew to her ears, covering a noise that Lucifer couldn't hear.

"Satan, put on some soothing piano music, something to drown out the silence," he whispered, not taking his eyes off her. He chanced sitting on the bed; it dipped beneath him, and he rubbed her arms, holding her. Soft melodies began to play.

Her muttering stopped, her breathing slowed, and she saw everyone's worried expression.

"A-are you all right?" Beelzebub asked in a concerned voice, low and raspy.

"There was a scream, it scared me. That can't be good for your complexion," Asmodeus added.

"Ya scared me there, not that I would care. It's just I was having a dream about money, and then I was interrupted by the scream," Mammon said.

She flinched as she felt the rubbing sensation. She saw Lucifer behind her. "It's just me," he said.

"I'm good, everyone, it was just a nightmare," she said, her voice cracking. Clearing her throat, she tried again. "I mean it, I'm all right—you don't need to be concerned. You can all go back to your rooms."

"Are you sure?" Satan asked. Their eyes met, and her silent plea reached him. He knew how important it was to be alone at times, often needing to be alone himself when his anger got bad. The others followed, except Lucifer. She looked over at him, and his terrified expression almost made her heart break. His eyes were filled with so much pain and desperation for her to be okay.

"Who's Franko?" he asked.

She burrowed into his chest, hiding her face.

"Did he hurt you? Is that why you flinch when people touch you?" Lucifer said, continuing.

"I don't. I . . ." Her arms gripped his neck. "I don't talk about it. Please, don't make me."

His eyes closed in pain, arms tightening around her. "Okay," he said. "Why don't you lie down and try to get some sleep. I'll be right here."

Her grip loosened, and she lay down. Lucifer began to stand up, and a death grip crushed his hand. "I'm just going to cover you up, and then I'm going to sit right here. Watch over you." The hand plopped on the bed, he tucked her in, and she scooted over, gesturing for him to join. He lay down beside her, and she nestled into his chest.

The next morning, she rolled over, stretching her arms out, connecting her hand with Lucifer's head. "Ow," he said.

"Hmm? Oh, oh yeah. I had a nightmare last night," she mumbled.

"Are you doing better?" He propped up on his elbow, and as he tried to stroke her cheek, she flinched. "I won't hurt you."

She searched his eyes, and he stroked her cheek, his red eyes showing how much he cared. "Simeon is lucky to have you return his feelings."

"We aren't dating. And besides, I thought you and Lord Diavolo were an item."

"You aren't? I thought you two had gone on a date," Lucifer said, clearly ignoring her observation of him and his lover.

"We have, but he hasn't officially asked to go on a second date or for me to be his girlfriend." Ashton averted her eyes.

"He will, he's just taking his time." He kissed the top of her head. "How're your classes going?"

"This early in the morning, and you want to ask about classes? Urgh ... they're going well. And I have a meeting with you and Lord Diavolo next week."

"You're right, come on, let's get up. You invited guests over for dinner tonight." They stood, and Lucifer left, letting her get changed in private.

Later that afternoon, she went to the kitchen and began preparing dinner. She placed each ingredient on the counter before reading the recipe she found online. Not much for seafood, but shrimp was delicious, and combining it with macaroni—*how could it go wrong?*

The oven preheated as she prepared the stuffed shells with shrimp. When ready, she opened the oven door and placed them on the rack. She chopped the vegetables, placing them in the garden salad.

She finished cleaning the counters and was just about to start the dessert when Simeon appeared in the kitchen. "Hey," she said with a smile.

"Hey, snowflake. Want some help?"

"No, you're my guest."

"I don't mind—it would mean I get to be close to you."

"Fine," she said with a laugh. "I'll ask if you can borrow Lucifer's apron."

She dragged him up the stairs to Lucifer's study, entering without knocking. Lucifer looked up, surprised. "Ashton, Simeon," Lucifer said.

"Would it be all right if Simeon uses your apron?" she asked as she side hugged him, nestling into him. Lucifer watched in amazement at how she didn't flinch with Simeon.

"Of course, just wash it afterward."

"Thank you," she said, making her way out the door with Simeon.

"Simeon," Lucifer said, raising his voice.

Simeon and Ashton stopped, looking at Lucifer. "If it's all right with you, I'd like to chat with you for a few minutes," Lucifer said.

"I'll be right down," he said, brushing the hair out of her eyes.

"Okay, I'll get the apron," she said.

She disappeared down the stairs, tending to dinner. Simeon closed the door behind him and approached Lucifer's desk. "Do you really like her?" Lucifer asked.

"Yes, I do." Simeon's forehead creased at the sudden question.

"I make it a point to not get involved in other people's business, but seeing how she has grown on me, I have to. You haven't made things official yet, why?"

"I've been trying to find the right time, and when I do, my nerves get in the way."

"She likes you, a lot. I see how she reacts to you and how she acts with everyone else, and it's different. She doesn't flinch with you."

"She does, usually when I make the first move."

"That's an interesting point. I wanted to let you know that she had a nightmare last night, but I'm not sure if it was a nightmare or a memory of something that's happened to her in the past. She was mumbling about a person named Franko and how she'd been good, not wanting him to whip her."

"Those must be the marks on her arms. When we were on a date, her sleeve came up, and I could see scars, white bumps, on her arms. I asked, but she shut me out. I'll keep an eye on her."

"And I also want to be up front that last night, when she had her nightmare, I did stay with her in the same bed. She clung on to me, and I helped her get back to sleep."

"Thank you for helping. I should get back to her—she's probably wondering where I am." Simeon stood up and left the study.

She mixed all the ingredients together and began to stir. When Simeon approached, she handed him the apron, and he put it on, asking, "Want me to stir?"

"Sure." She handed him the bowl, allowing him to take over. The timer went off, and she took the shells out of the oven, getting the pan ready with liners for the cupcakes. When she finished, she went over to Simeon, lifting herself onto the counter.

Her finger dipped into the batter, plopping a drop onto Simeon's nose as laughter filled the halls. "Hey," he said.

"Got you."

He dipped his finger in the batter, placing the bowl on the counter as he went in for his attack. She squealed, her hands and legs becoming a barrier to block the attack. His free hand tickled her while the other went in for the blow, streaking her cheek with cupcake batter.

"That's no fair," she said, giggling.

"There's no rule saying I can't tickle you," he said.

She leaned forward, hugging him. His hair tickled her neck and she pulled back, their eyes meeting, electricity flying between them. A magnetic pull brought them closer, their lips almost touching. "What's that smell? It smells good," Beelzebub said, sniffing the kitchen entrance. They pulled away, and Simeon stepped back, grabbing a towel to wipe the batter off his nose. "What were you two doing?" Beelzebub asked.

"N-nothing," they said with a stutter in unison. Beelzebub looked them over.

"Food's done, if you wouldn't mind getting everyone. Please," she said.

"Okay." Beelzebub headed for the stairs, yelling for his brothers.

She looked over at Simeon as he brought the towel to her cheek. She quickly kissed his cheek, hopping off the counter, and filling the cupcake liners. He froze. She placed the cupcakes in the oven, setting the timer and going to the fridge. With the salad bowl in her hand, she placed it in front of Simeon. "Sunshine, would you take over while I get the pan?" she asked.

"Sunshine?" he asked.

"D-do you not like it?"

"I do, yes, I do. It just took me by surprise, is all."

"You call me your snowflake, so I figured you could be my sunshine." Heat rose to her cheeks, shyness coming over her.

"I like it."

He brought over the salad bowl, she collected the pans, setting the table, and everyone filed in. They sat there, eating, reveling in the meal that she made. The flavors mixed majestically—the crisp snap of the shrimp when biting down, and the cheesy shell enveloping the taste buds with delight.

RING RING

"Vanilla cupcakes," Beelzebub said as he sniffed the air, sweet vanilla aroma meeting his sense of smell. "One of my favorites."

She went to check on them, taking them out so they could cool before she returned to the table. The demon brothers were arguing about how good the cupcakes would taste without frosting, while others agreed they would be good either way. They continued to argue, and Ashton looked over at Simeon. He smiled, and she leaned in, whispering in his ear, "When everyone is done, could you help me in the kitchen?" He nodded. "Thanks, sunshine." He flushed.

When they finished eating, they cleared the table, and Simeon helped Ashton in the kitchen. They brought out trays with different-colored frosting, sprinkles, candies, and marshmallows, placing them in the center of the table.

"What is this supposed to be?" Mammon asked.

"Build your own cupcakes. Everyone takes some of the toppings, and they decorate their cupcake however they want. I found the idea online, it looked neat."

"Wow, seriously? We get to design our own cupcakes? That's so cool," Seth said.

"Creative, I like it," Adrian said.

"Ooo, I'm going to make mine the most fashionable," Asmo said.

"Maybe I'll try to make a book," Satan said.

She watched as they created their own special designs. Idle chitchat filled the room, and laughter caught her ears. Her hand reached under the table, feeling for Simeon's, intertwining as he took a bite of the rainbow he made. She smiled, genuinely happy to have such amazing friends.

II

PORCELAIN

The streets hummed with chatter as demons passed, window shopping on the dimly lit streets of town. White vines and roses shone on the clear window, which read Devil Rose Teas with the catch line "Specialty in the devilishes tea," along with an image of a steaming cup of tea beside it.

The door jingled as Simeon held it open for Ashton. *Such the gentleman,* she thought. "Thank you," she said as she entered, taking a few steps forward. Simeon closed the door, stepping in and placing a hand on the small of her back. She leaned her forehead against his chest, closing her eyes for a moment, and sighed.

They looked around the store, which was split into three sections. Large clear bins were lined up ten in one row; a couple of feet above were another ten and then a third. Loose-leaf tea was visible in each container, the labels on top sporting the names. The stand beside them held small square tins, large circular tins, and boxes into which to scoop the loose tea.

Display lights hung from the ceiling on the back wall, which sported tea cupboards. The bottom held overstock while the top had one-foot squares, piled five high. Each cubby held its own version of bagged tea in metal and boxes.

Tea sets were spotted to their right. All kinds for afternoon tea, high tea, tea parties for children, special-occasion tea sets, and more. She was mesmerized by them, her mind taking her back to twenty-five:

"The house is all done, it's all yours. Just the way you wanted," the contractor said.

"Thank you," she said.

He dropped the keys into her hand and they landed lightly in her palm. She walked to the door and opened it. She sat on the couch, scrolling through things to buy for the house, when a tea set came on the screen.

Tea sets made from porcelain are delicate; they can easily break. Even so, they are tough and demand a certain elegance, respect. They were she, and she was they, she thought. With one click, the porcelain tea set was on its way.

"There's the perfect spot for them. Easily visible while I'm training, and I can get a new one each year. To remind me that I'm not my past," she said to herself in the empty training room.

Simeon watched as she stared at the tea sets. "Do you like them?" Simeon asked.

"Hmm?" She shook her head, coming back to the present.

"Are you all right? You look pale." He brought the back of his fingers to her cheek, sliding them across the warm skin.

Her eyes moved to his. "I'm good."

"Okay, well, I asked if you liked the tea sets, since you were staring at them." He pointed at the tea sets.

"I do like them. I just remembered the ones I got back in the Human Realm, that's all." She shrugged her shoulders and bit her bottom lip.

"Does seeing them make you homesick? We could take a trip to the Human Realm if it does."

"No, it doesn't make me homesick. It's just I get a new tea set each year on a specific date. I almost forgot that it was coming up. February fifth."

"Is there a reason you get a new one each year?"

Her voice trembled as she said, "It reminds me of how they and I are similar. But I don't talk about it, just like the white marks." She smiled and let out a deep sigh, making her way to the loose-leaf tea.

Simeon watched her. *I was always taught to be kind, to love, to be patient, to care for not just the angels but all species. Most of all, I was taught to be obedient, to follow the rules at all costs no matter how it made me feel. All these centuries, I was content with it, until I met her.*

He dropped the subject and followed her to the loose-leaf tea. He read the labels, eyes darting to her every so often. They were always close, almost touching when they were together. But here, she placed distance between them. *It must've been bad, her past. Why wasn't there an angel there for her?*

There was a teacup of an ocean-blue shade with dark-blue and pink flowers on it. The pink flower petals supported a small bee. Unlike the teacup and saucer, the teapot, sugar bowl, and creamer pitcher were white with blue and pink roses. The tops and handles were all lined with gold, crafting the perfect combination of colors. Very pleasing and captivating to the eyes.

He looked back at her as she picked up a small metal container and filled it with "Lavender me sleep." He caught a glimpse of the description, "gives off a calming sensation throughout the body. Relaxing it so much it puts you to sleep." *Hmm, Lucifer said she had been waking up with nightmares,* he thought as he read the labels.

Ashton looked at Simeon as she finished placing the lid on her tea. *Maybe I was too harsh. He didn't know it was a touchy subject. Nobody knows, except for what I tell them, which isn't much. I try to avoid the topic as much as possible. I should apologize, he looks really worried,* she thought as she watched him.

He collected two small metal containers, filling them with tea, when a soft thud landed on his shoulder. "I'm sorry. I shouldn't have brushed you off like that," she said.

He placed his index finger under her chin, lifting her eyes to his. "There isn't anything to be sorry for, you did nothing wrong."

"I did. I was curt with you and walked away. I could've used a more polite approach to let you know I didn't want to talk about it."

His thumb caressed her cheek. "I've had people do meaner things to me than being curt. In fact, there was this one time, before I became an archangel, that I was sent to help this soul. This soul was very angry and abusive, but he didn't mean to be, so I was there to help him get back on the right path. Well, I was about to place my hand on his shoulder to send a calming sensation through him, when his hand came up and whammed me in the nose—"

"So, wait, when you're on an assignment, then the soul you're helping can see you? Did you bleed? Were you okay?" Her mouth gaped with worry as she searched his sapphire eyes.

He chuckled and said, "The soul can't see me, because I'm like a hallucination. However, when I perform a charm, like my healing one, then I become solid for a moment. He just picked that precise moment and accidentally hit me. My hands flew to my nose 'cause it hurt, but I was able to perform a healing charm on myself, and then on the soul." He gave her a one-armed hug. "Why don't we move on to the next section?"

"Okay. And I'm glad you weren't hurt too badly." She blushed, and the edges of her lips curled up.

Simeon's calm demeanor was like nothing she was used to. It drew her in, and she wanted more. The moments they had were nice—yes, she flinched, but she still allowed them. They let them naturally happen and embraced them; she was always strong and by herself, and now she and Simeon were close. But the year anniversary of her escape was coming up. *Maybe I'll come back and pick up the tea set,* she thought as they made their way to the bagged tea.

"You look disappointed. Were you hoping they would have a specific kind?" Simeon asked, noticing her hunched shoulders.

"Yeah, I was hoping they'd have licorice spice. It's my favorite."

"I've never heard of that one before, which is unusual, since I've tasted a lot of teas."

"It's a rare tea to find, but it has a strong licorice aftertaste. I may have to go online and order some from the

Human Realm." She shrugged and placed her head on his shoulder, and his hand snaked around her waist. His heart picked up and he blushed. "Did you find anything you wanted?" she asked.

"I did, but I'll come back later for them. I think, for now, I'll stick with these two." He held the two metal containers up, and she smiled at him.

"Were we going to check out the tea sets?" she asked.

"Only if you want to." His insides shook with worry as he fought to keep a calm demeanor.

"Yes, I do want to check them out." She headed in the direction of the tea sets. "I saw one earlier, it was blue. It'd be a good addition to the others."

They stood in front of the blue tea set, and her eyes radiated from the sight of it. A pull connected her to the porcelain. She knew how it'd sound, but the symbolism between the porcelain and her identity was strong and real. She mumbled to herself, "I won't break"—her hand reached out, tracing the outline of a flower on the teacup—"and neither will you. We were made strong . . ." She trailed off, pulling her hand away, lost in the moment.

Simeon looked at her from the corner of his eye. He watched as she compared herself to the porcelain, not knowing what she truly meant by it. He wasn't sure whether she was aware he could hear her, but he didn't mention it.

Lucifer said there was a man named Franko in her nightmares. She cried out for him not to whip her, and the marks on her arms— she won't show anyone. And she flinches when she doesn't make the first move for physical contact. What happened to her, to make her that fragile, as if she could crack at any moment? Yet, here she is, speaking to an inanimate object, saying how the two of them are similar, repeating that they won't break. It makes me proud and shows me how strong she is. She won't let anything get her down. His thoughts raced.

"Are you ready for dinner?" she asked, her stomach growling, cheeks flushed from embarrassment.

He laughed, nodding. "Yeah," he said as he led the way to the register. He placed his items on the counter, reaching for hers. "Oh, I can pay for my own," she said.

"I want to pay for yours as well. Please, let me." He gave her a look she couldn't refuse, and she handed him the container.

"Thank you." *He always makes me feel special,* she thought.

Simeon held the paper bag with one hand, walking closer to the road. Their hands bumped several times, and she interlocked them together. Her butterflies were back, the ones that came out around only Simeon, and she smiled. He noticed her smile and bright cheeks, and he could feel the heat in his own. *She's so adorable,* he thought.

The waitress at the restaurant led them to a booth in the back. A rustic design with light and calming atmosphere made it pleasant. Booths lined the walls while tables filled the center. Electric lanterns hung from the ceiling, giving individual lighting to each table.

"Welcome to Devils' Cliff restaurant. Can I start the two of you off with something to drink?" the waitress asked.

"Ladies first," Simeon said and waved his hand in her direction.

"I'll just have a water, thank you," Ashton said.

"And for you?" the waitress asked.

"Coffee, please," Simeon said.

"I'll have those right out to you," the waitress said.

They were looking over the menu when the waitress came back with their drinks. In the distance, Ashton saw a rustic porcelain vase. "I have a past," she said. "It's not pleasant. I've had a lot of terrible things happen to me, and I've also been forced to do a lot of terrible things to others, as well." She paused, steadying her breath, her whole body shaking from nerves.

"I've never told anyone about it, and I really don't want to. I don't want to go into detail, but the tea sets back in the tea shop reminded me of how I compare myself to it. Well, not the tea set itself, but the material. It's made from porcelain. A material that is fragile, yet it can endure a lot by its strength. It's like me. Although, it's not alone—it has other teacups with it. I never had anyone to help me through it, it was always just me." She shook as a tear escaped her eyes.

Simeon scooted beside her, cradling her to his chest. His warmth, love, security, and protectiveness engulfed her. The motion of his hands combing through her hair was soothing, and it set her at ease. "Sshh, it's okay. You can lean on me, please, let me be here to help you and support you. You don't have to face whatever your past is on your own. Not anymore," he said.

"Please don't hurt me, don't leave me alone," she said.

"I won't. I'm not going to hurt you, and I certainly won't leave you alone. I'll always be here for you." He placed a kiss on the top of her head, resting his cheek where he kissed.

Archangel Michael would be mad if he knew I was holding her like this. Even though as an angel, it is our duty to help others, he wouldn't condone this physical contact. But I've never done anything like this with others. I've never held someone's hand, never held someone, never kissed someone's forehead—it's all forbidden outside of marriage.

His fingers continued to run through her hair, rocking her slowly in a comforting motion. The food came, but neither moved. A clank sounded as the plates met the table, the waitress rolling her eyes at the scene.

Ashton snaked her arms around Simeon's neck, fiddling with his hair as she snuggled into his shoulder. "I don't talk about my past. I have a past, but I'm not my past," she said.

"I don't want to push you into talking about it. I can see that something major happened to you, but I won't pressure you. But I do want you to know that I'm here for you, and I always will be. Whenever you want to talk about it— anything, anything at all—I'm here. You mean so much to me, and it pains me to see you like this. If there is anything I can do, I'll do it. You're always caring and loving, always willing to help everyone else above yourself. So, let me be here for you and care for you. I'll wait however long it takes, if that's what you need."

He pulled away, looking into her eyes and took in a shaky breath. "As an archangel, I know how to love and care for others. But this—what I feel for you—it's not like that. It's as if my life would end if I didn't have you with me."

The softness of his hand wiped away a tear, and in his eyes flowed honesty, patience, love, care, and truth. His words were sweet lullabies to her, ones that she longed to hear for so many years.

"I've never felt close to anyone before, like this, us." She averted her eyes and brushed her hair behind her ears. "I want to open up, but I don't know how." She turned to the food. "I'm sorry, I made the food grow cold."

He picked up his fork, taking a bite of his pasta. "It isn't that bad cold, I think it may taste better this way," he said, jokingly, smiling as he looked at her.

"A mistake worth making, it turned out better overall. My plan all along," she said with a chuckle. She kissed his neck, whispering, "Thank you, sunshine." He nodded and took another bite of his pasta.

"Will that be all today, or could I get you some dessert?" the waitress asked. Simeon looked at Ashton, and she shook her head no.

"We're all set, thanks," Simeon said.

"Here's your check." The waitress placed a piece of paper on the table.

Simeon fished in his wallet, retrieving the amount due and included a sufficient tip. "You don't have to pay for me, I can pay for myself," Ashton said.

"I certainly cannot let you pay, that would just be ungentlemanly of me. And then you may not respect me and like me very much."

"I don't think I would ever dislike you," she said.

"I'm paying," he said, placing the demon dollars on the table. The waitress came over. "We don't need the change," Simeon said.

"Thank you for coming to Devils' Cliff restaurant, I hope you two enjoy your evening, and please come again," the waitress said.

They made their way to the street, walking side by side, demons parting for them. A weight pressed on Simeon's shoulder, and he looked to see Ashton's head resting on it. His hand found hers, shocked that she didn't flinch. He slowed the pace, enjoying the closeness they were sharing. The moon shone bright, romance fluttering in the air.

The grand Victorian house came into view, and a coldness hit Simeon's shoulder as Ashton lifted her head. An audible sigh came from beside him; glancing over, he saw that her shoulders were hunched and a frown was present. "I also don't want this day to be over," he said.

"Come here." She sat on the step, patting the wooden step behind her. He stretched his legs out to her sides, and she leaned against his chest. "We should get together with Seth and Adrian for a study session soon. I don't know about you, but I've got some exams coming up."

"That would be a good idea. I also have a couple exams. It would also help Seth study better."

"Mmm . . . you mentioned earlier that you weren't always an archangel. What did you mean by that?" she asked as she watched the moon's glow; an orange tint mixed with musty clouds gave the atmosphere an ominous feel.

"All the archangels have started out as angels and been promoted to archangels. Seth is an angel, since he hasn't done enough training on souls to allow him to become an archangel. There are special requirements, a lot of which are helping souls find their way. But there's one big requirement for when you become an archangel, and that is dedicating yourself to the angels and the angels only." He paused for a moment, his hands trailing up her arms to massage her shoulders. "It's a great honor to become an archangel, since that's when we gain our wings. We also begin to form our powers as well, such as my healing charms."

She twisted and propped her elbow on his thigh. "Can I see your wings?" Her teeth showed as her bottom lips escaped them.

He leaned down and kissed her neck before closing his eyes. Large dove wings, ocean-blue to crystal-white ombré, formed behind him. Her mouth dropped open as she took in their gorgeous appearance. She reached out about to touch one when she pulled back. "May I?" she whispered.

He nodded and watched as her delicate fingers brushed against the velvety feathers. A chill went down his spine, and he shook at the tingling buzz. Her hand pulled away, and she looked at him. "Are they that sensitive?"

"Yes," he said. His heart still thumping from the buzz. He flapped his wings and engulfed Ashton and himself within them. His wings, like that, were a starry night, and she curled up in his arms, engraving the image in her mind.

12

CHEST TUBE

Ashton laughed with Seth, Adrian, and Simeon as they waited for their next class to start. She playfully pushed Adrian at the joke he told them and placed her forehead on Simeon's shoulder.

A loud uproar came from down the corridor. "He's not breathing," a demon yelled. Ashton peeked around Simeon, a frown on her lips as she saw a black demon lying on the cobblestone floor. She bolted down the hallway, screaming, "Get out of the way and call an ambulance!" Her knees hit the cold floor as she hovered over him, in sight of his heavy bleeding.

"Get away from him!" a demon that was close by said as they snarled at her.

"Hold his head steady," she yelled as she dodged the tail that came flying at her. From the raspy breath and enlarged chest, she knew that he needed a chest tube. *Without it, he won't make it before the ambulance gets here.*

She rummaged through her bag for her pocketknife and looked around at the demons for any kind of tubular object. "That—the straw in your drink, give me that," she demanded as her hand flew in the direction of the straw. "Does anyone have some damn alcohol in this place?" she screamed at the crowd, and a smaller demon with ram horns held a flask out to her.

She poured the amber liquid over the knife and doused the straw with it. "Hold him down and get the tail under control. This is already dangerous as it is. I don't need to be hit while I'm doing it."

Positioned over him, she ripped the clothes on his chest and held the blade over it. She took in a deep breath and pressed the blade into the hard skin. *Definitely tougher skin than humans! I'm having to use a lot of force here. Almost there, almost there. Got it!* She removed the knife and shoved the straw down the bloody hole.

Dark crimson-red blood spewed into the air, and the demons jumped back, but she stayed there, holding the tube in place while the blood hit her face. The black demon took a hard breath and said, "Ugh," as he blinked. Footsteps sounded down the hall, and she saw Lord Diavolo, followed by Barbatos, Lucifer, and the medics with a stretcher.

"What happened?" A succuba medic with black hair looked at her with wide eyes in shock at the straw.

"I don't know why, but his lungs flooded with air, so I found stuff to use as tools for a chest-tube thoracostomy," Ashton said as the succuba replaced her hand on the straw.

"Who are you? How did you know to do that?" the male demon with pale skin asked as he positioned himself to get the demon on the stretcher.

"I'm a neurosurgeon in the Human Realm, that's how I knew," she replied as she stood up. "Clear the way, let them get out."

The demons opened a path for the stretcher, and she had goose bumps. She watched as the stretcher disappeared, and the demons watched her. "Everyone get to class, it started twenty minutes ago," Lucifer said, his voice stern while he glared at them.

"That was amazing, I didn't know you could do that! Weren't you scared?" Seth asked as he gave her wide eyes.

"The only reason he's alive is because, thankfully, demon and human anatomies are similar. If it wasn't, then I would have killed him." She ran her hand through her blood-splattered hair.

"But wait, why did you do it, then?" Seth asked, confused. *I couldn't have done that. If I was uncertain, I wouldn't have. She's so powerful, I want to be like her.*

She knelt in front of Seth and looked into his deep ocean-blue eyes. "As a doctor, I took an oath to save people. I knew that he wouldn't make it to the ambulance if I didn't do something, so I tried. And if I failed, well, he would have died, anyway. But since I tried, he now gets to see another day. I was willing to take that chance, because any chance is worth more than none. Does that make sense?"

"Yes, it does," he said, nodding his head violently at her and smiling.

I knew she was a good choice, Lord Diavolo thought as he watched her explain to Seth why she did what she did. His arms were folded over his chest, and a huge grin was on his face. Lucifer looked over at his lover, bitterness forming in his veins. *Am I not enough? Why does he watch her like that? Get hold of yourself, he's probably just happy she performed well. Makes the exchange program look good.*

"Why don't I escort you home? That way, you can get cleaned up," Barbatos asked as he stood properly beside his master. "If that's all right with you, my lord."

Simeon's eyes darted to Barbatos, breathing becoming heavy as rage took hold of him. "I can escort her home!" Simeon stepped forward and held his hand out for hers. She looked up and smiled at him, placing her hand in his cool one. He tugged her up and she lost her footing, landing on his chest. His cheeks were freckled with shades of red.

"Seth, why don't we get going to class? We can bake something after school today," Adrian asked as he stepped forward and placed his hand on Seth's shoulder.

"Okay," Seth said, pouting, but he allowed Adrian to pull him away from the group.

"I guess that settles it. Simeon will escort her home, and I'll get the custodian down here to clean this up," Lord Diavolo said as he held his hands out and clapped them together. "I'll let the teachers know, and Ashton, that was . . . wow. I'm speechless," he said, laughing.

13

THE CALL

The glorious smell of turkey blended with potatoes, carrots, and stuffing. Baked yeast rolls met the senses, begging to be eaten. Conversations could be heard as Lord Diavolo, the seven devils, angels, humans, and the butler ate.

Jingle jangle, jingle jangle, jingle jangle.

Everyone stopped talking, some midbite, and stared at Ashton. "I'm sorry I forgot to turn my ringer off. It's a side effect from being a doctor. I'd always have to be available," she said.

"It's quite all right, go ahead and answer it," Lord Diavolo said.

"Are you sure?"

"Yes."

She checked the caller ID, jaw clenching as the name Collin Abbott appeared on the screen. "Hey, Collin, I hope you have a good reason for calling, or I'm hanging up," she whispered into the phone.

"Well, hello to you, Dr. Lure," Collin said.

"What do you want, Collin? I'm in the middle of something," she asked.

"I need your help with a patient."

"You do know that I'm no longer employed there? Right?"

"I'm well aware of that, but I have a twelve-year-old female with a butterfly glioblastoma on both of her back lobes of the brain. And the parents want to move her to a different hospital, thinking we can't do anything for her. Her condition is already bad."

"How bad? Has it already started to affect her cognition?"

"Not yet, but from the look of it, it won't be long, a few weeks if that," Collin replied.

"You can't let them move her. If she leaves the hospital in her state, she won't make it to the next one. She could very well die before she gets there. If there is any possibility that it could start affecting her, then it'd be catastrophic to move her to a different hospital." Her voice raised, becoming alarmed.

"I know that, but the parents won't listen to reason,"

"You must stall, she can't leave. Do whatever you have to do, but don't let her leave." Her hands flew through the air. *What do we do? She can't leave, how can we help her?* She thought.

"Even if she stays, what're we going to do? She still has a butterfly glioblastoma in her brain," asked Collin.

She leaned back in her chair, crossing her legs as she was thinking. *I was a well-respected neurosurgeon in the Human Realm, but I'm not in the Human Realm anymore. I'm in the Demon Realm now. What could I do in the Demon Realm to help this poor girl?*

"Talk to her parents and buy me some time. I'll try to find a way to remove the tumor, and I'll personally perform the surgery."

"You? You'd come back and do that?" Collin asked.

She looked at everyone at the table, who were all trying to discreetly listen in on the conversation, not giving her privacy. Her eyes landed on Simeon's. "If it'd save her life, then yes, I would. I want new scans on the tumor. I'll be arriving shortly."

"See you soon."

She hung up the phone, holding the corner of it to her lips, contemplating. "Lord Diavolo, Barbatos, Satan, and Simeon, pack your bags. We're going to the Human Realm. We'll probably be there for about a week, so make sure everything is set for that amount of time. I'll meet you in the main entrance within the next hour. Make sure you are ready to leave by then."

"W-why does Satan get to go and not the rest of us?" Leviathan asked.

"Lord Diavolo set up the exchange program, Barbatos is a well-rounded butler, Satan likes to learn, and Simeon is the only angel old enough to be allowed in the hospital under the circumstances. The exchange program was put in place to reunite the three realms. To allow angels, demons, and humans a chance to experience the diverse cultures. Well, in the Human Realm, I'm Dr. Ashton Lure, a renowned neurosurgeon who saves lives. It just so happens that there is a patient who needs the best, and that is me. So, congratulations, the four of you get to experience a once-in-a-lifetime opportunity to see me make the medical books. I'll meet you in the lobby in an hour. Be ready to leave," she said, finishing.

She walked out of the grand dining room, Satan catching up to her. "The others are staying there until we get back, and Lord Diavolo is setting Lucifer up to run the Demon Realm while he's away," Satan said.

"Okay, let's hurry," she said.

She packed only what she needed, knowing she had more in her house in the Human Realm. She knocked on Satan's door, and an annoyed "Come in" sounded from the other side. Satan's annoyance dissipated when he saw her, replaced with a bright smile.

"How's the packing going?" she asked.

"It's coming along well. I'll be done as soon as I find the book I'm looking for . . . ah, there it is!" Satan placed the book into his suitcase, zipping it up. He picked up his bag, walking over to her.

The brightest grin imaginable crossed his lips as he reached up, gently sliding his fingers across her cheek. Ba-bump—his heart picked up pace, beating faster as he looked into her hazel eyes. She flinched from his touch. "Let's head over and wait for the others," she said.

Ashton and Satan left the house, walking down the street to get to the castle. "Ashton, Satan," someone called behind them.

"Oh, hey, Simeon," Ashton said, smiling.

"Hello," Satan said, annoyed and rolling his eyes.

They made their way to the castle; Lord Diavolo and Barbatos were already waiting. "Are we ready?" she asked.

"Yes," they replied in unison.

Barbatos led them to the nearby portal, opening it for them. Darkness overtook them, spinning them before landing inside Ashton's bedroom. Simeon felt a coolness on his biceps, and turning, he saw Ashton clutching her stomach and holding on to him. "Are you all right?" he asked. She nodded, embarrassed as she noticed everyone watching her.

"Kaname," she said.

"Yes, Ashton?"

"Disarm the security system. I'll be here with these four for the next week or so."

"Of course, Ashton."

"Were there any intrusions while I was away?"

"No, everything proceeded smoothly and securely."

"Thank you, that's all for now."

"You're welcome, have a good day."

Everyone looked at her with confused expressions, and she proceeded to tell them about "Kaname." She led them from her room, allowing them ample time to look around, awestruck expressions on all their faces. *Lucifer tried to describe the place, but his description didn't do the place justice,* Lord Diavolo thought as he walked around.

"I know it's not much, but this is my house. It's where I lived before going to the Demon Realm," she said as she shrugged her shoulders. "These are the guest rooms. Unfortunately, I have only three. I'll let the four of you decide who wants to room with whom, and anyone is more than welcome to take the living room." She jabbed her finger in the direction of the sectional. "I'm going to put my luggage in my room and get ready to go to the hospital."

She headed for her room, turning on her heels. "I just remembered. Satan, upstairs there's the library. I think you'd like it. You can check it out if you want, or I can show everyone before we head out. Just pointing it out," she said.

"I'm sure we'd all love to see it," Satan said.

"Okay, I'll show it to you guys when we're done settling in," she said.

She walked into her room, seeing her bed, and she remembered the nights over the past ten years:

Deafening screams pierced the darkness. Body rocked back and forth rhythmically. Curled into a tight ball, she tried to ground herself back to reality. WHOOSH! Whipping noises sounded, as if she were still in the dampened cold chamber. Hands covering her ears at the sound that existed only in her mind. Nobody ever came at her cries of pain. Frozen in the past as the nightmares made her relive it.

She flopped down on her familiar mattress, bouncing a few times. The room held shadows as she turned on the lamp. The dresser, nightstand, vanity, and bed were dancing with night and light from her lamp. *Bittersweet being in the house that I designed, my new beginning,* she thought.

She opened the drawer, retrieving her favorite lab coat. She begged the chief of surgery to let her take it home with her, and because she was well respected, he agreed. She held the pearly-white lab coat up and, in the corner, it read:

Dr. Ashton Lure

Neurosurgeon

She pulled the lab coat on, her reward for becoming a full-time surgeon at the hospital, and walked to the mirror. She inhaled, fingering the golden letters, and remembered why she got into the line of work to begin with. Her mind flashed to seventeen:

"Your new target is Jordan Alcove, and this is what he looks like," Franko said. "Kill him."

The car sped down the highway, racing past cars as her GPS took her to the destination. "Your destination is up ahead," a female's voice sounded through the car. She pulled up into a parking lot and walked up to the dance club.

Music blared, bodies bumping her as she walked to the counter. "I'm looking for Jordan Alcove," she said.

"And who are you?" a man asked.

"Come closer," she said as she beckoned him with her index finger. He leaned forward. "I'm here for his lap dance—he specifically requested me because of my special talents." She winked.

The man blushed. "R-right, of course, right this way."

He led her down a carpeted hallway, opening a door to a private room. "Here you go, sexy." He spanked her ass as she walked in.

"Well, look at this sexy thing, who might you be?" Jordan Alcove asked. He sat on a couch, his legs spread open with two naked women on each side of him.

No emotions, no hesitation, and no mercy, she thought, repeating the words Franko drilled into her brain. BANG! BANG! BANG! She pulled the trigger, watching the blood drain out of their lifeless bodies. She exited the building, and nobody heard a thing over the blaring music.

Ashton took the lab coat off, placing it on her bag to take with her. She exited her bedroom and made her way to the kitchen. The tea kettle whistled, sure to alert the others she was ready. She filled a mug with steaming hot water and grabbed a random tea bag.

She sat on the barstool, taking a sip as she noticed Simeon walking toward her. "Would you like some tea?" she asked.

"Yes, please," he said.

She filled a mug with tea, setting it on the counter in front of him before reclaiming her seat. He took a sip, reveling in the warmth. "You look pale. Are you feeling all right?" he asked.

She looked at him, elbow on the counter. "No." She sighed in defeat.

"Do you want to talk about it?"

She shook her head. "No."

"Okay. I'm here if you do." He tucked a strand of loose hair behind her ear. "I like the house, by the way. You really designed it yourself?"

"Yeah, I did."

"Now that is impressive! I've never been one for designing, but I'm pretty good at whittling and pottery."

"Wait, really? I never knew that."

"You never asked."

"True," she said with a giggle. "Maybe I'm just too self-centered."

"Never."

Her head dropped onto Simeon's shoulder, both hands wrapped around the warm mug as she closed her eyes. He looked down at her, smiling, and placed a kiss on her forehead. He gained her trust; she didn't know how, but he did. She was comfortable around him, and she liked it, and a smile formed on her lips.

A door creaked and alerted them to others being present. Ashton and Simeon turn their heads, a shiver going down Simeon's spine from the cold spot on his shoulder. She placed three mugs on the counter and filled them with tea. She handed Lord Diavolo, Barbatos, and Satan a mug and led them toward the stairs. "What's that door?" Satan asked.

She looked to where he pointed—the door behind which was her porcelain, in her training room, the secured location. "That's just the basement," she said. They climbed up the stairs and reached the top, opening up to the library.

Most of the books were limited edition, ranging anywhere from manga to documentary to science fiction. There were three moderately sized bay windows, overlooking a lake. Two of them had thick, cozy cushions to sit on with oversize pillows to contentedly prop herself on while reading. The center window bay was rounded like a booth, an oak table in the middle for holding drinks or working on projects.

Bookshelves lined the walls, floor to ceiling, rose-and-vine designs carved into the sides and tops. Each was filled with books, leaving little space for new ones. An oak table sat beautifully in the center of the room. Four e-readers were evenly distributed in the middle. Each one was labeled on the back, the first being *A-F*, the second *G-L*, the third *M-R*, and the fourth *S-Z*.

A couch was beside the oak table, while two chairs and a small oak table between them were on the other side of the oak table. Red rugs with white rose-and-vine designs covered the floor, matching the bookshelves flawlessly. In the corner, a desk held her filing cabinets, laptop, papers, pens, printer, and financial supplies.

There was no main light in the upstairs, just lamps scattered strategically around for all the enjoyable reading spots. A mood light setting was what she preferred for a cozy reading time while looking out over the lake. The entryway to this extravagant library upstairs was a spiral staircase in the far corner, opposite the window.

Satan's eyes went wide as he jumped from one bookcase to the next. The others walked around, amazed at her collection. Ashton made her way to a window bay, pulling her legs up underneath her as she sipped her tea, watching them.

She enjoyed the time that she had to herself, but since she had been in the Demon Realm, she loved the company even more. They'd opened her up immensely, and that was something her past never allowed her to do. She took another sip of her tea.

"This is amazing, I had no idea you were so into books!" Satan looked at her, a huge grin on his face, eyes twinkling brightly. "Are these all your medical books that help you with your research? Some of these have your name on them! Did you help write them?" Satan asked.

Satan's question compelled them all to look at her. "Yes. That section is for all the medical books I own. Some of them have helped me study, and others I collaborated with other doctors to help write."

"Wait, so you actually helped write medical books?" Lord Diavolo asked.

"Only a couple," she said.

"That is amazing! Um, what are these? And how do you use them?" Lord Diavolo asked.

She stood up, walking over to the e-reader. She showed him how the digital device held hundreds of books, and he got a kick out of it. She made a mental note to get one for his birthday, and Satan as well.

"I hate to cut this short, but are you guys ready to head to the hospital?" she asked.

"Sure," they replied in unison.

They placed their empty tea mugs in the sink as Ashton led them to the door. She clicked the Unlock button on her car, and they filed in. Lord Diavolo sat shotgun, while the others squeezed into the back seat. "Sorry for the tight squeeze, guys," she said, only now realizing angels and demons are built larger than humans.

"Don't worry about it, my lady," Barbatos said.

"We're fine back here, snowflake," Simeon said.

"Okay," she said.

She connected the Bluetooth from her phone to her car, pressing the Shuffle button. "Camouflage" by Brad Paisley came through the speakers.

14

THE SURGERY

Ashton closed her eyes, taking in a deep breath, and walked toward the hospital entrance. Lord Diavolo, Barbatos, Satan, and Simeon followed as she entered an elevator, pressing the third-floor button.

Nurses scurried by while patients were being moved down the halls, interns and residents chatted about their days, and the door ahead read Chief of Surgery. She opened the door without knocking, and a man looked up. "I've been expecting you, doctor. How've you been, Ashton?" the chief of surgery asked.

"It's all right, what about you, Chief Cooney?" she asked.

"Still trying to find a good replacement for you. Do you know how hard it is to find talent like yours?" Cooney asked.

"Apparently not. Oh, and the next time you have a neuro case for me, call me yourself, don't have Collin do it."

"He was so thrilled to talk with you again, but I'll remember that for next time. I have your temporary badge right here, and this is her file with her most recent scans."

"Thanks." She took the scans and headed for the door.

"By the way, Ashton. Who do you have with you?"

"They're here to watch me perform the surgery. I thought it'd be a great opportunity for them to learn more about me. This is a teaching hospital, after all, Chief. Is there going to be a problem with me teaching them?" She raised an eyebrow at him.

Simeon walked over to the chief of surgery and held out his hand. "Hello, sir, my name is Simeon. It's certainly a pleasure to meet you." Chief Cooney shook Simeon's hand, and a warm, calming sensation filtered through him. "We're delighted to see what you have to offer here in this program. Would it be all right if we stayed? I know that you're very busy being the man in charge, but we wouldn't be a bother at all," Simeon said seductively.

"W-well, if you put it that way, then yes. Just make sure that you stay with Ashton," the chief said.

They exited the office, and Ashton placed her hand on Simeon's biceps. "What was that in there?"

He leaned down to whisper in her ear, "As an angel, I do have some abilities. Most of them were put on hold when I became an exchange student, but I do still have some of my charm powers."

"Did you use them on me?"

"Never, I wouldn't do that without your permission."

"Hmm . . ." Entering the image room, she placed the new scans on the lights, turning them on. Her eyes glistened with excitement and determination as a clear view of the tumor came into view. She carefully looked through each scan before moving to the next film.

"You look so serious," Satan said.

"Mmm, thinking. I'm thinking about how I'm going to remove this tumor, and it's not going to be easy. In fact, it's going to be my most difficult surgery I've ever done," she said.

She sat down at the desk, opening the file on her patient. "Okay, so she's a twelve-year-old female by the name of Mary-Ann. There's no history of disease or illness in her family. Except her grandmother, who had kidney failure. And her reason for being here is a butterfly glioblastoma pressing into the two back lobes of her brain. It also says that she has been to seven different doctors, who have told her it's a lost cause," she said.

She closed the file and put the scans back in their envelope. "All right, let's go meet the patient."

They walked to room 309, and she managed to place a big smile on her face. "Hi, my name is Dr. Ashton Lure. You must be Mary-Ann, and you two must be her parents."

"Yes, I'm Mary, and this is Don. Thank you so much for looking at her. It means a lot to us," Mary said.

"Are you going to remove the tumor from my brain?" Mary-Ann asked.

"Right down to business, I like it," Ashton said. "Well, there are no guarantees, but I'm going to try."

"None of the other doctors would remove it. How will you?" Mary-Ann asked.

"There are some doctors out there who think that it's impossible because it's never been done before. But I have a unique perspective. I'm not someone who turns patients away," she said.

"But if you do the surgery, won't I die?" Mary-Ann asked.

Ashton looked around the room, Mary and Don shook their heads, and she looked back at Mary-Ann. "There is a big possibility that you will die, but I'm going to do everything I can to make sure that you do wake up. But I do need something from you," she said.

"What do you need from me?"

"I need you to keep smiling—that helps the doctors do a better job. Do you think you can do that for me?"

"Yes, I can do that for you. I'm good at smiling."

"Good, I thought you were," Ashton said. "Hey, do you like chocolate?"

"Yeah, I do."

"Is it all right if she has this?" Ashton pulled a normal-size Hershey bar out of her lab coat.

"That'd be okay with us," Mary said.

"Here you go. Just don't tell the nurses I gave that to you," Ashton said, looking back at the door.

"Thank you, Dr. Lure."

"You're welcome. Now I'm going to have a look at the images, and I'll give you updates as soon as I know anything, okay?"

"Thank you, again," Don said.

Ashton and the others made their way into the hall, stopping when she heard her name. "Did you have a question or anything I could do for you?" Ashton asked the mother.

"Why did you do that?"

"What do you mean?"

"I mean, why did you go and tell her that she's going to die? We don't want her to spend what little time she has left in misery. Why didn't you just lie?" Mary asked.

Doctors and nurses stopped, watching the scene. "I have an obligation to my patient, not the parent. I've built my reputation as a neurosurgeon on not lying to my patients, and I'm not going to start now. I didn't tell her that she was going to die. I specifically told her that the possibility was high. But what I do know is that you're scared and hurting, and it's hard watching your daughter go through that and not being able to do anything about it. This is my job, though. It's what I was trained to do. And I'm going to do whatever I can to remove this tumor so that she can live a long and happy life with you. I need you to trust that I have your daughter's best interests at heart, okay? But the more time I spend here, arguing with you over what I did or didn't say, is less time that I have to figure out how to remove this tumor from her brain. So, I'm going to go now, I'm going do my job, and I'm going to do my best to save her life."

Ashton walked away to the research room, leaving the mother speechless and everyone watching her. The next few days were long. She spent every second going through textbooks, online sites, and scans—everything of which she could think. She consulted with other doctors, going through every angle, but a gut feeling told her something was missing. She leaned back in the office chair, looking at the scans, thinking.

"How long has she been like that?" Chief Cooney asked.

"Awhile," Satan replied.

"Come on, Ashton, what's going through your brain?" Chief Cooney asked.

"Something's missing. I'm missing something, but I don't know what," she said. She got up, pacing the room, eyes darting around.

"When's the last time you slept?" Chief Cooney asked.

"She hasn't slept since she got here," Barbatos said.

"Are you serious? Ashton, you need to sleep. Everything will still be here in the morning," Chief Cooney said.

"No, I don't need sleep. I need to find out what I'm missing," she said.

"You're of no help if you are sleep deprived. Now, get to one of the on-call rooms and go to sleep. The images will still be here when you wake up," Chief Cooney said, demandingly.

"THAT'S IT!" She snapped her fingers. "Does the hospital still have the three-dimensional printer?"

"Yeah. I'm surprised you remembered that it arrived a few days before you resigned. I don't even think you had the chance to use it."

"I need to use it. We're going to get a three-dimensional design of the brain and tumor. Then I'll be able to see every possible mistake that could be made."

"Well, do you remember where it is? It's down the hall, on the right-hand side."

"I remember." She led the way down the hall, looking at the picture of flowers that hung before entering the room. She sat down at the computer screen, typing in what she needed it to print. When the machine clicked, she picked up the model. The material was like durable plastic, but her fingers traveled each fold and crease, allowing her access to what the scans never could.

She used the model to help enhance her earlier knowledge of the tumor, to have a concrete plan in place. She walked to her patient's room. "Hi. How're you feeling, Mary-Ann?"

"I'm doing good today," Mary-Ann said.

"Good, I'm glad. So, I have some news. I've been looking over all the textbooks available, online resources, consulting the other doctors in the hospital and other resources. I can officially say that I found a way. I can remove the tumor without damaging your cognitive functions."

"Are you serious? That's amazing," Mary said.

"But I do have to warn you, the surgery is extremely difficult. One wrong move, and you could end up blind, deaf, unable to speak or move, or dead."

"Do it," Mary said.

"Are you sure you don't want to take some time to think it over?"

"She said do it, so do it. Anything so we can have our baby girl with us longer," Don said.

"Okay. Get a good night's rest. Tomorrow is going to be a long day."

"Okay, thank you."

Ashton and her entourage made their way back to her house for the evening. She unlocked the door; the wall was hard on her back as she leaned against it. Her eyes dipped closed as she slid to the floor; all energy left her as the weight of the last few days began to take its toll and sleep took over.

Her entourage smiled at her, and Simeon picked her up, carrying her to her bedroom and tucking her in. "You worked hard this week, and you'll do amazing tomorrow." He placed a kiss on her forehead. "Sleep well, snowflake."

The next morning, they drove to the hospital. News vans formed a line outside the building; reporters with big cameras filmed the hospital. The reporters rushed to Ashton as she made her way inside. "Dr. Ashton Lure, are you nervous about the surgery today?" "Why did you decide to take on this case?"

"What did you find that was different from the other surgeons?" "Are you making a statement that you are better than all the other neurosurgeons out there?"

She breezed by them, leading her entourage to the observation room. "You guys will be able to see everything from here. I'm going to go get ready," she said.

The soap slid over her skin, lathering her arms before she held them under warm water. The scrub nurse placed her fashionable blue gown on her, tying it in the back. "Is the three-dimensional model in there?" Ashton asked.

"It was disinfected earlier and placed on a metal tray," the scrub nurse said.

"Good. When I get in there, could you play a song on my phone?"

"Are you sure that's appropriate?" the scrub nurse asked.

"Probably not, but I'm going to have you do it, anyway. If you pick up my phone, it should be ready to play."

"Okay."

Ashton entered the operating room and the scrub nurse pressed play, "Let's go, girls." "Man! I Feel Like a Woman" by Shania Twain began to play. Ashton swayed to the beat, dancing around the others in the room, beckoning them to join her. She saw their eyes light up as they began dancing to the music with her. They laughed as the music ended.

"How's everyone feeling? A little more loose now?" she asked.

"Yeah," one of them said.

"Good, that's what we need. This is just like any other surgery. We do the best we can no matter what. To your stations."

She walked to her patient's head, sweeping her eyes up at the observation room filled with nurses, doctors, her friends, and a few news reporters. She took a deep breath, put on her safety glasses, and looked to her residents. "Let's make the medical books."

A nurse handed her the bone saw; she gripped it, testing it before nodding. "Start the timer."

The beginning hours went without any complications, the chief of surgery popping in and out throughout the day. She stopped working, running across a complication on how to remove the tumor. "Could I have the three-dimensional model?" she asked. The medical staff in the room with her turned the model in every direction that she directed, until it clicked, and she was able to get past the block.

The timer was nearing the nineteenth hour when she finished removing the tumor. "We're ready to put the radiation pieces in," she said. The scrub nurse retrieved the protection apron, placing it on her as she held her hands out. "All nonessentials, please leave the room for this process," she said.

She began placing the radiation pieces inside the brain in their correct locations. The first few went in without a problem, but the last few weren't reaching. The squashy brain only gave so much room, and her gloves were too thick. "How much time do we have left?" she asked.

"Two minutes for minimal radiation exposure. You've been at it for six minutes already."

She dropped the utensils on the tray, removed the gloves, and picked up the radiation pieces with her bare hands. She worked fast to place them, able to reach the proper locations. "What do you think you're doing? Get those gloves back on.

Do you know how much you're risking right now?" Chief Cooney's voice rang through the speaker from the observation room.

"I can't reach the correct locations with the gloves on."

"So, you're risking overexposure? Get them back on!"

"I'm fine, I'm almost done." She continued to place the radiation pieces inside the brain.

"What does that mean, overexposure to radiation?" Lord Diavolo asked the chief of surgery, and the others' thoughts were mirroring his exactly.

"High exposures to radiation can be extremely dangerous. By taking off her gloves, she triples her chances of getting radiation poisoning. It's unbelievably bad and could kill her."

Their eyes were now glued to her, concern etched on their faces. Simeon's heart pumped fast as he tried to remain calm.

"Done! It's done!" Her arms flew above her head as her breathing evened out. *Twenty hours, now the only thing left is to replace the removed bone, sew the wound back together, and have the nurses take her back to her room,* she thought.

The nurses rolled Ashton's patient out of the operating room. *Twenty hours of an overly complicated surgery with high risks that could've killed the patient. With the help of the well-trained medical staff, we managed to remove the butterfly glioblastoma from her brain,* she thought.

Her surgical gear was discarded into the proper container as she made her way to the observation room. Everyone clapped when she entered, but she stood in front of the window, her favorite surgical cap in her hand.

"The news reporters are outside, waiting for you to give a statement," Chief Cooney said.

"I'll be right out, after I let the patient's parents know," she said.

The waiting room was filled with loved ones. Some were crying while others paced, concerned, and waiting for their own news. She found Mary-Ann's parents and walked over to them. They stood up as she approached. "Please," Mary said.

"I have successfully removed the butterfly glioblastoma from her brain. She's in recovery now and should wake up soon. It's now up to her to fight. She's completely tumor free, and I've placed the radiation pieces inside to keep it from returning."

"Thank you so much." Mary pounced on Ashton, hugging her.

"You're welcome. You can go into the room with her, just keep it quiet until she's awake."

Ashton found an empty room, pressing her forehead against the wall as relief overtook her. Tears poured from her eyes. Simeon brushed his fingertips over her arm, and she buried herself into his chest. It was the hardest surgery she had ever done. She was proud of herself; she'd made medical history. Everyone in the medical world would know her name. Something that any doctor would ever want, but she didn't. She didn't do it for the glory or the fame, she did it to save people. To show others nothing is impossible until it has been attempted.

Lord Diavolo, Barbatos, and Satan watched as Simeon held Ashton. She held a tender spot in their hearts. They thought she was fragile and could break since she was a human. But, after what they saw, they knew it wasn't true. The long hours, sleepless nights, racking of the brain, and creative thinking to save someone else's life showed them she was anything but fragile.

15

CODE BLUE

Ashton stood behind the podium outside the hospital as cameras, microphones, reporters, and crowds of people awaited her statement. "Thank you all for joining the hospital for this surgery. It has been a long week. We've been working around the clock to supply the best care for our patient—"

"Why did you remove your gloves? Did you know that would bring overexposure to you? What about the patient? Isn't that unsanitary to have your hands on her brain with no gloves on?" a reporter asked.

"The butterfly glioblastoma was pressing into the two back lobes of her brain. With the help of many of the doctors here, we were able to produce a plan on how to remove the tumor safely," she said.

"Is it true that you used a three-dimensional printer?" a reporter asked.

"Yes, that is correct. We did use a three-dimensional printer to give us a model of the brain and tumor."

"Did you have to use it inside the operating room?"

"I did use it inside the operating room. When I was inside her brain, the tumor was different from what the images showed. By using the three-dimensional model, I was able to view areas of the brain and safely remove the tumor."

"Does she have any cognitive issues?"

"That is unknown as of this time."

"Why?"

"The patient is still asleep. Going through a surgery as drastic as that can be draining on the body. She needs time to rest."

"Why did you remove your gloves? Could that affect the outcome of her surgery? Who are the people you have with you? Why have they been following you?"

"No comment. Thank you for your support in this surgical case—it was much appreciated." Ashton turned, and a man in the distance caught her eye, and her step faltered. Her mind took her to twenty-two:

"Aren't you good for anything?" Franko asked.

Ashton lay in a pool of blood, pain shooting through her body as she miscarried. She lost track of how many abortions and miscarriages she had endured.

"You get pregnant when you aren't supposed to, and now, when you are supposed to have my child, you can't even do that," he said.

The unzipping of pants resonated in her ears; she was unable to move. Her uterus screamed, setting her on fire as he thrust into her seemingly lifeless body. "Ah, yes, that's right, squeeze my cock. It's so tight," Franko moaned.

He thrust harder and faster into her; hips whammed against the rigid stone, becoming erratic. Hot cum squirted into her and he pulled out, leaving her there. Her body shivered in the dark chamber as she fought to keep consciousness. Sangchul stood motionless as he watched his boss defile her.

"Ashton?" Simeon asked.

"Hmm?" She faced the entrance to the hospital, entering the sliding doors.

"Who was that man? He was staring at you, like you knew him," Simeon said.

"Let's just head to the on-call room and get some sleep," she said.

"Was that Franko?" Simeon asked.

"Who's Franko?" Lord Diavolo asked.

"No one," she said. She glared at Simeon, and he nodded, backing off.

The on-call room held bunk beds against the back wall, couches on the sides, and a table in the middle. She sat on the couch, closing her eyes. "I know it's not the comfiest place to sleep, but I can't leave until she's awake."

"I call top bunk," Satan said. He climbed onto the top bunk, looking down at everyone.

"Where would you like to sleep, my lord?" Barbatos asked.

"I'll take the lower bunk," Lord Diavolo said.

"Then I'll take the other couch," Barbatos said.

Simeon started to walk over to Ashton, when the door swung open, flooding the room with light for a moment. Collin barged in, practically sitting on Ashton's lap. His arm draped on the couch over her shoulder while the other rested on her leg. "Get out," she said, demandingly. Satan sat up on the bed with his legs dangling down, his grip denting the metal on the bed frame. Lord Diavolo crossed his arms in disgust and was ready to tear him to shreds if she needed him to. A frown was present on Barbatos's lips as he watched the scene unfold. *This is the moment I saw in her future when she first became a student. When I looked into the doorways of her future and alternate universe, I saw him. I know that she will be all right, but it sets me on edge to see it unfold in person,* Barbatos thought.

"Don't be like that. I just wanted to talk about the surgery," he said.

"Get out, or we will find a different room to sleep in." She tried standing up, but his hand caught her shoulder, pulling her to the couch.

"Is this about the pizza?" he asked.

"Pizza? No. This is about how you were feeling me up, and when I told you to stop, you didn't."

"I was messing with you, come on."

"Like now? You won't even let me stand up," she said.

"I don't get what your problem is. It's a huge turnoff for us guys to have women be like this."

You're wrong. It's not a turnoff for guys, it's a turnoff for you. I love her just the way she is, and if she doesn't want to, then I won't force her to, Simeon thought as his fists balled.

"Then I don't need a guy. Now remove your hands from me."

His hand crept farther up her thigh, and her hand tightened on it. "She told you to remove your hands," Simeon said. *He's tried to hurt her before. I've never felt anger like this—I just have to protect her!* Simeon's blood boiled as he took her hand and ripped Collin's off her as he helped her up. The grip on her hand tightened as his body blocked her from Collin. Simeon glared daggers at Collin. "Whatever, she's a worthless bitch, anyway," Collin said, exiting the room.

Simeon's body shook with anger. He tried to gain control when a heaviness came onto his back. He twisted and pressed his forehead to hers. "Are you okay?" She nodded. Ashton removed her lab coat, placing it on the table, and put her pager on the stand beside the couch. She took off her shoes, bringing her legs to her chin on the couch. She motioned for Simeon to sit. He brought his leg behind her back, lying down, and held her tightly while the anger subsided. He nuzzled her neck, and she placed a comforting hand on his cheek. "I'm okay."

They all lay asleep, and all that could be heard was the bustling in the hallways outside the door as they slept.

BEEP BEEP BEEP.

Ashton's pager rang in the room. "Mmm," she mumbled. Half-asleep, she reached over Simeon for the pager. Simeon opened his eyes, and his grip around her waist tightened. He watched as her head dipped to his shoulder, eyes closing before she looked at the pager. *Code Blue Room 309*

Ashton blinked, reading the pager again. "Shit!" She clambered off Simeon. "What's wrong?" he asked. She didn't respond, grabbing her lab coat and running down the hall. "Move," she said as a nurse stood in the middle of the hallway.

Mary-Ann lay motionless on the hospital bed, flatlining on the monitor. "What's happening? Is she okay?" Mary cried, frantic.

"Get them out of here, now," she said. A nurse removed them from the room.

"We gave her an epi and shocked her, no response," a nurse said.

"Give her another epi. Up the charge . . . Clear!" Everyone cleared the way as Ashton brought the paddles onto Mary-Ann's chest. Still flatlining.

"Come on, Mary-Ann, you have more fight in you than this. Give her another epi. Up the charge again. Fight, Mary-Ann, come on, you can do this! Clear!" She brought the paddles to Mary-Ann's chest, shocking her again. A heartbeat arrived on the monitor. "She's back."

Ashton made her way to Mary and Don. "This can happen. The brain went through a lot, and it can cause patients to flatline. She's still with us, though, which means she is fighting."

"So, she's okay?" Don asked.

"She's okay," Ashton said.

"Oh, thank you," Mary said.

"You can go back in, and the nurses will alert me if anything new comes up. I'm right in the on-call room." Ashton made her way back to the room. She couldn't tell which one snored louder, Lord Diavolo or Satan. She placed her lab coat on the table, and Simeon readjusted his position on the couch.

She sat on the couch, and the delicate feather touch of Simeon's hand brushed her arm. She hovered over him and nuzzled into his neck, placing silent kisses on his smooth skin. Love and caring kisses trailed to his chest, and she snuggled into him. His eyes closed, and he stroked her hair while he placed kisses on her forehead until she fell asleep.

Ashton stirred, sitting up as something fell onto the floor. She went to pick it up, noticing Lord Diavolo's red jacket. She looked at Lord Diavolo, who was sitting up on the lower bunk. "I woke up and you looked cold, so I covered you with it," he whispered.

"Thank you," she said.

They went to check on Mary-Ann, who was lying down with her eyes open, talking with her parents when Ashton walked in. "Hello there, Mary-Ann, how are you doing?"

"I'm doing okay."

"That's good. If it's okay with you, I would like to check your functions."

"Okay."

"Clearly, you can hear me, since you are replying to what I'm saying. Can you squeeze my fingers?" Ashton picked up Mary-Ann's hands; a light pressure enclosed Ashton's fingers. "Good job, that was fantastic. Now can you follow my finger with your eyes only?" She placed her finger about ten inches from Mary-Ann's eyes, moving it slowly in different directions. Mary-Ann's eyes followed.

"How did I do on that?" Mary-Ann asked.

"You did everything just as you were supposed to do. There doesn't seem to be any residual damage. Your cognitive functions seem to be working. Now, you may feel off or like something is missing. This is normal. It happens because you had an object in your brain for so long, and now it's not there. That is going to take some getting used to."

"See, I told you, Mom, it feels different in there." Mary-Ann pointed to her brain.

"It'll get better, though. Everything looks perfect, and all you need to do now is your physical therapy, and rest, of course. You think you can handle that for me?"

"I can do that, definitely."

"Good, I want to be around for your full recovery, but you will be in very good care with the chief of surgery, Dr. Cooney."

"Dr. Lure, thank you for coming back to help me. I wasn't ready to die yet."

"You're welcome." Ashton smiled, looking away so no one could see her tear up. "Do your physical therapy, rest, and get better." She patted Mary-Ann's arm before leaving the room.

The light shone from the ceiling, bouncing off the bright white walls of the hospital hallways as they made their way to an elevator. "Leaving already?" Chief Cooney asked.

"Yeah, she's in capable hands with you," Ashton said.

"Well, I certainly hate to see you leave. I don't think I'll ever find a neurosurgeon as good as you."

"You will, eventually."

"Always optimistic, that's what I like about you." The elevator doors opened. "Take care, and I'll be sure to call if I have any more cases that need your attention."

"I'll be looking forward to them, Chief."

16

THE INCIDENT

Lord Diavolo, Barbatos, Satan, Simeon, and Ashton sat in the living room. "You did an amazing job, my lady. How'd you learn all of that?" Barbatos asked.

"Years of medical school. Studying, late nights, things like that. Similar to what I'm doing with the exchange program, although I don't have to stay up as late," she said, laughing.

"I can't believe there weren't any residual effects after the surgery. It was as if you performed that surgery a hundred times," Lord Diavolo said.

"First time. That was the hardest one I've ever done," she said.

She rolled her neck and went to her room, changing into walking clothes. "I'm going to go for a walk, I'll be back in a bit."

"Do you want us to go with you?" Lord Diavolo asked.

"No, I'd rather be alone for a little while. But please, feel free to help yourselves to anything in the house."

Ashton mindlessly walked down the street, not surprised when the local park came into view. Trees were spread out, billowing in the light breeze. People sat, talking as they ate at the picnic tables; dogs playing fetch barked in the background, mixing with the chirping birds flying by. Dribbling and friendly shouts could be heard on the pavement as friends played basketball on the fenced-in courts.

She walked over to the open basketball court, picking up one of the loose balls. She began dribbling it, taking it over to the foul line. Basketball was a coping skill she had picked up over the years; not that she played with others, but she found the repeated motions of shooting to be soothing, relaxing.

She continued shooting hoops, some missing, while in amazement she managed to make a bunch. It's all overwhelming, the surgery was difficult, but she had managed to succeed. Collin feeling her up—Simeon, her love, protecting her. Franko showing up at the hospital, bringing back the memories. She spent many years trying to suppress the memories, and he wouldn't leave her alone.

She missed a shot, jogging over to where the ball landed. Her whole body was shaking from the adrenaline, or maybe it was nerves as she tried to settle down. She gave a point to both adrenaline and nerves, not sure which outweighed the other. She knew her nerves often took over after a lot of stress, which was present that week. *Just focus,* she thought. She took another shot, making it, and decided to push everything out of her mind. She took a deep breath, focusing on the next shot, making it.

She managed to focus on the shooting, her accuracy increasing significantly. Now making more shots than she missed, her confidence was boosted, and she was feeling good. Sweat dripped from her body as she tired herself out, running for the rebound. She looked at her watch, realizing two hours had gone by. "I better get back before they start to worry and come out looking for me," she said to herself. She retrieved the ball, placing it back where she found it, and began walking home.

Ashton stopped in her tracks; fear gripped her insides as Franko stood ahead of her. "Let's talk," he said, demandingly.

"No," she said.

He grabbed her waist, bringing her to his front as she tried to walk past him. Her lower back felt something grow on it as he pressed her against him. Balmy air hit her neck, her hair standing straight up as his hand went to her privates. "Get your hands off me, NOW!"

"Now, why would I do that, when you're just so delicious?" he smirked, whispering in her ear.

She closed her eyes, channeling her mind to the switch, and flipping it—the switch she wished she never had to turn back on. It was better if she hid that person, but Franko just wouldn't let her go.

Her right leg lifted, slamming down onto his foot. It then bent up, kicking him in the privates with the heel. She spun around and leaned back, missing the punch that would have landed a direct blow to her face. She spun again, planting her foot square on his chest and sent him flying backward.

He flew several feet, rolling on the ground before his back hit a brick building. "You son of a fucking bitch, you whore!" he said with a snarl as he got back to his feet. A malicious look appeared on his face as his anger took over.

She stood rooted; her posture showed determination and willpower as she held back everything she could from really hurting him. "Might I remind you that we have a contract," she said.

"Fuck the contract, you slutty whore. I don't give a rat's ass about the contract," he said, his voice dripping with anger.

"I'll ask you once more. Do you wish to terminate our contract?"

"You and following the fucking rules, yes, I want to terminate our contract. It was already invalid."

Franko waved his thugs, or businesspeople, as they liked to be called, out into the open. "Get her," he commanded.

She placed one knee on the concrete sidewalk. Her fingertips felt the heat radiating off the concrete, and her eyes closed as she focused on her surroundings. The men walked closer to her, and Franko scoffed.

Her eyes zoomed open; the once-bright hazel that was kind and sweet was gone. Her aura switched from calming blue to raging red. Fierce, she reached into her knee-high boots, pulling out a dagger. She stood up, tossing it into the air, and caught it after several twirls.

She glowered at the men she trained with every day for twenty-one years; they knew she was serious. Her head held high, she took a step forward, and the men lowered their heads in submission. They backed away from her, nothing more than cowards who feared the prodigy that their boss created.

In their world, the underground, she was the one they called "White Walker," someone who was feared by all. Franko stared with disapproval at what he thought were his most loyal and talented men. "I told you to get her," he yelled.

"Even they disobey their master when they are facing death. You should've known that they would back down at my presence, since they watched you create me to be nothing more than a killer. No emotions, no hesitation, and certainly no mercy. That was what you taught me," she said, her voice and eyes dripping venom as she spoke.

Franko walked toward her, and she advanced toward him. "So now the mutt goes and growls. After ten years you want to bite me?" he scornfully said, taking another step.

"I never wanted to growl or bite. Instead, I made a choice that day. A choice to walk away," she said. She met his step. They were like circling cats waiting to see who would pounce first.

"You were always weak—you never would have made it if you stayed," he said.

He lunged forward to grab her wrist. She managed to sidestep, swiping him with the dagger, grazing his arm as a small trickle of blood dripped down onto the concrete.

She stepped back, repositioning herself so she had a full view. He lunged at her again, grabbing her wrist, and squeezing it till she dropped the dagger. He twisted her around, and she kicked the dagger away from them, struggling to get loose. She slammed her head back, head butting him on the cheek. He took several steps backward, reaching for his lips. Blood covered his hand as he pulled it away from his lip.

He snarled and charged after her. He grabbed her waist, slamming her against a brick building. An audible gasp escaped her; reaching her hand out, she grasped his neck. He gasped for air, releasing her. She stood firm, lifting him off the ground a few inches. His legs flailed out, kicking her in the shin. She dropped him to the ground as she reached for her knee.

They noticed the dagger at the same time, thrashing to get to it before the other. Still hurting from his powerful kick, her knee refused to move quickly. He twirled around when he got the dagger, sending it gashing into her side. She doubled over in pain. She realized, with a second to spare, that he came for another attack, missing her. Her hand reached for his wrist, twisting the dagger into his side.

He stumbled backward. "You slut. You think that will stop me?" He lashed out, grabbing her arm. His hand clutched her waist as the dagger pressed into her throat. "How do you like this, baby doll? Huh, you like this?"

"Don't, mm, call me mm that," she tried to reply, but her words were muffled by her mouth being covered.

"Aww, but you used to love that. It was my nickname for you. Don't you remember?" Bile came up from her throat at the thought of that nickname. "How'd you like seeing me every day outside the hospital? A constant reminder that your mine."

"Mmm . . . argh," she struggled to speak, wiggling to get away but failing.

"What's the matter? Got a speaking problem? Or should I help you make other sounds?" His hand that once pinned her waist moved to her breast. She squirmed, trying harder to get free, but it was no use. The blade cut into her skin at each attempt as she tried to break away from his grasp.

"Mmm . . . no" was all she could get out.

"You like that, don't you?"

"Stop!" His hand squeezed her breast, slipping down her shirt as he ripped her bra.

"Now why would I do that, when I got you right where I want you?"

A muffled and tangled "Stop" escaped her. She strained her wrist, digging her nails into his thigh.

"You're a fucking cunt," he said, swearing. His hand moved to grasp his thigh.

"What did you expect me to do—let you rape me again?"

"You liked it!"

"I was four when you started raping me. I didn't even know what sex was, you pedophile!"

With the dagger no longer on her throat, she slammed her head back against his again, catching him in the chin. He released his grip completely, and she turned around, striking his face hard with the back of her hand. He wasn't fazed, looking right back at her, prepared to fight.

"You think that you can take me?" he said, putting his hands up, ready to fight.

"Do you think I want to do this?"

"Why wouldn't you? Everyone wants to kill their leader, it's the territory. We can live only so long."

"So, you have a death wish? Is that why you keep attacking me and stalking me? Because you want me to kill you?"

"I don't want you to kill me, but eventually, you will. It's what every prodigy does in this business. And you are my prodigy, my successor."

"I never wanted to kill you. Didn't you piece it together when I came to you to sign a contract? I wanted to walk away and stay away. I don't want to be an assassin, and I certainly don't want to kill you or anyone else anymore."

"And that's exactly what makes you so weak. You let your emotions get in the way of your life, of what you were made to do," he said, angrily.

"I never had any choice but to kill, thanks to you, and I didn't let my emotions get in the way of it. Because I knew the consequences if I did." Her voice was raised, just as angry as his.

"What a weakling you are. Pathetic." He lunged at her with fisted hands, but she blocked them with her arm.

"I'm not a weakling—I just don't want to hurt others as you hurt me."

He took another swing at her and got her rib cage. She swung her leg, managing to strike the back of his knee, and he dropped to the ground before regaining control.

"Anyone who walks away is weak. You just proved to me that you can't handle this line of work." He swung the dagger at her, scraping her cheek before she could get back far enough. The red blood was slick and smooth as it sank to her lips, leaving a foul taste in her mouth. "All you were ever good for was the sex. And even then, you couldn't manage to do it correctly!"

His constant stabbing of words cut worse than the dagger. She lunged at him, trying to gain control of the blade, but he slipped out of her grasp. Her nails dug into his arm, leaving long red marks. The badgering continued as he baited her with his words. Each word stung worse than the last as old memories bombarded her brain.

"You couldn't even bear my child when I wanted you to. You even managed to fuck that up. I bet you were sleeping with several hundred guys. Dirty slut." His eyes never moved from hers as he lunged at her again. She moved back, grabbing his wrist with such force that he dropped the dagger. She kicked it away. He spun around, kicking her right in the ribs. He grabbed her, throwing her into a brick wall.

Her back hit the bricks before sending her to the ground. The pain was excruciating. *Keep fighting, just keep fighting,* she thought. Shakily, she picked herself up, staggering to the side, missing his attack. She sent her knee soaring right in between his legs, hitting his groin. He tumbled to the ground in pain as she picked up the dagger.

"So, now you want to kill me? Is that it? Didn't you just say that that isn't what you wanted to do?" He spat the words out at her.

"Yes, I'm going to kill you and finish this once and for all." She walked toward him as he scurried backward until his back pressed against the brick wall, still holding on to his crotch in pain. "I'm through with this torment, everything that you have put me through. You stole my past. You took everything from me. My parents, my past, my childhood, my child, and my gift—everything. And this time, it is my turn to repay you for all of it." She looked him in the eyes as she plunged the dagger into his heart, twisting it to the side.

His hand shot up around her neck, holding it in a death grip as he faded. The more he faded, the looser his grip got, until his body no longer sat up, but lay fully on the ground, and she could breathe again. She stumbled backward, landing on her knees on the ground, shaking and covered in blood. She checked his heart rate, wanting to be completely sure he was gone. It pumped a few more times before coming to a complete stop. She sat there on the concrete, too shocked to move.

"Here comes Blade. He's not going to be happy," said Gage, one of the stronger of Franko's men.

Sangchul looked down the busy street, cars and people passing, and their boss's friend coming. *He'll certainly kill her if he sees her,* he thought. He went over to Ashton. "Get up. You must go, Blade's coming," he said.

She looked up at him, eyes glazed over, hollow inside. Sangchul grabbed her arm, forcing her up. "You must leave now. Blade will kill you if he finds you here," he said. He shoved her out onto the busy street.

"Why the hell did you do that?" one of the men asked.

"Franko put her through hell, she doesn't deserve to die for it," Sangchul said.

"You and your heart, pathetic."

Covered in blood in broad daylight, the pain showed her that her ribs were damaged. Beads of sweat popping out on her forehead and grime stung her eyes. She started to walk back to her house. People stared at the disheveled sight of her, but no one cared enough to ask if she was okay. No one cared enough to call the police. Not that the police would do anything, anyway; that's just not how it's done in the underground.

Blade passed Ashton on the sidewalk; he knew right then what she had done. He looked ahead of him, retrieving his only friend, the one she killed.

17

HER STORY

Lord Diavolo, Barbatos, and Simeon sat in the living room watching a movie, passing the time. One of the characters said something funny, and they burst out laughing. The door opened, and they looked up from their movie, freezing at the sight of Ashton's mangled body. She was barely able to stand, covered in blood, shaking, breathing heavily, and crying.

"Kaname, unlock secure location," she said with a squeak.

"Of course, Ashton."

She clutched her side, hitting the floor as she struggled to stay conscious. Lord Diavolo, Barbatos, and Simeon ran to her side. "We have to get her to the hospital. We need to see how bad her wounds are," Barbatos said.

"Basement, the basement," she said.

Barbatos bent, picking her up. She yelped at the sharpness that rocketed through her body.

"She said the basement, open the door," Barbatos said.

"Of course." Lord Diavolo ran ahead, opening the door as Satan appeared at the top of the library stairs.

"What happened?" Satan raced down the stairs to her side, only now noticing the blood. Fury radiated off him. He was the avatar of wrath, losing control quickly, but since she came into his life, she helped ground him better than anything or anyone else ever had. Of course, his unrequited feelings for her helped.

"We don't know, she just came home this way. It's difficult for her to speak at the moment," Barbatos said. He carried her down the stairs.

"How could this happen? One of us should have gone with her—we should have fought her on this." Satan's voice grew angrier and angrier.

"You need to calm down. Getting angry won't help her now. And there was no reason for us to go with her," Lord Diavolo said, snapping at him.

Satan inhaled deeply, trying to get hold of himself, enough to help them. Barbatos reached the bottom of the stairs. "Kaname, open medical bay," she said. There was a click over in the corner; it resonated in the empty room. Barbatos made his way over. The medical bay was as big as a hospital room, holding only medical equipment, supplies, and a small bar.

Barbatos placed Ashton onto the medical bed, and her head bobbed from side to side. She couldn't grasp the fact that she killed the man who had hurt her for twenty-one years. She opened her mouth, but all that came out was pitiful sobs.

Simeon remained by the door, shock rendering his body motionless. His mind wouldn't let him stop long enough to help her. *She means so much to me. I know that angel-human relations aren't allowed, but I would give up my angel heritage to be with her. If that's what she wanted, then I would become a human if it meant I could stay by her side forever. But now, I might not even get the chance. There is so much blood on her, and she isn't talking. I need, I need to get to her.*

He pulled himself together long enough to realize that he was alone in the living room. He searched for the door, walking in a trance, as if someone else were controlling his body. He reached the bottom of the stairs, the light reflecting perfectly on the glass display case. He looked in the direction of the shine, noticing the collection of tea sets.

In his stupor, he stopped walking and became fixated on them. He recalled the day in the tea shop. *She was talking about these when we went to the tea shop and then out for dinner. There was the blue floral one that I couldn't resist going back and getting for her. She said that they were important to her, but I couldn't fully understand it back then; all I could do was comfort her.* He took another step closer to the tea sets and got lost in his racing thoughts again.

These were what she had been talking about. Each one of them is porcelain; she had specifically mentioned they had to be porcelain. It didn't matter whether they were pretty or not, the most important thing to her was what they were made from. They had to be made of porcelain! A fragile glass that symbolized her soul. The porcelain can take a lot of damage, just as she had, and both the porcelain and she can withstand a lot of hurt. She was trying to tell me that she had never broken even after all that she had endured. That's why she had chosen all-porcelain tea sets to identify with. I now understand what she had been trying to tell me. Simeon opened his eyes wide as he realized the truth.

"Simeon! Simeon!" Satan yelled at him to get his attention. "Simeon!" Simeon snapped out of his thoughts long enough to look at Satan.

"Hmm?"

"She's asking for you, she needs you," Satan said in a raised voice to make sure Simeon was still paying attention. *I don't see why she needs him; why couldn't it have been me? I wouldn't have been looking at some useless piece of glass instead of being by her side,* Satan thought as he yelled.

"Right." Simeon regained his sense of reality, moving to the medical bay. She looked over at him from the gurney. Their eyes locked, and he could sense her pain. Salty water collected in his eyes, threatening to spew over. He stepped to her side out of Barbatos's way. "I'm right here, snowflake. Everything is all right." His hand found hers, caressing it.

She was lying on the medical bed in a daze, Barbatos giving Lord Diavolo orders on what to place on the counter for him. Her voice was a soft noise, one they weren't even sure they heard, but then Satan realized that she called for Simeon. He was the one person she wanted by her side. The one whom she came to love and trust over a brief period. Now, he stood there caressing her hand.

"Simeon, you should try some of your healing spells on her," Barbatos said.

Simeon placed his hands over her knife wound, straining for the white cloud of mist to drift above his hands, but it never came. "It's not working, I can't use it," he said. *Of course, that would be one of my powers I can't use in the Human Realm; I'm utterly useless,* he thought.

"That's okay, you tried. Ashton, I need to remove your clothes to gain access to some of the wounds. Is that all right?

I'll do my best make sure your parts are covered," Barbatos asked. *The wounds are so deep, it's going to take a lot of tending to care for them.*

She gave a slight nod, and Barbatos ripped her clothes, exposing her body. Their audible gasps filled the room. Her body was naked, marred, and soiled with raised white scars. Rage emanated off the demons, bursting into the already damaged atmosphere. Satan changed into his demon form, curled horns extended from his head, a long tail whipping out from his rear.

Satan smashed the mirrored glass with his white-knuckled fist, shattering it to the ground. Lord Diavolo formed into his demon self, black with gold-tipped horns extended from his head and magnificent wings expanded from his back taking up a large portion of the room. He pinned Satan to the wall as Satan thrashed and lashed out at him, the wall caving in from the force.

"That man hurt her, let me go. I'm going to kill him," Satan said.

"That's not going to help her right now. She's injured. We need to tend to her first, now calm down," Lord Diavolo said.

Ashton's gaze was on Simeon—hollow, pained, wounded. He didn't know how he managed to control his anger, perhaps because he felt her pain? *Who could hurt her in such a way?* he thought, the salty water spilling from his eyes as he looked over each mark on her body.

"I'm going to start working on your wounds now, okay, my lady?" Barbatos asked. She nodded.

"The man you asked me about earlier, his name was Franko. He hurt me for twenty-one years. The look in his eyes was mischievous and dangerous when he looked into mine at four years old. I heard someone come into the house and a scream from my mom, which made me run from my room. Stopping in the doorway of the hall is when I saw him holding the gun to their heads. Point blank, he looked over at me as I stood wide eyed and crying. BANG! And they were gone. He stared at me as he killed my parents." Her voice trembled as she remembered the moment that changed her life.

"After that, all I knew was pain. After so much, you can't feel it anymore. He took me to a place called the 'underground,' where assassins live and train. Killing one another on the commands of others that are higher up. But the beatings from him were severe. The repeated motions of him defiling my body were even worse. I learned quickly to keep my mouth shut and not do anything. But that never stopped him, though. Even when I did nothing wrong, he would still beat and rape me. Not just once or twice, countless times."

Her tears now flowed freely, the grip Simeon had on her hand stiffened, and Satan and Lord Diavolo stared at her with pained expressions. She kept her voided eyes on Simeon. "Training twelve-hour days in combat and weaponry, stealth, and hunting to kill the prey. Emotions weren't allowed, feelings were nonexistent, the hesitation was futile, and mercy was never heard of. I was not a human. I was something that he designed to kill on his command and his command only. In twenty-one years, I was forced to murder thousands of people, most of whom were innocent.

"I was shackled to the wall in a chamber by my wrists, ankles, and neck. Beat with whips, cat claws, chains, and balls with spikes. Whatever he could think of, he would use on my body. I was numb and bleeding out. Often, I would pass out because of the pain." She whimpered at the memory, sobbing as she remembered the pain and what the scars were to her—a constant reminder on her body.

"And then there was the rape. It didn't happen a few times, it happened every day. The older I got, the worse it would get. I've endured countless abortions and miscarriages. From the first one when I was ten and the last when I turned twenty-five. That was how many times he got me pregnant.

"During the abortions, the doctor would come into the room as I lay there in stirrups, and he would operate. He never said a word to me, just did what he had to do and left. The man who was at the hospital during the news conference, that was Franko. He never even entered the room as I had the abortions on his command. When he wanted me to have a child, my body was too marred and damaged to carry over the first trimester." She let out a heavy breath and tried to stabilize her voice. It became shakier the more she remembered and with what she spent years trying to forget.

"When I was twenty-five, I finally found a way out. I had walked up to him and decided that I wanted out. And all he did was laugh at me. He was about done with me and decided that he would give me a chance. An impossible task that was designed to kill me, and if I succeeded, then he would grant me my freedom. The task was the hardest thing I had ever done when it came to killing, but I had been programmed into not having emotions. So, I completed the task and walked back into his office, and we agreed on a contract.

"**Since** I completed this impossible task, I was allowed to leave, and he could make no contact with me at all, not even be near me or look at me. And in exchange, I'd relinquish all rights to overthrow him as the leader. He knew the day would come when the one they call the mutt would eventually growl or bite the master. Which is exactly why he wanted me dead. Events didn't turn out how he planned, and he was surprised when I walked back in there. I was barely hanging on, but I made it.

"That was the day that I made a choice—a choice to walk away and forget everything that he did to me. Or so I thought. AAHH," she yelped as Barbatos pressed the bandage to her ribs.

"I'm sorry, my lady. I'll try to be more careful," Barbatos said with a panicked expression.

"The very next day, I felt him lurking in the shadows. Even though he thought I couldn't see him, I could feel him. For the past ten years, I'd find him following me, stalking me wherever I went. Instead of doing something about it, I made yet another choice to turn a blind eye. Just like I chose to walk away instead of killing him. My patience and my mercy can go only so far. I don't want to be that person anymore. I don't want him to hurt me anymore.

"I constantly thought: Do I let him continue to follow me and hurt me? Or do I add one more kill to the list of names that I've taken from others?" she said, continuing in a whisper.

"That is why when I broke free, and I became a surgeon so that instead of killing people, I could do everything in my power to save them." She let out a strangled sob, and Simeon began stroking her hair.

The atmosphere was tense; the time dragged as Barbatos cleaned her wounds. Being a demon, he could do more in the medical field than the average human, but under the circumstances, she got lucky that none of her wounds needed extensive care. He was able to wrap them up, working as quickly as he could. "I'm all done—I've done the best I could," he said.

Simeon and Barbatos helped her sit up, and Barbatos wrapped a blanket around her. Simeon snaked his arm around her waist, placing soft kisses on her head. Satan and Lord Diavolo changed back to their human form, kneeling on the ground before her. She felt their caring hands on her knees as she welcomed Simeon's embrace.

She reached up, her fingers firmly grasping Simeon's biceps. Her voice was barely above a whisper, almost strangled. "I thought that by leaving, I could be free from him. That I would be able to move on with my life, but all that happened was I was alone. I went night after night reliving what he did to me. Curling up in my bed with the blankets wrapped around me, my face stained from streaking, salty tears. I would try to ground myself, but it would take hours before it would let up and I could see where I was again.

"The first five years, there were multiple nightmares each night, and then after the fifth year, it became one, and it wasn't until the eighth year that it went down to five days a week. It's relentless, there's no escape." The strangled cry that came from her filled Lord Diavolo, Barbatos, Satan, and Simeon with pain and made them crumble inside. They were doing everything they could to hold back their own feelings as their own tears had welled up in their eyes.

"But then, I found a place where I was at least a little safe. Somewhere far away from him, where he couldn't follow me. He couldn't follow me to the Demon Realm." Her eyes wandered to Lord Diavolo in a desperate plea to understand as she placed the side of her head to rest on Simeon's chest.

"In the Demon Realm, I was surrounded by demons that I was supposed to be afraid of, afraid that I might get hurt or eaten by them. But I wasn't scared of them. I didn't shake with fright because I'd already been staring at death my entire life. You brought me to a place in which I could heal. I didn't have to be afraid. And slowly, within the six months, the nightmares went from five a week to barely any at all. I was getting sleep without constantly waking up. Sleep deprivation had become something of the past, and with it, the memories. They started to get stored in a compartment that I could leave them in. I could finally be free." She closed her eyes, exhausted from the events and sharing her story with others for the first time. Mentally, it took a lot out of her, and she let Simeon support her as she leaned on him. He obliged, tightening his grip around her as he stroked her hair.

"Today, on the way back home, I ran into him. I killed him." The words tumbled out of her mouth as she looked up at Simeon. Her eyes held fear, the fear that Simeon would despise her and hate her for what she had done. She didn't want to kill the man, but her patience had worn thin. He had kept pushing her and pushing her. After what he had done to her and what she'd had to go through, she didn't want to kill him, but she did want him gone for good.

"Did he attack you, Ashton?" Barbatos kept his voice quiet and low as not to startle her.

"Yes. I never thought that I would be able to be so close to someone like this. I've spent my entire life having no one there for me and having to endure all the pain myself. And now . . . now I have not just the four of you, but many others as well. I'm not alone anymore. I feel like for the first time I can trust. Please don't leave me—I didn't want to kill him."

"We aren't going to leave you at all. You don't have to worry about that," Lord Diavolo said.

"You're strong, and it takes a lot to kill someone. We know you didn't want to. It's not your fault. None of this was your fault, my lady," Barbatos said.

"I would never leave your side," Simeon said.

She tried to stand up, but the pain was too sharp, and she sat back down. Simeon helped her stand up, gripping her waist as she walked. He started to lead her to the stairs with a secure grip on her waist, but she caught sight of the glass case. "I won't break, I'm made of porcelain." Simeon barely heard her, but he knew exactly what she meant.

When she reached the bottom of the stairs, she glanced up at the top. She felt they were impossible to climb up; the pain in her ribs was already excruciating. Simeon noticed the overwhelmed expression on her face and gave her a light hug. "I'm not going to leave your side. I'll help you every step of the way."

She knew that Simeon's words had more than one meaning, and it was exactly what she needed to hear. Simeon lifted her up over the stairs, bridal style, giving her a feeling of assurance—a feeling that he would pick her up when she couldn't do so herself, reassuring her that he would stay with her. Even though she killed a person, Simeon hadn't passed judgment on her, and neither had the others.

Lord Diavolo and Barbatos stayed down in the medical bay to clean up. There were a lot of bloody rags, since Barbatos used them to clean all the blood off her. And Satan followed behind Ashton and Simeon just in case she needed any extra help.

Simeon managed to get her to her bedroom. He laid her down on her left side, and each of them sat on the bed beside her. Simeon felt a moment of jealousy at how close Satan sat to her, but he didn't say anything, since he knew she needed all the support she could get. "Satan," she said, her voice raspy from telling them her past; she could barely speak.

"Yes?"

"Water." Her voice was low and raspy, but he understood exactly what she needed.

"Of course, I'll be back in just a moment." He walked out of the room to grab a glass of water. Ashton tried to sit up, wanting to rest her back against the backboard, but it was harder than she thought. Simeon supported her weight to help her and ended up with her forehead on his chest. "I'm sorry I killed him," she said, her voice cracking from the pressure it had been under earlier that day. "Please, sunshine, don't hate me, I didn't have a choice anymore." She broke down crying as she clung to Simeon's clothes. She kept her forehead pressed to his chest as she cried.

Simeon wrapped his arms around her to give her the support and comfort she needed. "It's all right, snowflake. I'm not upset with you, and I understand what you had to do. You don't have to worry. I'm going to be right here with you. I won't leave your side. Shh . . . It's okay." Simeon's words came out in soft lullabies of comfort as Satan reentered with the water for which she asked.

Satan made his way over to the bed, and they felt it dip under his weight as he sat down. "The water's right here for when you want it," he said. He held the glass of water in his hands. Satan believed that if he placed the water down, he would smash his fist through the wall, and the water was the only thing that kept him from doing that. He was about to lay a hand on her back, but the look that Simeon gave him made him second-guess the idea.

Lord Diavolo and Barbatos went to check on Ashton after they finished cleaning up the medical bay. They started to approach her, but Simeon let out a growl as a warning. Satan shook his head at them not to touch her. Lord Diavolo met Simeon's eyes, and he could see that Simeon was no longer acting as an angel, but as someone who was going to lose a loved one. Simeon wasn't just comforting her, he was protecting her from everyone, including them. Lord Diavolo gave a small nod of understanding before he and Barbatos went to sit on the floor beside the bed.

Soft feathers enclosed around her and Simeon as he protected her. *I'm not going to leave her. Never. The archangels can do whatever they want to me, but I won't leave her side. Why didn't an angel get assigned to her? She shouldn't have had to go through any of that, especially alone!* "I'll never leave your side," he whispered in a stern, loving voice.

As time passed, all they heard was Ashton's intense cries from pain and hurt. Everything she suffered from her whole life spilled out in all her tears. Losing her parents, every beating, every rape, every abortion, every miscarriage, every person she was forced to kill, every patient she saved, every patient that died, all the life she had spent alone and suffering, all of it came out that day as she spent the rest of it crying in Simeon's arms.

I didn't know that the one we chose for the exchange program has gone through so much. This must've been what she meant when she said that she had faced death her whole life. I can't even imagine what she's been through. I know that my father wasn't the greatest and would often hit me at times when he was angry, but he wasn't that bad. Not like the men in her past, Lord Diavolo thought as he put his arm around Barbatos.

Barbatos's head dipped onto his master's shoulder as the weight of what happened was too much for him to bear. *I knew she had a past, because I saw it in her future, but to hear her speak the words and see the scars up close. It's harder to take—I can't even imagine. And to think that I inflict whip marks on demons in the dungeons under the castle when permitted.*

Lord Diavolo and Barbatos sat there holding each other as if to comfort themselves from the pain they felt from her crying. Silent tears stained their cheeks.

Satan sat on the bed, still holding the glass of water that kept him from snapping. *I don't even know, because all I feel is hollow inside.* Tears still flowed silently and heavily from his own eyes. And Simeon's eyes were closed, tearstained, and still whispering sweet lullabies to the top of her head as he patted her hair.

After a while, Barbatos and Lord Diavolo faded off to sleep, heads resting on each other. Satan placed the water down as he began to nod off. Ashton's crying slowed, becoming less frantic. The grip she had on Simeon loosened as she drifted off to sleep, and Simeon kept his hold on her. He loosened the grip but didn't remove his hands. He stayed awake for a while longer while everyone else rested, just to make sure she wouldn't wake up. He had to be sure she was going to be okay. He managed to stay awake for an extra hour after everyone else had drifted off. Then, he placed his cheek on the top of her head and drifted off to sleep himself.

18

FIRST KISS

Ashton moaned as her hand went to her eyes, rubbing them. Pain shot through her side as she tried to readjust, falling onto Simeon's chest as her body gave out. Simeon jolted awake as he searched for Ashton. His eyes caught her as her body weight came down onto him. "Are you all right?"

"I—." Her voice cracked, coming out in a raspy scratch.

"I'll go get you a fresh glass of water," Simeon told her as she slowly moved from his body, leaning against the headrest.

She rubbed her eyes more thoroughly, removing the crusty bits from them. Slowly, she nodded as Simeon scooted to the edge of the bed. She watched as her protector left the room. Carefully, she made her way to the edge of the bed, looking down at Lord Diavolo and Barbatos sleeping.

Hmm . . . Satan's blocking the other side of the bed so I can't get off. And Lord Diavolo and Barbatos have their feet in the way. There's no way I'd be able to make it over their feet without being in more pain. It already hurts a lot. But I really need to clean up, she thought as she looked at the feet blocking her way.

Simeon silently opened the door, pausing when he saw Ashton was sitting up, hair a tangled mess. He chuckled, a smile crossing his lips. He made his way over to the side of the bed, holding the glass of water out to her. Shaking hands greeted the glass of water, sending droplets flying onto the bed. He reached his hand out, cupping hers to steady them as she took a sip.

She slowly drank the water, closing her eyes as the icy water swept the soreness away. Her hands loosened around the cup, letting Simeon have full control. "They look peaceful," she said, speaking softly as she looked down at the demons.

"Yes, they do," Simeon replied.

"Thank you," she said.

"For what?"

"Staying with me after what I did."

"Ashton, what you did wasn't your fault. You didn't have a choice."

"I didn't. I didn't want to kill anyone ever again."

"I know," he said as he brushed a strand of hair behind her ear.

"Hmm . . ." Barbatos stirred as he lifted his head off Lord Diavolo's shoulder. Barbatos's eyes opened, closing after a second.

"Where are you going, pillow?" Lord Diavolo mumbled. His head dropped as Barbatos moved.

Ashton burst out laughing as a huge grin spread across her face. She continued to laugh despite the pain radiating from her ribs. Simeon looked at her as she laughed, his heart feeling lighter at the sound.

"What's so funny?" Lord Diavolo asked as he looked up at Ashton, puzzled as he continued to wake up.

"The two of you," she replied in between fits of giggles.

"What about us?" Barbatos chimed in, smiling when he saw her laughing.

"You're just too cute, the way you two are sleeping in each other's arms," she said, continuing to laugh.

"Huh? What? What is it?" Satan bolted straight up. "Who made that noise?" He rubbed his eyes as he tried to wake himself up.

"That would be Ashton. It seems she finds Barbatos and me *cute*?" Lord Diavolo filled Satan in.

"How are they cute?" Satan asked, perplexed.

"They just are. The way they fell asleep in each other's arms." She shrugged her shoulders as she smiled. "Um, could I get the two of you to move your feet? I can't get around them, and I didn't want to wake you up," she asked Lord Diavolo and Barbatos.

They retracted their feet, letting her get by. Her hands reached for the bed as she tried to steady herself while walking. She felt an arm around her waist, looking up to find Simeon smiling down at her. "Let me help," he told her, and she nodded in reply.

"I think I'll go get cleaned up," Lord Diavolo said as he stood up.

"I think I'll do the same," Satan said.

"Why don't I start preparing some breakfast while everyone gets cleaned up?" Barbatos asked.

"Barbatos, if you would like to use my room, you are more than welcome to," Simeon told him as he stood outside the bathroom door waiting. "I'm going to wait till Ashton is taken care of, so please feel free."

"Well, in that case, thank you, Simeon. I shall get what I need from the room and head over to yours. Thank you again," Barbatos said, giving him a slight bow.

"Of course, you're welcome," Simeon said with a nod, watching the three demons leave the room.

Ashton placed a hand on her messy hair. *Wow, I have scratches all over my face, and my clothes are bloody and torn. I really need a shower. I ended up not taking one after I spent hours at the basketball court. But how am I supposed to support myself in the shower? It's way too slippery; I can't even walk well on my own. I'm sure Simeon would help, but am I comfortable with that? We've had physical contact, which has been okay. But being naked in a shower is different. I don't have a choice, though. I can do this!* The thoughts ran through her head as she looked in the mirror.

Her heart pounded in her chest as she opened the bathroom door. Simeon looked over and smiled at her as the door opened. His smile vanished at her expression. "What's wrong?"

"N-nothing, i-it's just . . . could you possibly h-help me t-take a s-shower?" she said, stammering nervously as she kept her gaze on the floor.

"Of course, I can," Simeon's eyes closed as relief filled his body.

He turned the knob in the shower, adjusting the temperature until it was right. He turned back to face Ashton, who hesitated to remove her clothes.

"I won't look, and I don't have to get in if you don't want me to. I can have my back turned and stand beside the shower in case you need me," Simeon said, reassuring her.

"I won't be able to stand by myself—it'll be too slippery. I want you in there. You should close your eyes, though," she told him apprehensively.

Ashton carefully removed her clothes after Simeon closed his eyes. "I'm done, you can undress now," she told him.

Simeon removed his clothes, hesitating at his form-fitting boxers. "Would you like me to leave my boxers on?" he asked her softly.

"It's okay, you can take them off if you want," she responded after a moment of hesitation.

Ashton walked over to Simeon, placing a soft, delicate hand on his chest. He kept his eyes closed as his arm snaked around her waist, helping her into the shower. The warm water hit their skin as they stood there embracing its warmth.

"I'm going to wash your hair with some shampoo now, is that okay?" he asked as he kissed the top of her head.

Her head moved up and down slowly as she whispered a simple yes.

She reveled in the sensation of his massaging the shampoo onto her scalp. Her eyes closed as she dipped her head under the water, washing the dirt away. He reached for the conditioner and used his hands to massage it into her hair, taking his time as he tried to make her feel relaxed.

Her shoulders dropped as she let out a contented sigh, leaning back onto Simeon's chest, her head on his shoulder. "That felt wonderful, thank you." Her eyes opened as she looked at him, noticing that his eyes remained shut.

"I'm glad you enjoyed it." He tilted his head in the direction of her voice, smiling.

Her pounding heart raced at the movement, gravity pulling her toward him. Her lips brushed against his as she kissed him for the first time. The sensation of her kiss sent his heart soaring; his eyebrows raised with surprise, as he had longed for that kiss for a long time.

"You can open your eyes, sunshine," she said. Her nerves shook at her words, heat rising to stain her cheeks.

"Are you sure? I don't want to make you uncomfortable." His fluttered voice mixed with the pitter-patter of water droplets.

"Yes, I'm sure," she said.

His eyes opened, meeting hers. They stared into each other's nervous eyes, faces flushed. She dipped her head back, allowing the steamy hot water to run over her hair, washing away the conditioner. A tingly sensation sent goose bumps over his body as he kept his gaze on her face.

"Did you want to use the shampoo and conditioner? I know it's cherry-blossom scented, but it's all I have," she asked.

"If you are okay with that, then I would like to use them," he replied.

"Of course, I don't mind."

Her hand reached for the shower wall, leaning her back against the cold wall as she covered her chest. His eyes didn't stray from hers as he reached for the shampoo. "You haven't looked down . . . at my body," she whispered.

"No, I wouldn't do that. You're putting a lot of trust in me, and I wouldn't do anything to break it." *Although it is hard not to, but I'm trying my best because I love her so much.*

Ashton's stomach filled with butterflies as she watched the water run over Simeon's hair, washing away the shampoo and conditioner. His eyes blinked the water droplets away, meeting her gaze. Her hands reached for him, landing on his shoulders as his arms wrapped around her waist. Her bottom lip caught between her teeth nervously, waiting with expectation of another kiss.

His head moved toward hers, stopping as his eyes closed, letting out a breath. "Did you not want to?" she asked, her expression frantic.

"I want to. I just don't want to push you into something you aren't ready for." His breath came out strangled as he tried to control his urge.

The lump in her throat swallowed hard as she took in a deep breath, closing the distance between them, kissing him. Her lips were soft, and the kiss was delicate yet rough. He deepened the kiss, tilting his jaw toward her as his hand cupped her neck.

They pulled back, gasping for air, and Simeon couldn't control himself. He leaned down, stealing another kiss, longer and more passionate. His hand caressed her cheek as his jaw moved back and forth. Her hands snaked around his neck, further encouraging him. He pressed his forehead against hers as he gasped for breath, looking into her hazel orbs.

"Are you okay with me using the loofah to wash your body, or would you prefer to do it yourself?" he asked as he pulled himself back together.

"Would you do it for me, please?"

"Of course."

His thumb brushed against her cheek, sending a sensation coursing through her as he reached for the loofah. The loofah moved over her skin as he avoided sensitive areas that could hurt her. She placed her head on his chest. "Thank you."

His hand stroked her hair as he kissed the top of her head. "You're welcome."

A shiver went down her spine as he turned the water off; stepping out, he wrapped the towel around her. Goose bumps laced her arms; his hands rubbed them, giving her warmth. She kissed his cheek, causing a light shade of red to appear on his face.

Her hand moved across the countertop as she walked, supporting her. Brushing her teeth, she noticed Simeon's gaze. "It's every inch from the neck down."

"I-I'm sorry I didn't mean—I didn't realize. I'm sorry," he said, stuttering.

"You didn't know. Anyone would be shocked when seeing them."

Her body trembled as she made her way to the bedroom. Nails dug into her side as pain shot through her body. Her head bore down on the dresser as her eyes closed, tears stinging her eyes.

Simeon grappled with himself as he followed her, hurt resonating through him at her pain. "Would you like me to help?"

"I just can't open the drawer."

"What would you like? I can get it for you."

"The gray sweatpants and the blue zip-up sweater." She pointed to the drawer they were in, waiting for him to retrieve them. "Thank you. You should change yourself, or you'll catch a cold."

"If you're okay with it, I'd like to stay just in case you need any more help."

"Don't look."

19

WOODEN FLOWER PETAL

Simeon and Ashton exited the room, making their way to the kitchen. Heads turned as the bedroom door opened, eyes going wide. They stopped; Simeon sported only a towel as water droplets dripped from wet hair, landing on smooth skin.

"What? Did I do something wrong?" Ashton's voice was concerned as everyone stared at her.

"I think I'm going to go change now," Simeon said. His face went beet red as he quickly made his way to his room.

"I forgot I was the only one who changed into clothes," Ashton mumbled to herself as she realized why they were staring.

"Well, I guess we know what took you so long." Satan rolled his eyes angrily as his voice dripped with annoyance.

"What Satan is trying to say is we were starting to get worried. You'd been in there for a long time, but we didn't want to interrupt." Barbatos attempted to ease the tension hanging in the air as he gave Satan a warning glare to control himself.

"Oh, um . . . Yeah, I, um, wanted to take a shower since I was messy, but I wasn't steady enough on my own. So, I-I, um, asked Simeon if he could h-help me." The heat rose in her cheeks as she became flushed. "Sorry," she mumbled. Her hand found the wall for support as she made her way to the empty barstool beside Lord Diavolo.

"You don't have to apologize, there's nothing wrong with wanting to get cleaned up," Lord Diavolo told her as he stood up, pulling the stool out and holding it steady for her.

"Thank you, AHH," she said, her voice barely audible. She grunted in pain as she went to sit down.

"Are you okay? Does it hurt?" Panic was eminent in Lord Diavolo's voice as he asked.

"I'm okay, it just hurts a little," she said, trying to reassure him, but her face betrayed her.

"If you'd like, I saw some pain medicine down in the medical bay. I could go retrieve it for you." Barbatos's forehead creased with worry. He saw the pain she tried to hide, and he longed to take it all away from her.

"Don't be silly, you're busy. I can always get it later, thank you, though," Ashton said, smiling.

"Nonsense. I'm never too busy to tend to your needs," he told her as he headed for the stairs to retrieve the medicine before she could tell him no again.

Lord Diavolo stepped over to the stove, finishing the food that Barbatos had started. "It looks like the shower helped. You look like you have more color," Lord Diavolo said, noticing as he glanced over at her.

"I feel a lot better, especially after the shower. It made me feel refreshed." A small smile crossed her lips as she watched Lord Diavolo cook. *I'm so glad that I have all of them,* she thought to herself. *I know they try to keep their distance so that Simeon doesn't get jealous, and I appreciate that. But, knowing that they're all on my side gives me a lot of solace, even though I'm trying to grip the feeling of that emotion.*

"Good, I'm glad that you feel refreshed." A smile grew on his face as he turned the burner off, placing the food on platters. His reply brought her out of her thoughts as the door opened and Simeon entered the room.

"Is no one going to talk about what happened?" Satan's voice blurted out incredulously. The grip that he thought he had had slipped away. "I mean, that's a lot to go through, and here she is, pretending it didn't even happen. Like she didn't come home stained in blood yesterday with broken ribs. As if she didn't spend all day crying and—"

"That's enough." Barbatos ran up the last few steps as Satan's voice grew louder.

Ashton's face drained in color as her mind shut down. In her peripheral vision, she thought she saw Lord Diavolo shaking his head, but she wasn't sure since her sight was off. Simeon's steps were quick as he made his way to her side, noticing the change in her demeanor. He placed his hand gently onto her shoulder, eyebrows furrowing with worry. She shrugged his hand off the moment she felt the touch. He drew back, giving her space as she went to her room.

They watched as she went to hide in her room. "You can't lose control like that around her. She just started letting us in about this," Barbatos said, reprimanding Satan.

"What am I supposed to do? Sit back and do nothing?" Satan's voice grew louder.

"You can just be there for her. If she wants you to, like with the glass of water yesterday." Barbatos attempted to keep his voice calm.

"But this anger, I just want to smash stuff and set it on fire." Satan's voice boomed through the kitchen walls.

Their argument ceased as they heard Kaname's voice saying, "Yes, Ashton." They couldn't hear what she asked the system, but they heard a click sound. Their eyes moved around, searching one another's for the answer, but none came.

Simeon's eyes were on the ground as he walked over to her bedroom door. He placed his warm hand on the coolness of it, sighing as he sat down on the wooden floor. He stared ahead, but he didn't see anything as his thoughts darted in his mind. *I know why she shrugged my hand off her shoulder, but it hurts to have her do that. Seeing her get upset like that yesterday, I don't know how I kept myself together as well as I did . . .*

"Satan, why don't you take a break in your room or go outdoors and try and calm down? I'm going to make a phone call to Lucifer and let him know that some of us will be staying longer." Lord Diavolo's voice left no room for argument as he tore his gaze off Simeon, giving Satan stern eyes not to argue with him.

Satan flew off the barstool, storming up the stairs to the library. Lord Diavolo and Barbatos stared after him, waiting till Satan was out of the room before Lord Diavolo asked, "How long do you think she'll need to rest before she's well enough to use the transportation device again?"

"At least another week, maybe even two. But it's hard to tell until her ribs start healing. I won't know more until then," Barbatos said.

Lord Diavolo nodded as he made his way to his room, leaving Barbatos in the kitchen. Barbatos eyed the food that he made, sighing as he went to put each of the items in the fridge. He had turned to the counter to pick up the last item when the dessert case caught his eye.

Hmmm, I remember her telling me that she loved brownies. We made them when she first came to the Demon Realm. Asmo had abandoned her, so I invited her over to the baking lesson. I bet she'd love some right now. And it looks as if Simeon needs to be with her as well. I'm going to make some for her. The thoughts crossed Barbatos's mind as he put the last platter in the fridge.

Barbatos gathered all the ingredients for the brownies, putting them together and mixing them. He preheated the oven as he poured the batter into the greased pan, putting them in to bake. He cleaned up the kitchen as they baked, waiting for the timer to go off. Pulling out the brownies, he looked over at Simeon, but he wasn't there.

He searched the room and found the sliding glass door partly open, with Simeon sitting at a table. He walked over, and Simeon looked up at him while he held a wooden flower petal. "Did you whittle that?" Barbatos asked.

"Yes, I couldn't just sit there doing nothing, and I thought that she'd like this," Simeon said. "It's not my best work, but with the only knife I have and the amount of time, it's better than nothing."

"I made her some brownies, you could take them into her when you take her the petal," Barbatos told him. *As much as I want to be the one to take them into her, I know she'll accept them better from him,* Barbatos thought.

"Are you sure that that's okay? Since you made them," Simeon asked. His eyes met Barbatos's with a pleading, desperate look.

"It's perfectly okay with me. I'm sure she'd enjoy receiving them from you a lot more. If you're done, we can go to the kitchen and wait for them to cool."

"I just finished when you came out," Simeon said as he stood up. He placed the petal in his pocket along with his knife and cleaned up the shavings the best he could.

They made their way to the kitchen, preparing a serving tray with two glasses of milk. "I'll check them, make sure they're cooled down enough," Barbatos told Simeon as he held his hand over the brownies.

He grabbed a knife, cutting into the brownies as he placed several of them on the platter. "The platter's ready for you, Simeon," Barbatos said, gesturing as he brought Simeon out of his trance by placing a hand on his shoulder.

"Thank you," Simeon whispered as he took the platter, making his way over to the bedroom.

He knocked gently on the door, careful not to spill anything. His breathing grew more anxious as he waited for the door to open. "Hi," she said, speaking in a quiet voice as she opened the door, seeing that it was Simeon.

"Hi," he said. "Um, Barbatos made you some brownies. He wanted me to take them in to you," Simeon told her nervously, as he looked at the tray.

She followed his gaze, eyeing the tray over. She stepped back from the door, opening it farther to allow Simeon in. Immediately, she closed it right after, and she made her way back to the bed. "I'm almost done with this chapter." She held the book up, showing Simeon. "You should come sit." She bit her lip nervously as she patted the empty space beside her.

He nodded as he made his way to the other side of the bed. He placed the brownies down on the stand before he climbed into the empty spot beside her. He looked at her from the corner of his eye as she read her book. Restlessly, his fingers fiddled with one another as he waited impatiently.

Ashton read to the end of the chapter before she reached for the bookmark on her stand. She placed the bookmark in her book as she thought to herself, *I still want to be alone, but that smell is delicious. The chocolaty goodness that is drifting to my nose, mmm, it's making my stomach rumble.*

A growl sounded beside Simeon as Ashton craned her neck to see the brownies. "Would you like one?" Simeon asked softly as he retrieved the brownies and milk. She nodded as she bit her lip, embarrassed that she got caught.

She looked at each brownie carefully before her hand reached for a middle piece. Quickly, she took a tiny bite out of the corner. "Mmm." She couldn't help the moan that escaped her lips as her eyes closed from the taste.

A smiled tugged at Simeon's lips as he watched her enjoy the ecstasy that she got from eating the brownie. "Is it that good?" he asked.

"Mmmhmm." She took another bite, nodding as she swallowed before she continued. "How could it not? The sweet chocolate flavors that melt in the mouth chased down by the cold silkiness of the milk. The combination sends the taste buds soaring, like a shooting star. They complement each other perfectly."

"They do," he said.

His hand moved to caress her cheek, but she flinched, making his hand stop. "I'm sorry," he told her as he pulled his hand back, fear evident in her eyes.

"No." She shook her head as she tried to get hold of herself. "No, you, you didn't do anything wrong. I did. I-it's a reflex, from always being alone. I like the physical contact we have, but I'm still trying to adjust to it."

"Don't blame yourself, I should've known better," Simeon told her, pausing before he continued. "I know this is hard for you. I should've known better. And I want you to understand that I'm not going to hurt you. I would never do anything you don't want me to do."

"You wouldn't, but Satan—"

"Satan cares deeply for you. In fact, his feelings mirror my own when it comes to your love. And it's hard to watch someone you love go through so much pain. To know that they experienced a lot of suffering, and you weren't there to do anything about it. Satan's trying the best he can to control his wrath, but that isn't always easy. It's his way of showing how much he cares about you and how he wants you to be all right," Simeon told her as he cut her off.

"If you and Satan feel the same way, then how are you able to control your wrath?" she asked as she looked at him.

"I'm angry, but for Satan, it's harder since he's the avatar of wrath. That means that the wrath is more prominent to him, making it harder to control." Simeon paused, meeting her gaze before he continued. "My one focus is *you*. I can't imagine what it was like for you to go through all of that alone. I-I don't know how you dealt with it all those years, I don't. Knowing what you went through, it makes me not want to leave your side. It hurts me to leave your side because

I never want to make you feel alone. It brings me great pain to hear and see you cry, shutting me out. I understand why you do, though. It's your way of handling all of it, it's your way of protecting yourself. But I want you to know that I'm right here waiting for you, whenever you're ready to let me in. Even if it's just a small amount, I'll never take more than you are willing to give." His voice was shaky as he told her how he felt.

"I killed him, though, and not just him. I've killed thousands of people. How can you care for someone who has done that? Someone who has murdered?" Her voice and eyes held the guilt that she felt in her soul.

"I can see the guilt that you carry, but you don't have to carry it all. You can let it go and be free. It wasn't your choice to kill all those people, you didn't want to. As for him, you did what you had to do. He attacked you, which makes it self-defense." He searched her eyes, hoping she would grasp that it was not her fault.

"You don't hate me for it? But you're an angel," she questioned.

"No, I don't hate you for what you did, and yes, I'm an angel, and I would do anything for you," he whispered to her, reaching into his pocket to retrieve the flower petal he had whittled. "I made this for you. I know it's not the best, but I hope you like it."

She stared at the wooden flower petal in his hand as the truth of his words sank in. *He isn't going anywhere.* Her lips twitched as she tried to keep herself from crying. She took the petal and wrapped it in her fingers as her arms went around his neck, placing kisses on it. A warm, gentle hand caressed her back as his other hand stroked her hair.

Her lips trailed a path to his lips, kissing them softly before she pulled back. The bed creaked as she lay down on her back, waiting for Simeon to follow. She scooted closer to him, her head resting on his chest and her hand resting on his shoulder. Her contented sigh filled the quiet room as she snuggled into him, feeling his arms embrace her. "I'm tired, sunshine," she told him.

"Why don't you sleep? Your body is trying to heal itself," he whispered to her.

"I think I will . . ." she mumbled as her eyes drifted closed.

"Sleep well, snowflake," he whispered into her hair as he kissed her head. He emerged into his angel form, letting his wings bring her protection.

20

THE PLAN

Lord Diavolo paced his room as he held the phone in his hand. His thoughts raced as he searched for Lucifer's number. *I've already been gone a week. Lucifer always does pristine work when I'm away, but I can't leave him there for much longer. I trust him, but the pressure is a lot to handle. Other demons have often told me how easy I have it as the demon prince, but it's the opposite. The responsibility that I have is far greater than they'll ever know. The sacrifices that I make for my kingdom . . .*

I don't want to leave Ashton in this state, but I don't have a choice. I must return to my duties, at least to check up on how things are. And it's a good thing that Barbatos is always prepared in non-magical ways, since Simeon couldn't use his healing charm in the Human Realm. Come to think of it, I've never known Simeon act so out of character. He's always one of the top angels. He knows that having an angel-human relationship is forbidden; he must have strong feelings for her. I'm glad they found each other, tho—

"Hello?" Lucifer answered the phone, interrupting Lord Diavolo's thoughts.

"Hi, Lucifer, it's me Lord Diavolo," he answered.

"Lord Diavolo, how are you? You haven't said much during the trip," Lucifer asked.

"Yes, I know I've been more quiet than usual, and I'm sorry. It's been a rough week," Lord Diavolo said.

"Dia, are you well? Your voice sounds like you're tired." Lucifer's eyebrows furrowed with concern.

"I'm well, but after the surgery, there were a couple of incidents," Lord Diavolo told him.

"Incidents? What do you mean?" Lucifer asked curiously.

"Ashton . . ." Lord Diavolo was slow to answer, pausing as he took in a deep breath.

"What happened to Ashton?" Lucifer's voice grew a few octaves as panic went through his body.

"She got hurt, and she can't use the transportation device until she's healed," Lord Diavolo told him, his voice laced with defeat.

"What do you mean she got hurt? How bad? How did it happen? Simeon's with you, didn't he use his healing charms?" Lucifer's questions tumbled out one after another.

"She fractured her ribs, but she's doing well. She just needs time to heal. Simeon can't use his healing charms in the Human Realm. He tried, and they wouldn't work. And it's not my story to tell, how she fractured her ribs. That's something she'll have to share if she chooses to." Lord Diavolo's steps quickened as he answered each of Lucifer's questions.

Lucifer's audible gasp sounded through the phone as Lord Diavolo continued: "Barbatos fixed her up the best he could, but she needs a lot of rest. He said it could take a couple of weeks, if not more, depending on how fast her body decides to heal itself. She's in her room now, resting. And Satan isn't taking it very well. He keeps snapping, making everything worse."

"I keep telling him he needs to learn more self-control!" Lucifer said, growling into the phone.

"We can't blame him, since we're all on edge about the situation. And it's worse since he has feelings for her. I think the best choice would be for me to take Satan back to the Demon Realm. That way he can take out his anger and get a grip on his emotions. And I can check on how things are going, while Barbatos and Simeon stay behind to help Ashton." Lord Diavolo put the thought out there, waiting for a confirmation.

"I agree that Satan should come back. He shouldn't be around her if he is exploding like that. And things are going fine here in the Demon Realm. I've been doing exactly as you told me to do," Lucifer replied.

"I don't doubt that you would, Lucifer, and I thank you for taking on such a big responsibility. I'll let them know about the plan and be back tomorrow with Satan as planned. We need to talk about finding a way to help her through. She experienced a great deal, and I want to help her the best I can. Her residency will be permanent should she choose to go that route. She's more than welcome to stay however long she likes in the Demon Realm," Lord Diavolo said.

"Is it that bad? That you'd have her take up full residency down here?" Lucifer asked.

"Yes. It's that bad," Lord Diavolo started saying as Lucifer's thoughts sped rapidly through his mind. "Normally I wouldn't allow a human to take up full residency, but under the circumstances, I must give her that choice. I don't want her to feel as though she's stuck in the Human Realm forever." Lord Diavolo let out a breath. "I miss you, Luci."

"I miss you too, Dia," Lucifer whispered into the phone.

"What do I do? I feel like I can't do anything to help her!" Lord Diavolo's frustrated voice went through the phone as he placed the palm of his hand on his forehead, rubbing it.

"You're doing something, Dia. You're going to make it so that she has an out. By granting her full residency in the Demon Realm," Lucifer said, comforting his lover.

"But I feel like that's not enough. Like I must do more to protect her and keep her safe." Lord Diavolo's voice cracked.

"Hey, it's okay. She's alive, that's what matters. They're just bones, and they can heal," Lucifer said, trying his best as he whispered comforting words through the phone.

"It's simply hard seeing her like that. She's always so bright, and this is the opposite of how she is," Lord Diavolo said.

"Dia, you'll be back home tomorrow. We can get a drink, or I can hold you. I'll be right there waiting as you exit the transportation device," Lucifer told him.

"You're right. She's alive, and I'll be going back home tomorrow. I can't wait to see you. I'd love to have you hold me." Lord Diavolo's voice cheered up as he thought of Lucifer's arms around him.

"I'll be waiting at the transportation device, ready to hug you the second we're alone," Lucifer said as he continued to describe the positive feelings of holding his friend.

"I can't wait, I've missed you. I'll see you tomorrow," Lord Diavolo whispered into the phone.

"I've missed you as well. I'll be waiting," Lucifer responded before hanging up.

Lord Diavolo tossed his phone onto the bed as he made his way to the bathroom sink. "Time to go get everyone together for a meeting," he said with a sigh as he looked in the mirror at his tired eyes. He turned the water on, a chill going down his spine as he splashed the icy water onto his face.

Barbatos thought to himself as he sipped his tea, waiting for his lord to need him. *My lord is trying his best to be strong, just like the rest of us. We demons and angels always feel a stronger pull toward the female species. We even value them as greater than ourselves, wanting to do whatever we can to protect them and make them happy at all costs. Although, humans don't feel as strong a pull. The pull is always greater when it is someone with whom we have become close to.*

Barbatos turned his head as the creak of a door opening filled the room. He caught his lord's stressed expression as he made his way to the bar. "We should all discuss the plan over the next few weeks." He hovered beside his butler as he spoke.

"I believe that'd be a wise choice," Barbatos stated.

Lord Diavolo spoke loudly up the stairs to the library: "Satan? Can you come down here?"

Satan dropped the book he was reading as he raced to the stairs, his thoughts flying through his brain. *Is she all, right? Did something happen? What did the book say about dealing with trauma again? I just read it. I should be able to remember! I found a book that could specifically help me help her, and now I can't even remember what it said.*

Satan's words rushed out of his mouth: "What is it? Is she okay?"

"Yes, Ashton's the same as she was before. I'd just like to discuss with everyone what our course of action will be over the next few weeks," Lord Diavolo replied before he made his way to Ashton's bedroom door. His hand hovered over the doorknob nervously before he finally knocked.

Simeon rolled his head on the pillow in the direction of the door as he blinked his eyes awake. Even with his eyes closed, his senses were on high alert in case she needed him. He looked down at her as she slept peacefully in his arms. The corners of his lips played to a smile as he grudgingly and carefully stood up. He brushed her hair out of her face, leaning down to kiss the tip of her nose before he made his way to the door.

Light flooded through the crack of the door that Simeon had opened. He saw Lord Diavolo, waiting patiently for a response. "Hey," Simeon greeted him lightly.

"Hey," Lord Diavolo spoke in a normal tone. Simeon raised a finger to his lips as he made sure she was still asleep. "How's she doing?" Lord Diavolo kept his voice low as he asked.

"She's doing better. She fell asleep an hour ago," Simeon said, shrugging his shoulders as he replied.

"Good, I'm glad," Lord Diavolo smiled as he continued. "I was hoping that all of us could have a meeting, but if she's sleeping, then I don't want to wake her up."

"What did you want to talk about?" Simeon asked, his brows furrowed.

"I produced a plan, but I wanted to get everyone's input, so that we can discuss further what will be best for her over the next few weeks," Lord Diavolo said.

"I don't want to wake her, either. We can always ask her opinion later." Simeon let out a heavy sigh as he leaned his forehead on the door looking at her. "I don't want to leave her side, but it's important that we do talk about the next few weeks. Especially since the Demon Realm is a lot safer for her than the Human Realm, and I never thought I would say that. No offense, Lord Diavolo," Simeon said with a smile as he finished speaking his thoughts.

"None taken," Lord Diavolo said, grinning at Simeon's last words.

Simeon took a final look at her before stepping out and closing the door. They made their way over to the barstool, sitting down as Barbatos placed tea and brownies on the counter.

"As I mentioned, I have a plan, but I want to run it by everyone," Lord Diavolo started saying as he placed a brownie on a dessert plate.

"What's your plan?" Simeon asked as he took one of the tea mugs.

"As much as I don't want to leave her in this vulnerable state, I can't leave Lucifer in charge of the Demon Realm for much longer. So, I propose that I go back with Satan and take care of business in the Demon Realm, while Barbatos and Simeon stay and tend to her needs," Lord Diavolo said.

"Why do I have to go back? Why can't I stay? I don't want to go back if she isn't coming, too!" Satan said, snapping at the demon prince.

"That's exactly why I want you to go back with me. Because you can't control your wrath right now. As soon as you can gain control of it again, then you can come back. Not until then." Lord Diavolo gave Satan a stern look, not intimidated by him.

"I know that Simeon isn't going to leave no matter what anyone says. I respect that decision, and I'm not going to force him to leave her side." Lord Diavolo made eye contact with Simeon as he nodded, showing his understanding of Simeon's desire to be with her. A silent thank-you exchanged between their eyes.

"As for Barbatos, I feel his services would be of better use here. He can tend to her broken bones, help with her meds, fixing meals, and anything else that she may need. That'd give Simeon more time to be by her side for emotional support." Lord Diavolo looked around at the demons and angel. "What does everyone think?"

"I'm perfectly okay with that, if that's what you'd like, my lord," Barbatos replied to Lord Diavolo's question. "But are you sure you will not need my assistance back in the Demon Realm?"

"I don't plan to stay away for long. I plan to work only on things that need my dire attention. That should take only a day or two," Lord Diavolo replied.

"I can tend to her alone if you do need Barbatos to go back with you at any point," Simeon told them, hoping that would take any added pressure off them.

"No, no, like I said, it should only take a couple of days . . . Now, the other things that I want everyone's opinion on is I plan to set up full residency for her in the Demon Realm. If she chooses, of course. I don't want her to feel like she must stay in her world, alone. And I want her to know that she'll have all the support she needs in the Demon Realm," Lord Diavolo told them.

Their eyes snapped to him in shock at what he'd just mentioned. "Are you sure you want to do that, my lord?" Barbatos asked.

"Yes, I've given it a lot of thought, and I wouldn't suggest it if I didn't think it was better for her. I know that it's a risk to have her there since she's a human, but no demon would even consider harming her. Not with me as the prince. They'd shudder in fear as I turn into my demon form showing them their gravest mistake." Lord Diavolo's answer came out in a fierce tone.

"That's a big decision to consider. If my opinion is worth anything, I think it'd be a wise choice. She'd be around all of us who care about her," Barbatos agreed after he gave it some thought.

"As I mentioned earlier, I also agree that she'd be better off in the Demon Realm than here in the Human Realm. And Barbatos is correct—she'd have all of us to watch over her and protect her," Simeon said, pausing as he took a sip of tea. "I also know that this isn't a decision that we can make for her."

"We can always give her the choice when she wakes up," Satan chimed in.

"I agree, we let her know what her options are when she wakes up. The final decision will always be hers," Lord Diavolo said as he took a bite of his brownie.

"As I mentioned to you earlier—" Barbatos started to say something, but the noise of a door opening made him stop.

Ashton rubbed at her tired eyes, holding her side as she made her way into the kitchen. Everyone's gaze was on her as she walked over to Simeon, laying her head on his shoulder. "Sunshine," she whispered.

"Did you sleep all right, snowflake?" Simeon asked her as his hand snaked around her waist.

"Mmm," she nodded, clutching her side tightly.

"Let me get you some pain meds. I brought them up earlier," Barbatos said and walked over to where he left the pain meds, taking them to her.

"Here, sit down, I can stand," Simeon said. He tried to move but couldn't. Ashton buried herself farther into his shoulder, pressing her hand against him, pinning him gently to the chair.

"Here are the pain meds, my lady," Barbatos said as he placed them on the counter in front of her.

She placed the pain meds in her mouth, chasing them down with water. "Thank you." Her voice came out in a groggy, hoarse tone.

"You're welcome, my lady," Barbatos replied.

"What was everyone talking about as I came in?" she asked as she nuzzled back into Simeon's shoulder.

"We were discussing how to move forward until you can use the transportation device," Lord Diavolo said.

"Am I not able to use it now?" Her head snapped up as she looked at him, her eyebrows furrowed.

"No, not in your condition," Barbatos said. "I was just talking about that. It'd be detrimental to your health if you used it right now. It'd cause your already fractured ribs to break even further. Because of the pressure."

"So, I'm stuck here?" She pressed for more information as her thoughts raced: *I like my house, but it's nothing like the Demon Realm. Over the last six months, the Demon Realm has become more of a home than the Human Realm. I'm going to be alone again. I let them in, and now they're just going to leave, like I was nothing to them. How can I ever get used to this feeling of loss? At least before, I never felt it because I never knew what companionship was.*

"It's only temporary," Barbatos quickly added. "It'll be only until your ribs are healed."

A stabbing pain hit their hearts at the fear they saw laced within her eyes. "How long should that be?" Her voice broke as panic filled her. "Fractured ribs can take months to heal. I don't . . ." she said as she trailed off, turning away so they wouldn't see her cry.

Simeon's hand guided her head to his shoulder as he stroked her hair, wiping the tears away. "It shouldn't take that long, not to be able to use the transportation device again. The bones just have to heal enough for you to be able to use it." Barbatos reassured her. "It should take only a week, maybe two."

"I'm guessing all of you will be returning tomorrow as planned?" Her words came out barely audible.

"No, it'd be just Satan and me returning tomorrow," Lord Diavolo said. "We were also discussing that before you came out. We thought it'd be best if Barbatos and Simeon stayed with you, while I go back to take care of things in the Demon Realm and Satan gets hold of his anger."

"I told you that I wouldn't leave you, and I don't plan to. If you're staying here, then I'll be right here for as long as you want me," Simeon whispered sweetly into her ear as he comforted her.

"We also have something to propose to you, a choice to make . . ." Lord Diavolo started saying. "Being the demon prince, I can get away with a lot of things, including the exchange program. I know it was supposed to be for only one year, but I'd like to get your thoughts on being a full-time resident of the Demon Realm." Lord Diavolo sat there, fidgeting with his brownie.

She stared at him as she tried to think of what to say, but she couldn't. She opened her mouth several times, trying to speak, but nothing came out. "What, wow, um . . ." was all she could manage.

"You don't have to decide right now, but I did want to put it out there. I'd do anything to keep you safe," Lord Diavolo added.

Simeon's eyes darted to Lord Diavolo, jealousy seeping into his veins at what he told Ashton. Lord Diavolo noticed that Simeon was glaring daggers at him, so he gave him a look to convey silently that he wasn't imposing. Simeon moved his eyes back to Ashton, placing his cheek on her head.

"I'll keep that in mind," she said, her words coming out slowly as she spoke. "I like the idea, but I don't want to be hasty in my decision. I'll consider the pros and cons before I make a final decision."

"Okay." Lord Diavolo looked at her with defeated eyes.

There was a moment of silence before Ashton's stomach growled. She placed a hand over her stomach, hiding her face deeper into Simeon's shoulder with embarrassment. "Oops, I guess I should probably get something to eat," she mumbled to herself.

Barbatos flew to the fridge, reheating what he cooked that morning. He worked quickly as he set plates on the counter. Within minutes, the smell of eggs, toast, sausages, French toast, and bacon filled the air.

"My lady, the food is ready for you," Barbatos told her as he placed the last item on the table.

Her eyes darted to each of the food items, lighting up with joy as she took a plate to fill. She noticed that none of the others were moving to fill plates, so she paused and asked, "Are you all not going to have some?"

"We will, but we're waiting for you to get your fill first," Satan said, answering her question, and the others nodded in agreement.

Her cheeks flushed. *Why do they all have to be so damn adorable? Always the freaking gentlemen, but that's what makes them special.* She kept her face as calm as she could as the thoughts filled her mind; she placed the last item on her plate heading to the dining table.

She waited for the others to fill their plates, making their way over to sit with her. They talked with one another as they ate. Ashton smiled as the air that had been heavy the last few days lifted.

21

FUN DAY

"Is there anything specific that everyone would like to do?" Ashton asked as they sat in the living room.

"What about a movie? Or a game?" Lord Diavolo offered his ideas.

"I believe that a movie may be the better choice. It'd require the least amount of movement from Ashton," Barbatos chimed as he sat in the recliner.

"The DVD collection's over there in the corner." She pointed to the corner before continuing. "Why don't you all pick? I'm good with any movie."

Ashton smiled as she turned the TV on and set it to the DVD player. They filed in, and Satan put the disc in before taking his seat. She looked at Simeon as he sat down beside her. Her eyes went to the screen as she pressed play on the remote. *IT* by Stephen King was on the title screen. *They picked my least favorite genre, but hey, I can't complain, since all of them look happy,* she thought to herself as she reached behind her for the throw blanket.

The sounds from the movie filled the living room as she offered Simeon the blanket. He smiled at her, happily covering himself with part of it. He placed his hand between them, hoping that she would want to hold it. Her hand found his as the movie continued.

She flinched at a scary part, hiding her face in Simeon's shoulder. He looked down at her, placing a warm kiss on the top of her head. The pressure on his hand tightened as she gripped it tighter. "It's all right, you're okay," he whispered in her ear, his other hand caressing her cheek. Her eyes met his, and he saw the fear they held. His arms wrapped around her shoulders in a warm embrace as he kissed her cheek. "I'm right here." Her body deflated as she let out the breath she was holding.

Demon's laughter echoed through the room as the end credits came on. She met Simeon's eyes, smiling as she placed a tender hand on his cheek. Her eyes moved around the room as she watched each of the demons wipe away tears from laughing so hard.

"You do know that most people wouldn't laugh at that?" she asked as their laughing died down.

"Why not? It's hilarious," Lord Diavolo said with a smirk as he turned his head to look at her. His face flushed as he saw Simeon and her cuddling.

"It's a horror movie. Most people would get a thrill out of it, some type of fear. They wouldn't laugh throughout the movie like it is a comedy," she explained, smiling at him.

"Well, we've lived through worse than clowns wanting to kill people," Lord Diavolo said, chuckling.

"Of course, you have. What was I thinking? I should've known that demons wouldn't find a horror movie terrifying." She laughed before continuing. "It was an excellent choice, though."

Simeon kept his hand on her arm, caressing it as he suggested, "Why don't we play a board game?"

His hair brushed against her neck as he whispered in her ear, "As much as I like cuddling with you, I think a game would help your body rest better. You wouldn't be tensing as much."

The demons watched in envy; their jaws dropped as her face flushed red and she ducked her head under the blanket to hide.

"Ahem," Barbatos said, clearing his throat and gaining everyone's attention. "I haven't played many board games in my time, but I certainly wouldn't mind trying them. What games do you have, my lady?"

"I have a variety—they're down there. Underneath the stand." She pointed. "You're more than welcome to look through them."

"Thank you, I think I will," Barbatos replied as he knelt beside the table, looking through the games. "There's Monopoly, Clue, Trouble, Sorry, and many more, if none of those catches our eyes," he said as he placed them on the table.

Lord Diavolo knelt beside Barbatos, looking through the games, and said, "Hmm . . . which one is your favorite?" he asked as he looked up at her over the pile.

"I don't know, I haven't actually played any of them before," she admitted.

"Wait, you have all of these games, but you've never actually played them?" Satan asked curiously, his brows furrowed.

"Well, I got them to play with other people," she said, shrugging her shoulders before continuing. "All of you are the first visitors I've had. Because of my past, I never got to asking other people to visit. I meant to, but then my life as a doctor became very demanding," she replied as she bit her bottom lip, avoiding their eyes.

"We can all learn together," Simeon chimed in beside her.

"I agree, a board game would be a lot of fun," Lord Diavolo added as he looked through the games. "Hmm . . . let us see. How about this one?!"

Everyone looked at the game that he held up—Monopoly.

"That looks like a fun one, what does everyone else think?" Barbatos asked.

"Sure," Satan agreed as he sat down on the floor.

Barbatos and Lord Diavolo looked up at Ashton as she nodded and smiled.

"I can set it up while you read the instructions, Barbatos," Lord Diavolo suggested.

"Okay, my lord." Barbatos took out the instructions as Lord Diavolo waited to be told where each piece went.

Ashton sat on the couch trying to listen to Barbatos explain the rules, telling Lord Diavolo where each piece went. Simeon distracted her as he whispered in her ear, "It'll be fun." She looked over at him, smiling. "Sshh, I'm trying to pay attention," she whispered back in his ear as she held her index finger to her lips.

"That's all for the rules, does everyone think they got that?" Barbatos asked as he looked around at everyone.

"I think I understand," Satan replied.

"Yes, I got it. Thank you, Barbatos." Ashton turned to smile at him.

"I'm ready," Lord Diavolo said. "Why don't we pick our tokens?"

"I call the ship!" Ashton blurted out as she wiggled out of Simeon's arms, sitting on the floor.

"Very well, my lady," Barbatos replied, placing the ship on GO.

"I guess I'll take the cat," Satan added.

"I'll go with the dog," Simeon told them as he joined Ashton on the floor.

"I think I'll choose the race car," Lord Diavolo said.

"Hmm . . . I guess I'll go with the wheelbarrow," Barbatos said as he placed all the tokens on GO.

The game continued for several hours, Lord Diavolo and Barbatos claiming most of the properties. Satan, Simeon, and Ashton tried to keep up but were unsuccessful. Ashton was the first to take bankruptcy, closely followed by Satan. Ashton watched as Simeon tried to regain control, ultimately landing on one of Lord Diavolo's big hotels in the end.

Ashton, Simeon, and Satan watched as the game progressed; neither Lord Diavolo nor Barbatos was showing any signs of giving in. "I'm going to go get dinner started, it's beginning to get around that time," Satan told them as he stood up.

"I can make dinner if you want," Ashton said, trying to be useful.

"My lady, moving around that much wouldn't be good for your ribs," Barbatos chimed in after he took his turn.

"I have it taken care of." Satan winked at Ashton, and with a smile, he made his way to the kitchen.

Ashton let out a heavy sigh, disappointed that she couldn't be of use. "Who do you think is going to win?" Simeon asked, trying to distract her.

"Umm . . . Lord Diavolo," Ashton replied.

"I don't know, I think that Barbatos will win." Simeon gave her a wink as he smiled at her.

Ashton and Simeon bickered back and forth as to who was going to win the game. Ashton would loudly cheer every time Lord Diavolo got ahead, sticking her tongue out at Simeon as she did. She watched as Simeon pouted at her reaction, and she leaned over, kissing his cheek in response. His eyes went wide as he looked at her, blushing profusely.

"Dinner's ready," Satan said, calling from the kitchen.

"Oh no, I don't like this roll," Lord Diavolo told them as he landed on Barbatos's hotel.

"Pay up, my lord," Barbatos told him as he held his hand out.

"Ah, I'm ten dollars short." Lord Diavolo recounted his money as he tried to find a way to pay.

"Looks like Barbatos won," Ashton said.

Lord Diavolo handed all the money over to Barbatos, sighing in defeat. "Oh well, that was still a fun game! I'm glad that we decided to play," he told them as he started to put the game away.

"Want me to help you pick up?" Ashton asked Lord Diavolo.

"No, I have it. Why don't all of you get ready for dinner? Including you, Barbatos," Lord Diavolo told his butler.

"Thank you, my lord, I appreciate it greatly," Barbatos replied with a small bow as he made his way to the sink, washing his hands before dinner.

"Let me help you up," Simeon told Ashton as he held his hand out for her.

"Thank you." She took his hand as they made their way over to the sink.

They started eating as soon as Lord Diavolo joined them. "Thank you for cooking, Satan, it looks delicious. And it's one of my favorite meals. Hamburger, corn, and potatoes—such a great combination," Ashton told them as she took another bite.

"You're welcome, and I'm glad to hear you say that. I was hoping it could help me redeem myself, since my behavior hasn't been the best," Satan replied.

"Satan, you haven't done anything wrong," Ashton said.

"I have—" Satan started to say.

"NO, I won't let any of you blame yourselves for not knowing how to handle a situation you were thrown into by mistake," Ashton said, her voice stern as she cut Satan off.

She went back to her food as they ate in silence the rest of the meal. She finished eating, remembering that they were leaving the next day. Before she could stop herself, she asked, "How long will you be gone?"

Lord Diavolo stopped midbite at her sudden question, and he placed his fork down as he answered, "I'm hoping for just a day or two. But I'm not sure, to be honest."

"Okay," she replied as the smile fell from her lips.

"We'll be back as quickly as possible, I promise," Lord Diavolo said, trying to comfort her as he placed his hand on her arm. "We aren't going to abandon you—we'll be back soon."

"Ha, I know that. I-I wasn't worried . . ." she said, trailing off as she quickly placed a smile on her face. She stared at her plate before she continued: "It's, um, it's been a long day. I'm going to head to bed." She didn't wait for their replies. Getting up, she made her way to her bedroom.

She lay on her bed, looking up at the ceiling as her thoughts wandered. *What happened to me? I used to be this strong and fierce person, but now? Now I'm getting upset and worried because they're going back to their home. I don't get it. I've always been alone. I've always dealt with everything by myself. When did I start relying on others so much? Can I even truly rely on them? Or will they end up hurting me like everyone else?*

She swiped away a tear that trickled down her cheek as her thoughts continued. *Yes. I can rely on them. Simeon alone has proved that to me. He didn't even look at me in the shower until I told him he could, and even then, he kept his eyes on mine. And how could I forget how they all cried for me? You don't cry unless you genuinely care for the person. You don't just show that type of emotion if you plan to leave. Besides, Lord Diavolo and Satan acted as if they didn't want to leave. They'll be back—I hope they come back.*

She sighed in relief as she spoke aloud, saying, "They've more than proved themselves to me, and I can let them in. None of them have taken more than I was willing to give, and they didn't push me into anything, either. Instead, they've changed me. All of them have changed me. I don't want to be alone anymore. Franko took my past, but I'm not going to let him take my future, too!" Ashton lay in bed as the realization sank in. Smiling, she got up and moved to the vanity.

"This sucks," Satan said as they watched her close the door to her bedroom. "Seeing her like this and not being able to help her."

"But we are," Barbatos started saying, hoping his explanation would get through to Satan. "We are helping her by being here for her. Ashton chose to let us in on something she's never told anyone else about. That isn't easy. She spent her entire life fighting this on her own, and now, for the first time, she doesn't have to. She has other people there for her, and that's a tremendous change. All of this is unfamiliar territory for her. I'm sure that she's trying to cope and adjust the best way that she can."

"That's true. I believe she's made a lot of effort these past few days to show us what she's been dealing. Showing us her scars, letting us see her crying, and telling us what had happened. Those are big steps for her. Yes, it hurts to have her walk away from us, but she's given us a lot already," Simeon said, agreeing with Barbatos as he finished talking.

"Mmm, I agree with both of you. She's given us a lot over the past few days. As much as it hurts for us to hear it and see it, we must remain strong for her. I believe that when she's ready, she'll come to us and let us know what she needs. I don't think I've ever met someone who's as strong as she, and I'm genuinely surprised that she's not broken," Lord Diavolo chimed in, looking at Satan as he finished.

"Satan, this is hard for all of us. We know how much it hurts to see her like this, how she pushes us away. If you genuinely want to help, then just be there for her. Help make her smile. Show her that she can rely on you and that you'll be there for her. But I don't think you can do that if you can't control your wrath. I'm also finding it hard to control my wrath, and I'd love nothing more than to hurt someone. But that isn't going to help her, and that isn't what she wants," Lord Diavolo said. His voice was soft, holding no judgment as he spoke to Satan.

"I don't like seeing her hurt. I don't like how she keeps shutting us out, keeping herself alone and isolated. I don't want her to feel that way," Satan said, his voice low as he bowed his head in defeat.

"We know. That's why tomorrow you'll be going back to the Demon Realm. You'll have a safe environment to let your wrath out in. Once you have that under control, you can come right back here," Lord Diavolo said, reassuring Satan.

"Ashton is correct—it's been a long day. It'd be wise if all of us went to bed?" Barbatos asked.

"Yeah, that'd be good. I'll just put the leftovers away before heading to my room," Satan replied.

"Simeon, would you care to take her some pain meds? I can fetch them for you," Barbatos asked.

"I'd like to take them to her, thank you," Simeon said with a smile as he turned to Lord Diavolo. "Lord Diavolo, could I speak with you alone?"

"Of course, is something wrong?" Lord Diavolo looked at Simeon with curious eyes.

Simeon gestured for him to follow as they made their way to the patio. "Lord Diavolo, could I ask a favor of you?" Simeon inquired when they were alone.

"What's the favor?" Lord Diavolo replied with furrowed brows.

"Would you check on Seth for me? Make sure that he's doing all right. It's been awhile since I've heard from him," Simeon asked as he stared into space.

"For you, I'll make sure that he's nothing less than perfect," Lord Diavolo replied with a smile as he continued. "You have something else you would like to ask, don't you?"

"Well, yes there is something else," Simeon said, rubbing his neck as he turned to face the water, watching the waves and moon dance with each other.

"What is it?" Lord Diavolo questioned.

"I have a gift for Ashton back in my room in the Demon Realm. It holds a lot of significance, and I was planning to give it to her next week on this specific day. C-could you bring that with you when you return?" Simeon asked hesitantly.

"I can do that for you! I'm glad that you trust me with something so important. I'll do my absolute best to bring it back to you when I return," Lord Diavolo responded as he, too, watched the waves and moon dance.

"Thank you so much, it means a lot to me and Ashton. When you go into my room, it'll be in a medium-sized box. Be incredibly careful because it's breakable." Simeon let out a sigh as he sheepishly hugged the demon prince. "Thank you."

"You're more than welcome." Lord Diavolo's eyes went wide with shock as he returned the hug. "I'll bring it back in perfect condition. When do you need it by?"

"February fifth is the day I plan to give it to her," Simeon answered as he pulled back.

"Then I'll get it to you before then." Lord Diavolo leaned against the railing as the cool breeze hit his face.

"I should go back in. I'm sure Barbatos has her pain meds ready," Simeon said as he headed for the door. Lord Diavolo watched as Simeon went back inside, turning back to face the water.

Simeon knocked gently on Ashton's bedroom door, waiting for her to answer. He lightly sighed in relief as she opened right up. "I brought you some more pain meds—in case you wanted to take some before bed."

"Thank you." She chased the pills down with water as she placed the glass on her stand. Her hand found Simeon's as she led him to her vanity, picking up her hairbrush. "Would you?" she asked as she held it out to him limply.

He took the brush, gesturing for her to sit. His hand rested on top of her head as he carefully brushed all the tangles out. His humming reached her ears, making her eyes close as she listened to the soft melody. She reveled in the feeling of his fingers running through her hair as he finished brushing.

"Sleep well tonight, snowflake," Simeon said as he placed a gentle kiss on her head.

"Simeon," Ashton said, her voice low and mischievous.

"Hmm?" Simeon smiled as he turned to her.

"Do I get a goodnight kiss?" She bit her bottom lips as she asked.

"I did kiss you, snowflake," Simeon said teasingly as he caressed her cheek.

"But what if I want the kiss somewhere else?" she asked, hopeful.

"Where would you like me to kiss you?" he asked as he kept her in suspense.

"Here, sunshine." Her index finger slid across her lips as she gave him her best puppy-dog eyes.

He leaned down, brushing his lips against hers in a delicate, loving kiss. "How's that, snowflake?" Simeon questioned as he met her eyes.

Words left her as she stared at his crystal eyes, nodding her head in reply. He closed the distance between their lips, kissing her again. His breath was hot against her lips as he whispered, "Goodnight, snowflake."

"Goodnight, sunshine," she whispered.

22

ENVY IN THE AIR

Ashton's eyes fluttered open the next morning. She blinked as her eyes became focused and the ceiling came into view. *Today's the day,* she thought to herself. *It's the day that I must learn to face these new feelings. I've finally let Lord Diavolo, Barbatos, Satan, and Simeon in, and now I must face that Lord Diavolo and Satan are going home. I feel sad about that, and it's weird that I feel that way. I've never felt that way about other people. Have I truly become close to them? At least I'll not be alone, like before. Simeon and Barbatos are staying. I can do this.* She finished her thoughts of encouragement before sighing, scooting to the edge of the bed.

She held her side with closed eyes as she adjusted to the pain. Slowly, she stood up, making her way over to the dresser to change for the day. She sat down in the vanity chair as she combed through her hair, placing a blue butterfly barrette in the back to hold the hair out of her face. She applied some light makeup, and the eye shadow she chose illuminated her eyes, allowing them to shine even more brightly than they already did.

She smiled and made her way out into the kitchen. She could smell French toast, the scent of maple syrup wafting to her nose. Barbatos was in the kitchen cooking breakfast for everyone, even though no one else was out there with him.

"Good morning," Ashton said.

"Well, good morning," he said, turning, and his breath hitched in his throat as she made her way to the stool. She was positively gorgeous as the sun shone through the window, catching her hair perfectly in the glistening rays. "W-would you like for me to get you some tea, my lady?" he said, stuttering, as he tried to regain his posture.

"Licorice spice flavor, please," she smiled at him as she sat there.

"I'll get that on right away." He glanced over at her before he filled the teakettle with water to boil.

Ashton stretched her arms over her head before she splayed them across the counter. Barbatos stole a second glance at Ashton. "Did you sleep well last night, my lady?" he asked as he noticed her tired behavior.

"Kind of," she mumbled. She shivered at the memory of her silent tossing and turning.

"Kind of? Is that good or bad?" he said, chuckling as he asked her.

"Both, I guess." She crossed her arms on the counter in front of her, laying her chin on the softness of her sleeved arm. Her eyes drifted over to Barbatos, who had turned slightly, and she laughed to herself. The apron that he wore had cupcakes on it that sported brightly colored sprinkles. She enjoyed the sight with a smile before she answered him completely. "I had several small nightmares, but they weren't that bad. There are a lot of times when I'd wake up, but this wasn't one of those times. Instead, I tossed and turned a lot before settling back in . . ." She drifted off in her talking.

"You're the strongest person I know," he told her as he grabbed what he assumed to be her favorite cup. It was a dark-blue mug with a whale-tail handle, and she'd used it each day that she'd been there, so he could only assume it was her favorite. He filled the mug with steaming hot water, placing the tea bag in afterward. "I'm not just saying that, either, my lady. I've seen a lot of people go through difficult things, but I've never seen anyone handle a situation as well as you," he said as he took her tea to her.

She lifted her head from her arm, taking the hot mug from Barbatos's hands as she met his green-tinted eyes. He reached across the counter, placing his hand lightly on her cheek. His thumb slid softly over her lips before whispering to her, "You are amazing."

Their eyes stayed locked as her heart picked up pace and her cheeks flushed bright red. "Barbatos," she whispered after a moment.

"Yes, my lady." His reply was smooth as his hand moved to brush her hair behind her ear.

"I have feelings . . . for Simeon," she said, swallowing hard as she kept eye contact with him, speaking to life what she felt for Simeon.

"I know, and I accept that. But it will not stop me from caring deeply for you, as a close friend," he said, purring to her as the back of his fingers grazed over her cheek.

She didn't know it was possible for her face to grow even redder than it already was. Her bottom lip caught between her teeth, and she averted her eyes by taking a sip of her tea. He leaned across the counter and cupped her face in his feather-like hands as he placed a sweet kiss on her forehead.

Barbatos leaned back, uncupping her face as a glimmer caught his eye. Looking down, he noticed two feathers that fell around her neck and landed on her chest. "You're wearing the necklace that I got you," he said, his voice sounding astonished.

"Oh, ha, yes, um. I wear it all the time, it's my favorite necklace." Her eyes moved to where the necklace was as her fingers found the two feathers instinctively, gingerly twirling it.

"I'm glad that you still find joy in it." His eyes shone from the feeling he got, knowing that he got her something that after months she still enjoyed. They smiled at each other as a creaking sound filled the room. Their heads turned to face the noise and watched Satan enter the room.

Satan yawned loudly before noticing a seat beside Ashton was available. He made his way over, occupying the seat, placing his elbow on the counter, leaning his head against his knuckles as he looked at her. "You look stunning," he whispered to her.

"Would you like some tea?" Barbatos kept his smile, but it became strained at how Satan was acting toward her. He could understand and accept her and Simeon, but this made him feel a twinge of jealousy.

Satan pulled away from Ashton, not realizing that he had drawn close to her. He cleared his throat, looking at Barbatos with embarrassment. "Ahem, mm, yes, please. That'd be much appreciated, thank you."

Barbatos went to the cupboard to get a mug before pouring hot water into it. He grabbed a black tea bag, placing it into the hot water before setting it on the counter in front of Satan. "Thank you," Satan told him as he wrapped his hands around the hot mug.

There was a loud creak as Lord Diavolo and Simeon entered the kitchen at the same time. Lord Diavolo stretched as he made his way over to sit beside Satan, and Simeon rubbed the back of his neck on his way to stand beside Ashton.

Simeon closed his eyes for a moment as he stood there before he looked down at Ashton and saw her looking up at him adoringly. His mesmerizing blue eyes lit up as he looked at her, his heart picked up speed, and his stomach began to prickle with excitement.

"Would you like a sip?" she asked him innocently as she held the whale mug up between them. Her words sent a chill down his spine, and he shivered eagerly as he took the cup. He kept his eyes on her as he took a sip. His face scrunched up in disgust as he looked down at the cup. "What kind of tea is that?" he asked incredulously.

"Licorice spice." She put a hand over her mouth and tried to muffle her laughter from his response.

"That doesn't taste good at all," he told her as he turned his head away, holding the cup out for her to take.

"It's an acquired taste." She shrugged her shoulders at him as she took the cup back, taking a sip.

The others watched the scene as the sexual tension rose between the two. Jealousy laced each of them, and they longed for it to be them that she favored. Their breathing grew heavy as they tried to get a grasp on their sexual needs.

There were audible sighs of relief when Simeon broke eye contact from her, making her laugh with his expression.

"Since everyone is up . . ." Barbatos clapped his hands, further breaking the lustful atmosphere. "Why doesn't everyone move to the dining room for breakfast?" he asked everyone as he gestured to the dining room.

"You're very much appreciated, Barbatos! Thank you." Ashton's eyes flickered over to Barbatos, making him swallow hard. Simeon leaned down and whispered, "Let me help you," as he held out his hand to her.

Her head snapped around at the surprise of his whisper in her ear, and their faces were mere inches from each other. Her lips parted slightly as her body became pins and needles with positive nerves. Her eyes went wide, unblinking as she stared into his; she shook her head, placing her hand in his. She closed the distance between them, kissing his lips. His smile grew to a full grin, both becoming flustered.

He led her to the table where everyone else sat, watching them with lustful eyes. She kept her eyes to the floor, unable to meet any of their longing eyes, too embarrassed. Simeon pulled her chair out for her. Sitting down, she bit her bottom lip while she rubbed her arm nervously.

"Would you like for me to fill your plate with food, my lady?" Barbatos asked her, noticing her embarrassment as it dusted her cheeks.

"N-no, I-I-I can do it," she said with a stutter before moving a shaking hand toward the food.

The dining room was quiet except for the scrapping of silverware on the plates. The sexual tension that had been in the air had begun to dissipate, leaving the atmosphere with a contented satisfaction from the food.

"It'd be best if Satan and I leave right after breakfast," Lord Diavolo said as all neared their fill. "The sooner we get back and take care of what we have to, the sooner we can return."

"If that's what you want, Lord Diavolo," Satan said, speaking after he swallowed his food; his tone was unenthusiastic.

"I don't want to leave, either, but it will be for the best," Lord Diavolo said.

Ashton lost her appetite. Placing her fork on her plate, she sat in silence, waiting for everyone else to finish. *Why do they have to go? I just opened up about my past! They're the first ones I've ever told, and now even though they're just going back home, it feels like they're going to abandon me. Like I'll be left alone. I need to get a grip on myself and adjust to this new hurt. I've never felt this before—I need to just get a grip on myself. They'll be back,* she thought to herself as she tried to slow her quick-beating heart.

They sat there with empty plates before Barbatos stood, picking up each of the plates as he walked to the sink. "It's time," Lord Diavolo said, speaking the words she'd been dreading. "Would you care to join, Barbatos?" Lord Diavolo asked his loyal butler.

"I'm sorry, but I'll not be joining the departure. I'd like to finish the dishes," Barbatos said, speaking professionally to his lord.

"Very well," Lord Diavolo said, smiling at his butler as the rest of them made their way to Ashton's bedroom.

Simeon and Ashton stood off to the side as Lord Diavolo and Satan disappeared. Her eyes went to the floor, a frown present in her expression. Simeon's eyes flickered to her as her demeanor changed. He placed a caring hand on the small of her back, lifting her eyes to his with a finger. "They'll be back soon." Softness and assurance were eminent in his tone as he looked into her downcast eyes.

"I know, I'm just . . . I'm not used to this feeling." She averted her eyes before bringing them back to his. "I'm still trying to get a grasp on this new emotion," she whispered.

A hand brushed across her cheek as he leaned his forehead on hers. "You're amazing and breathtaking." His voice was a whisper that she could barely hear over her pounding heart. He leaned down, closing the space between their lips, kissing her. Instinctively, her hand went to his chest for balance, and he deepened the kiss even further, bringing a hand to the back of her neck for support.

They broke free, gasping for air as their foreheads met. She forcefully kissed him, her fingers becoming entangled in his hair and tugging. A moan escaped his lips, and his hands slid down her curves to her ass and thighs. He dipped and picked her up, her legs wrapped around his waist. Their lips never parted, and her hands continued to comb and pull his hair, causing his lust to grow. He walked to the bed, and her back landed on softness. His body hovered over her as he trailed kisses to her neck, nibbling on her sweet spot.

"Mmm, Simeon," she moaned in pleasure as electricity coursed through her body. Her hands became brave, moving from his hair to his torso, exploring the unfamiliar territory. He bit down on her neck and sucked, leaving his mark. He nuzzled his head against her and caught her earlobe between his teeth. Her nails dug into his sides at the sensation, and she kissed his shoulder.

His cock grew in his pants, creating a bulge that pressed against the inside of her thigh. Hands continued exploring her body and he leaned down, planting tender kisses at the top of her breasts.

Nerves got the better of her, and her body began to shake. He pulled back, looking into her eyes while he caressed her cheek. "I won't hurt you, it's okay. We can stop," he whispered to her as he removed his hands from her body.

She turned her head to the side, nodding as she bit her trembling lip. "I should go and take some pain meds," she whispered between breaths.

"Okay, snowflake." He stood up and helped her stand. She made her way to the bedroom door, looking back over her shoulder at Simeon. He smiled at her, staying where he was. She closed the door behind her, making her way past the kitchen to the doorway downstairs. "I have your pain meds right here, my lady." Barbatos broke her trance. *She has a red mark on her neck from him,* he thought as he strained his smile and he kept his envy in check.

She looked over at him, chuckling as he held the water and pain meds out for her. "How do you anticipate my every need?" She made her way over to him, taking the pain meds and chased them down with water.

"A butler must always be prepared." He winked at her.

Simeon sat on the bed and unzipped his pants. He stroked his cock, remembering the feeling of her pulling his hair, how it sent a powerful force through him. The thought of the force made his cock pulsate and he gritted his teeth as he released on his hand, dripping to the floor. He cleaned up and entered the kitchen, leaning against the wall.

"What's on the agenda for today?" Ashton asked no one in particular.

"You, my lady, should be in bed resting. The more rest you get now, the quicker you'll heal, and the sooner you can return to the Demon Realm," Barbatos said, answering her question as he washed the glass.

"Isn't there anything else I could do instead? Something that would be more entertaining than just lying in bed?" Her shoulders fell in displeasure.

"You do have an extensive DVD collection and library. Perhaps those could be of use?" Barbatos suggested as he noticed her attitude toward his earlier response.

"How about we all watch a movie?" Simeon spoke from the other side of the room. He remembered how she clung on to him as the scary parts came on, and he wanted to cuddle with her more.

"Sure." Her eyes flashed to his with a grin on her face.

They made their way to the DVD collection, collaborating with each other on which movie they wanted to watch. Their movie of choice had been *Scooby-Doo*, one of her favorites. She loved how funny Shaggy and Scooby acted, and that made her relaxed.

She placed her back against the cozy cushions after she set up the DVD player. Simeon claimed the spot to her right, holding his arm up welcoming her to his side. She glanced over at the gesture and curled her legs underneath her, snuggling into Simeon's arms. "I'm sorry. I can't, yet," she whispered into his ear.

"You don't need to worry about it. That was my fault for pushing you too much," he whispered. "I'm the one who needs to be sorry."

"You're okay with just cuddling and kissing, though, right?" she asked as she hid her face in his shoulder.

"Of course, I'm okay with that—those are the best parts," he said with a chuckle and kissed her.

Barbatos turned after placing the DVD into the player, noticing the lovestruck expression on their faces as they whispered to each other. He grabbed a throw blanket from the top of the recliner, holding it out to Simeon for them to use.

Simeon looked over at the object before taking it. "Thank you," he replied as he took the blanket, covering them up with it.

"Of course." Barbatos smiled, bowing before he took his own seat in the recliner.

23

LUST

Lucifer stood in front of the portal fiddling with his phone as he waited for Lord Diavolo and Satan to arrive. The portal opened as he finished reading an article from the hottest news company. He turned his eyes to the portal and said, "Welcome back, you two!"

"Hello, Lucifer. It seems like it's been longer than it has. Especially with what happened," Lord Diavolo said as he made his way over to his close friend.

"I'm assuming that Lord Diavolo filled you in on what happened?" Satan asked as he made his way over to his brother.

"He mentioned that Ashton fractured her ribs, but that he couldn't go into more detail. That it'd be up to her, if she wanted the rest of us to know," Lucifer replied as he gave his brother a stern look, an unspoken exchange not to mention any of it to their brothers. Satan met Lucifer's glaring red eyes, as he nodded in agreement. Lucifer continued: "How's she doing today?"

"Her spirits were higher today, a lot better than they've been the last few days. She didn't want us to leave, though," Lord Diavolo said, speaking as he remembered Ashton's expression during breakfast. "Why don't we head back to the castle? I'm sure there's a lot for me to catch up on," Lord Diavolo added as he gestured for them to start walking.

"Well, I'm going to be heading back to the house. The two of you have fun with all that paperwork." Satan rolled his eyes at them before walking off.

They stared at him as he set off in the direction of the house. "He's been short-tempered since she was attacked," Lord Diavolo said when Satan was far enough away.

". . . And how are you faring, Dia?" Lucifer's eyes moved to Lord Diavolo, noticing his frown. He brushed his fingers over the demon prince's hand. Lord Diavolo looked down at the feeling of Lucifer's hand against his. Lord Diavolo took Lucifer's hand in his own before he spoke. "I'd be lying if I said I was okay. I didn't know that a human could have such an effect on demons."

"She's certainly something special," Lucifer agreed, since she also held a tender spot in his heart.

"Different . . . She's special and different. After what she has gone through, I'm surprised that she can be the way she is," Lord Diavolo said, speaking in a soft voice, barely audible, and Lucifer had to strain to hear him.

"Dia, she means a lot to all of us—we all feel the need to protect her. You said that she was okay, you don't have to worry," Lucifer whispered as he placed his free hand on Lord Diavolo's biceps, brushing his lips to his neck.

Lord Diavolo nuzzled his head into Lucifer's shoulder, sighing deeply. "I should get back to the castle to take care of everything. She was upset that Satan and I were leaving, and if I can help it, I'd rather not be away from her for too long."

"Then let's get back to the castle, and I can fill you in on everything that's been going on here." Lucifer placed a feather-like kiss on the top of Lord Diavolo's hand before placing it back at his side. They broke their physical contact, making their way back to the castle.

The entrance to the castle was massive double wooden doors, which opened into a large entryway with a stone staircase leading to both wings.

Lord Diavolo led the way up the stairs to his study, and as they entered, Lucifer talked about the points that Lord Diavolo left him in charge of. Lucifer made his way to the ivory desk drawer, taking out the paperwork to show Lord Diavolo. Eyeing the paperwork, he knew that it would take more than a few days to complete. He sighed in defeat; the trip that was supposed to be quick would now take longer than he intended.

This stack is huge! I told her that I'd be gone for only a day or two, but with this, there isn't any way that's going to happen, Lord Diavolo thought to himself as his hand combed through his hair. *Well, there isn't any way around it. I can get away with a lot of things as the demon prince, but my duties aren't one of them. I need to push her condition out of my mind and focus.*

Lord Diavolo sat down in the chair behind the desk as he picked up the first sheet of paper. He looked over at Lucifer, who occupied the seat in front of the desk. "You don't have to stay, Lucifer. You should get some rest," Lord Diavolo said over the paperwork.

"Don't be foolish, you know very well that I'm not going to be leaving," Lucifer said, scoffing as he looked back at his lord.

They looked at each other before turning back to the paperwork; Lord Diavolo couldn't help smiling. There was an audible sigh, and Lucifer looked up from the paperwork. The stress lines were evident in Lord Diavolo's forehead as he worked. He stood up, making his way over to his lord. He placed delicate hands on the masculine shoulders, massaging them.

Lord Diavolo kept working through the relaxing sensation until Lucifer leaned down, placing tender kisses onto his neck, causing his hand to stop moving on its own. Lucifer's eyes noticed the reaction, and he tugged lightly on his earlobe, sending a shiver down his spine. His breaths became shallow, hitching in his throat as the heat rose in his groin. "Mmm, Luci," Lord Diavolo said, moaning in response.

"Yes, Dia," Lucifer whispered into his skin as he placed kisses on his neck.

Lord Diavolo closed his eyes as he tilted his head, giving Lucifer better access to his neck. "We should lock the door," Lord Diavolo said with a hiss.

Lucifer bit his neck, pulling lightly; a moan tumbled from his lips as he gripped the arms of the chair. "We should," Lucifer agreed as his lips caught Lord Diavolo's earlobe, sucking gently. His head tilted back against the chair, sensation coursing through his body the closer Lucifer's hand went to his clothed erection. Lucifer's lips curled into a grin as he rubbed his lover's excitement.

"I'll go lock the door," Lucifer seductively whispered into his neck between kisses. Lucifer stood up, pleased at the black-and-blue mark he left on his neck. Slowly, Lucifer made his way to the door, and Lord Diavolo watched him lustfully.

Lord Diavolo scampered over behind Lucifer, wrapping his arms around Lucifer's waist. He pressed Lucifer to his body, breathing heavily into Lucifer's ear as Lucifer locked the door. A moan escape from Lucifer's lips.

"You're mine," Lord Diavolo said to Lucifer as he bit down hard on Lucifer's neck. Lucifer let out a yelp.

"Do with me as you wish, Dia," Lucifer said, speaking through heavy breaths, his head turned to the side as his eyes met Lord Diavolo's.

The look Lucifer gave him made his cock twitch from excitement; it was all he needed to remove Lucifer's cape, tossing it to the ground. His lips never left Lucifer's neck as his hands fumbled with the buttons on Lucifer's shirt. Lucifer let out a moan, his hand resting gingerly on Lord Diavolo's shoulder.

Lord Diavolo's hands ravaged Lucifer's naked torso, and as he kissed his lips, Lucifer shrugged his red coat off him. Lucifer stripped him of his clothes as he led him to the couch. They stood there, staring at each other, gasping for air, before Lord Diavolo placed his hands onto Lucifer's chest, pushing him down onto the couch.

Lucifer sat there looking up at his lover as Lord Diavolo stared back into his eyes, stroking his own cock while moaning. Lucifer smirked, leaning forward, licking the massive cock from base to head. Lord Diavolo growled at the sensation that simple action gave him. Lucifer made circles around the head of Lord Diavolo's cock with his tongue as his eyes looked up to meet Lord Diavolo's.

Lucifer wrapped his lips around his cock, hitting the back of his throat, choking before pulling out with a POP. Lucifer's cock twitched as he gazed upon Lord Diavolo's sweet honey eyes, becoming more lustful and hungrier by the second.

"Are you going to simply tease, or should I take what I want?" Lord Diavolo asked in a strained voice as he tried to control his lust.

"You know I like it when you're forceful," Lucifer said, licking his bottom lip as he leaned back in his seat. Lord Diavolo leaned down, pressing his lips against Lucifer's hard-on as his hand pinned Lucifer to the couch. He gripped Lucifer's waist, flipping him over forcefully, pressing his erection against Lucifer's back.

A moan escaped Lucifer as he braced himself against the top of the couch with his hands. "I need you in me, Dia," Lucifer said through gritted teeth, his head slightly turned to view Lord Diavolo.

Lord Diavolo grinned, kissing Lucifer's back before he turned to open the drawer. They often had sex in his office, so he made sure to keep a supply ready for when they were excited. He squeezed the cold lube onto his hand, rubbing it in before applying it to Lucifer's hole. Lucifer waited in anxious anticipation.

A pleasurable moan sounded from Lucifer as Lord Diavolo slowly moved his finger in and out of Lucifer's hole. He inserted a second finger and then a third. He pumped his fingers in and out quickly as Lucifer's moans continued to fill the room.

"Dia! Oh, Dia, it feels so good," Lucifer said, moaning into the couch as he tried to stifle the loudness of his screams.

Lord Diavolo leaned down to Lucifer's ear, but did not show any signs of stopping. He demanded, "Beg for it."

Lucifer turned to meet Lord Diavolo's eyes; he knew what he wanted. Lord Diavolo was an amazing lover, but he had a submission kink. Lucifer often set aside his pride, since his love for Lord Diavolo was greater, but he would be lying if he said it did not hurt him to do it.

"Please, I beg of you, please." Lucifer bowed his head, submitting fully to his lover.

"Please what!" Lord Diavolo said demandingly as he moved his fingers harder into Lucifer's hole.

"Ah! P-please, I need your c-cock inside of me, p-please, D-Dia," Lucifer pleaded with half-lidded eyes.

"Good demon," Lord Diavolo said as he removed his fingers. Lucifer's hole clenched as the cool air hit it.

Lord Diavolo squirted the cool lube onto his cock, shivering as he massaged it in as he aligned himself to Lucifer's hole. Slowly, he pushed the head in, his head falling back in pleasure. He noticed Lucifer's grunt; he placed his hand on Lucifer's back, rubbing it softly to try to ease the pain as he inserted more.

"AAAHHH," Lucifer grunted as he gripped the couch tightly.

Lord Diavolo stopped, and he trailed gentle kisses up Lucifer's back as he made his way to Lucifer's neck. "Are you all right? Should I stop?" Lord Diavolo asked with concern into Lucifer's ear. As the demon prince, his cock was bigger than the average demon. He had barbs and bumps that would grow with his excitement, he had to be careful so that he didn't seriously hurt Lucifer.

"I'm okay, continue. Go slow, it feels good," Lucifer said.

† 221 †

Lord Diavolo placed a hand on Lucifer's cheek, turning his head to face him. He grazed his lips over Lucifer's before he leaned back, placing more lube on his cock. He pulled out slightly before he went back in, more of his huge, barbed cock sliding into Lucifer's hole.

One of his tender hands rested on Lucifer's waist while the other clutched the couch to ground him. The tightness gripped around his cock, sending fireworks throughout his body as he tried not to lose control.

Lucifer sighed in relief as Lord Diavolo bottomed out inside of him. Lord Diavolo stopped moving, allowing Lucifer time to adjust. As Lucifer's breath evened out, he moved his hips over Lord Diavolo's cock; a growl resonated from above.

Lord Diavolo began moving his hips at a rhythmic pace, his hands squeezed against Lucifer's waist.

"Oh, Luci, you're so tight," he said, moaning through gritted teeth, his head pressed against Lucifer's shoulder. His pace picked up the more he gave into the feeling that gripped his body. Lucifer let out a strangled moan as Lord Diavolo's hand gripped his throat.

"You like that?" Lord Diavolo asked with gritted teeth as his hand gripped Lucifer's neck tighter. His pace picked up with the stirring that filled his body; he rammed his cock into Lucifer as Lucifer's hand began stroking his own cock.

Lord Diavolo peppered Lucifer's back with bite marks; Lucifer cried out in pleasure from the pain. Lord Diavolo's mind grew foggier with each pleasurable cry Lucifer let out; he gripped Lucifer's neck tighter as his pace became erratic. He chased his own orgasm, slamming his cock into Lucifer's hole as it clenched tightly around him.

His head flew back with pleasure as his moan penetrated the walls of his office, thundering down the halls of the echoing hallway. His seed spewed into Lucifer's hole, his cock twitching violently. He pulled out when the last drop finished; flipping Lucifer over, he dropped to his knees.

Lucifer moaned as his hand worked over his own cock, chasing his own orgasm. Lord Diavolo pushed Lucifer's hand away as his mouth enclosed around Lucifer's thick cock. He bobbed his head quickly up and down on Lucifer's thick cock, sucking firmly.

A hand tightened in Lord Diavolo's hair; pain shot through his head unable to move. Lucifer lifted his hips at a fast pace, shoving his cock down Lord Diavolo's throat, causing him to gag. The gagging sound pushed Lucifer over his limit; he tightened his grip on Lord Diavolo's head, shoving his cock deep down his throat as his hot seed spilled out. Lord Diavolo swallowed.

Lord Diavolo's hair smoothed out as the grip on his hair loosened, taking the opportunity to slide onto the couch beside Lucifer. His head dipped onto Lucifer's shoulder as their breathing slowly evened out. "I missed you, Luci," he whispered as he placed a kiss to Lucifer's neck.

"I missed you too, Dia," Lucifer whispered as he held his lover.

Lord Diavolo sighed and said, "We should get back to paperwork."

Lucifer looked down as he also sighed in response and said, "Very well."

Lord Diavolo and Lucifer changed into clothes before they moved to the desk, beginning to work on the ginormous stack of paper. The stack grew smaller as Lord Diavolo looked up at the sound of light snoring, Lucifer's head resting on his arms as he slept. A smiled crossed his lips as he stood up, scooping his lover into his arms as he moved to the couch. He placed Lucifer's head on the cushion before he sat down beside him, caressing his cheek. "You did an amazing job taking care of the Demon Realm for me," Lord Diavolo whispered as he leaned down to kiss Lucifer's lips goodnight.

24

SATAN'S STRUGGLE

BANG!

The door closed loudly behind Satan as he made his way through the front door. He ran up the carpeted stairs to his bedroom, ignoring the commotion of his brothers. His heart raced as he violently ran his fingers through his hair, pacing back and forth.

What the hell was that? he thought to himself. *How could someone hurt her? She's so sweet and kind and loving. Her whole torso painted with old wounds. The story that she told us, that . . . that was horrific. It was worse than any horror movie I'd ever seen, everything that I encountered in my lifetime as a demon.*

His hip bumped against the nightstand; he reached to his side throwing whatever was on it. The glass globe hit the wall as it shattered, splashing water onto the floor. *Why wouldn't anyone stop that?! That abuse, the hurt that she faced, how could they let that happen?! Why wasn't anyone there for her?! She shouldn't have had to face it all alone.* He shook violently as his thoughts hurtled through his brain.

She's so wonderful, her smile, her laugh, the brightness that I get when she's around. That time that she helped me calm down after I sent a desk flying. She could have backed away in fear of me, as everyone else does, but she didn't. Her gleaming hazel eyes stood her ground as she looked at me, waiting for me to go to her. And when I did, she held me. I was glad that my lower half was not against her—she would have felt my erection.

Satan moaned as his hand went to his clothed excitement. His head fell back, remembering her closeness, her beauty. His belt buckle was cold on his shaking hands as he removed it from his waist. He unzipped his pants as he quickly stroked his cock, moaning loudly.

She was so wonderful as she calmed down my wrath, the only one who can do that to me. The way her perfectly rounded breasts bounce with each step she takes. Her alluring scent that I can smell when strolling beside her. He clenched his jaw tightly together as he continued stroking his cock.

Her scent would always grow more prominent when Simeon was around. That angel, that damn angel that won her over. Why couldn't she love me? Why did it have to be an angel? Satan grunted, twitching as his seed flew into the air. His breathing was heavy as he put his cock away, falling to his knees.

I'm no better than that man who hurt her. What did I just do? Jerking off to the thought of her, knowing what she went through. I'm a complete ASS! He gripped his hair tightly as he made a disgusted face.

A knock came to his door. "Yo, stop hiding in there. Where's Ashton?" Mammon's voice bellowed behind the door.

"Y-yeah, you can't keep her to yourself, where is she?" Leviathan said, stuttering.

"Let us in," Belphegor said.

"Oh, is Ashton back? I can't wait to paint her nails," Asmodeus said.

"I want her to come make food with me," Beelzebub said.

Satan's voice boomed throughout his room, leaking into the hallway. "STAY OUT!" He picked up a book and heaved it at the door with a loud THUNK.

The five demon brothers jumped out of their skin at the unexpected response as they looked around at one another. "Guess he needs alone time," Beelzebub said.

"U-u-um, why don't we check back tomorrow? H-he may calm down by then," Leviathan said, stuttering.

"I wonder what has him in this bad a mood? He hasn't been this bad since Ashton came here," Asmodeus chimed in with his hand on his cheek.

"Yo, you don't think something happened to Ashton, do you? She's supposed to be back, but she isn't," Mammon said, his face creased with worry as he spoke the thought that echoed in each of their minds.

Leviathan exited the hallway first, making his way back to his own room. He gulped as he turned on the most violent video game; he had to release his anxiety. The others followed his example, leaving the hallway to find their own ways of coping.

Those that stayed in the house that night heard the deafening sounds that came from Satan's room. There was no reprieve from the noise as their brother screamed in agony all night.

Beelzebub went to Satan's room the next morning, forgetting to knock. He entered with a tray of food, hoping it'd help ease his brother's hurt. He stopped in his tracks halfway in the room as he saw Satan twitching on the floor trying to control himself. "Satan, I brought you some breakfast. I ate only one slice of bacon, too, instead of all of them," Beelzebub said, timidly holding out the food. His brother's wrath was nothing to take lightly—in the past, he'd burned down the house, and they'd had to rebuild it.

Satan stopped rocking back and forth, muttering to himself as his brother spoke. His eyes followed the noise; he looked right at Beelzebub, but he didn't see him. His mind clogged with his vicious thoughts as he screamed at the noise, "GET OUT! GET OUT!" Satan picked up several books that were around him, hurling them at the noise that was his brother.

Beelzebub retreated, dodging the books, lucky that each of them missed him. He knew that if Satan had been on his game, all of them would've hit him.

☙♥❧

The days began to merge as Lord Diavolo and Lucifer worked on the stack of papers. Lord Diavolo focused on his duties, forgetting the request that Simeon asked him. Lucifer brought him back to the date when he asked about a specific document.

"What day did you say it was?" Lord Diavolo asked Lucifer after responding about the document.

"It is the third of February. Dia, are you feeling all right? Perhaps we should take a break," Lucifer said, his forehead creasing with worry as he looked at his lover.

"Yes, yes, I'm all right. I was so lost in all this paperwork that I forgot about a request that Simeon asked me to do for him," Lord Diavolo said, speaking as he leaned back in his chair.

"What'd he ask you to do for him?" Lucifer inquired, his curiosity piqued.

"The first was to check on Seth, and the other was to bring back a box," Lord Diavolo replied. "Would you care to join me in paying Seth and Adrian a visit? It'd be a good break from the paperwork."

"If I may, I'd like to join." Lucifer gave a curt nod as he stood up.

Lord Diavolo walked over to the door. Before opening it, he turned back to Lucifer. His smile met his eyes as he gave his lover a kiss before they exited the room.

They knocked on the door, waiting for someone to answer. "Who is it?" Seth's voice rang out.

"Lord Diavolo and Lucifer," Lord Diavolo replied as a smile crossed his lips.

The door opened. "Come in, come in. Here, sit over here," Seth said, taking them to the living room after closing the door behind them.

"Seth, who was at the door?" Adrian asked as he made his way down the hallway; he had just finished a potion. "Ah, you're back! How was the trip?" Adrian answered his earlier question as he reached the living room.

"Yeah, how was the trip? And where's Simeon? He should be here," Seth said, his voice holding excitement and curiosity.

"The surgery went amazing—she did a wonderful job. Being a neurosurgeon can't be easy, especially after what I saw leading up to the surgery," Lord Diavolo said. "She barely slept at all, and then the actual surgery took her twenty hours to perform. She even risked her own life with radiation poisoning to save her patient." Lord Diavolo's voice excitedly told them of the events from the surgery as his hands flew in the air as he talked. They sat there, sipping tea as they listened to each detail the demon prince enthusiastically gave them. "It was a fantastic opportunity she gave us!" Lord Diavolo concluded.

"That sounds like it was a lot to take in when you were there, but also very thrilling," Adrian said, speaking after he took a sip of his hot tea.

"Yes, it was," Lord Diavolo said with a laugh.

"Where is Simeon?" Seth asked.

"That's right, if you're here, then the others must be back as well," Adrian said.

"Well"—Lord Diavolo's deep sigh penetrated their nerves as they looked at him, perplexed—"after the surgery . . . there was an incident. I'll not go into detail, since it isn't my place to, but Ashton fractured her ribs. She can't use the transportation device because of it. Using the device would only cause more damage at this time. I told Barbatos to stay behind so he could help her with the healing, and as for Simeon . . ." he paused, remembering Simeon's reaction.

"What about Simeon?" Seth asked.

"Simeon refused to leave her side. In fact, he barely let the rest of us near her." Lord Diavolo's eyes looked at the carpeted floor, a frown appearing on his lips at the memory of his injured friend.

"Is Ashton all right? I hope she is. She makes the most delicious brownies. I was going to see if she wanted to make some with me when she got back," Seth said, his concerned voice filling the room as he spoke quickly.

"Her body will heal, but it'll take some time. I asked Barbatos how long he thought it would be until she could use the transportation device, and he said about a week or two," Lord Diavolo said. "I've been here for a week, so hopefully, by the time I get back, she will be well enough. And I'm sure she'd love to bake some brownies with you." Lord Diavolo paused as he looked around the room.

Everyone looked at Lord Diavolo and his downfallen expression with eyes that held no joy. Lucifer placed a hand on his cold, clammy one. Lord Diavolo met Lucifer's eyes before he continued: "Simeon specifically asked me to check on you, Seth. He was concerned about how you were faring without him."

"I'm doing okay. Adrian's been a tremendous help and keeps me busy with baking," Seth said. "Although none of the stuff he bakes comes out particularly good. We have to throw his version away." Seth spoke rapidly from his anxiety.

"That doesn't sound very pleasant." Lord Diavolo looked at Seth; his chuckle came out strained.

"Beelzebub came over and tried one of his cupcakes, which ended up making him sick," Seth said. "So, we started just throwing the food out instead." Seth's hands flew through the air as he talked.

"Wise choice." Lord Diavolo's tongue came out to lick his bottom lip before he asked, "Would you mind showing me to Simeon's room? He asked me to take something back to him."

"Of course, it's right this way," Adrian said, placing his teacup down as he led the way down the hall to Simeon's room.

"If you're going back, can I go?" Seth asked. "I want to see Ashton and make sure she's okay." He chased after Adrian, Lord Diavolo, and Lucifer, tugging on Lord Diavolo's sleeve.

Lord Diavolo halted in the hallway, kneeling in front of Seth. "Not this time, okay? She'll be back soon. Right now, she needs to rest."

"Aww, but I want to see her." Seth's eyes were like big puppy-dog eyes as he pouted.

"I know, and I'm sorry," Lord Diavolo whispered.

Seth's gaze went to the floor as he pouted back to his bedroom. Adrian's hand found a doorknob as he watched the scene. "This is his bedroom," Adrian said as Lord Diavolo stood up straight.

Lord Diavolo entered the room, his eyes scanning for a medium-sized box—it wasn't hard to find. He walked over to the box, and picking it up, he made his way back to the doorway.

"What's in it?" Adrian's curiosity got the better of him; he couldn't refrain from asking.

"I'm not sure, I didn't ask him," Lord Diavolo replied as he stood in the hallway facing Adrian and Lucifer.

"Hmm . . . mysterious." Adrian's lips curved in a mischievous grin as he closed Simeon's bedroom door. "I like it!"

"Yes, it's very mysterious," Lord Diavolo said, pausing as he gave Lucifer a look.

"Lord Diavolo, are you ready to head back to the office? We still have a lot of paperwork to go through." Lucifer didn't like the aura that Adrian gave off as Lord Diavolo looked in his eyes. They both wanted to leave as quickly as possible.

"You're correct, Lucifer. There's still a lot of work to finish in the castle," Lord Diavolo replied.

"Then, by all means, make your way back and let her know I hope she feels better soon," Adrian told them as he led them to the door.

"I'll do that, thank you, Adrian. And thank you for taking care of Seth in Simeon's absence," Lord Diavolo said as they made their way to the door.

"It isn't a problem at all," Adrian replied as he closed the door behind them.

Lord Diavolo and Lucifer made their way down the driveway, turning toward the castle. "I should go and check on Satan. He's supposed to be going back with you tomorrow," Lucifer said with a sigh as they stopped at the street corner, waiting for the Walk sign to turn on.

"If he's still angry, then I don't want him going back," Lord Diavolo told Lucifer as they waited.

"I agree, he shouldn't be near her if he's like that," Lucifer replied.

"If he hasn't regained control, would you like to go back with me and check on her?" Lord Diavolo asked as they walked across the street.

"Who'd run the Demon Realm with both of us gone?" Lucifer turned his head to look at Lord Diavolo.

"It wouldn't be for long, just a day or so . . . the Demon Realm isn't going to burn down over my being absent for one day and leaving no one in charge. They fear my power too much to go against me," Lord Diavolo replied as his heart rate picked up speed from Lucifer's look.

"Then if Satan isn't able to go, I'll join you." Lucifer smiled as he went to walk down the opposite side of the street; he stopped as a warm hand tugged on his. He looked back, his eyes wide, as Lord Diavolo stared at him. "What's wrong, Dia?"

"I don't like keeping us a secret," Lord Diavolo whispered in a melancholy tone.

"I don't, either, but with your title, we have to," Lucifer whispered as he gestured for Lord Diavolo to follow him. He led him to an abandoned building, where Lucifer made sure no one could find them. Lucifer's lips were on Lord Diavolo's as his hands raked over Lord Diavolo's body. His kisses were messy as they traveled down Lord Diavolo's neck, creating a moan from his lips. "Sshh, someone will hear us," Lucifer said with a hiss into his lover's ear.

"Luci, we can't. We must get back and finish our work." Lord Diavolo's protests slowly slipped away as Lucifer's hand slid down to the buckle on his pants.

"I'll make it quick." Lucifer's voice rushed with adrenaline.

"Let me set this down—I can't take it back broken," Lord Diavolo said, moving away from Lucifer as he set the box down by the entrance.

Lucifer pounced on Lord Diavolo, pinning him to the wall, his hand snaking down Lord Diavolo's pants. A moan echoed in the empty building; Lucifer stifled it with a kiss. Lucifer's hand worked around Lord Diavolo's cock as he exposed it to the air before taking his own out. His lips never parted from Lord Diavolo's as his hands wrapped around both cocks, pressing them together. He pumped his hand rapidly, catching their moans in rough kisses as they chased their orgasms.

Lucifer leaned his head against Lord Diavolo's shoulder as they stood there, panting heavily. "You never cease to amaze me, Luci," Lord Diavolo said, his voice purring into Lucifer's ear, and a chill ran down his spine.

Lucifer nuzzled his head into Lord Diavolo's neck as he wrapped his arms around him, hugging him. The warmth engulfed them as they stood there, embracing each other.

"I should get back, finish that paperwork. And you should check on Satan," Lord Diavolo told Lucifer defeatedly.

"Okay." Lucifer kissed Lord Diavolo before he continued, saying, "I'll see you tomorrow."

Lucifer's heart raced as he made his way to the door to leave. "Don't forget the box," he said, remembering on the way out.

"I won't," Lord Diavolo said. He leaned against the wall, catching his breath before he left the building.

Lucifer arrived at the house, climbing the stairs to his brother's room. He peeked in. He looked around at the destruction: furniture overturned across the room, papers strewn everywhere, books torn in pieces, glass spewed across every inch of the floor, and Satan in the corner mumbling to himself as he shook with anger.

Lucifer closed the door quietly behind him, knowing it was best to leave Satan alone when he was in that state.

25

SIMEON'S GIFT

Lord Diavolo opened the door to Ashton's bedroom, filling it with light from the living-room windows. He heard a movie playing as his eyes found Ashton curled up in Simeon's arms, hugging him tightly. He looked over his shoulder at Lucifer, a smile crossing his lips as he whispered, "They look cute." Lucifer craned his head to catch a glimpse before nodding his head in agreement.

Lord Diavolo tapped his knuckles on the wall. They turned to see what the noise was. Ashton's eyes widened, filling with excitement when she saw who it was. "You're back!"

"Yes, I'm sorry I took longer than I planned. There was a lot to finish before I was able to return," Lord Diavolo said, his lips turning into a bright smile at her reaction.

"That's okay." She unwrapped herself from Simeon, and he reluctantly lifted his arm as she stood up. She walked around the sectional, making her way to Lord Diavolo and

Lucifer. They watched her as she wrapped her arms around them in a warm embrace. "I missed you," she whispered.

"We missed you as well," Lord Diavolo and Lucifer replied at the same time, returning her hugs.

"Simeon, I have the package that you asked me to retrieve," Lord Diavolo said, raising the box slightly in Simeon's direction.

Ashton's eyes moved between Lord Diavolo and Simeon before staying on Simeon. He winked as he smiled, getting up to take the box from Lord Diavolo. "I'll just set this in the bedroom. Thank you for taking the time to retrieve it for me," Simeon told them as he took the box.

"You're more than welcome—it wasn't any trouble at all," Lord Diavolo replied as he watched Simeon leave the room. His gaze turned to Ashton. "How are you feeling? Any better?" Lord Diavolo asked.

"I'm not in as much pain, and I can move around a lot better. Barbatos and Simeon have helped a lot," she replied before pausing for a moment. "Did you . . . tell the others?" Her eyes flickered over to Lucifer as concern filled her voice.

"The only thing he told us is that you injured yourself. That's the only thing, he wouldn't go into any more detail," Lucifer said as his hand hovered over her arm with concern.

"It isn't my story to tell. I wouldn't do that," Lord Diavolo said. He met her eyes, pleading for her to understand that he did not hurt her.

Simeon walked back out of his room. Looking over, he saw Lucifer's hand close to Ashton, a throbbing sting of jealousy filling his body. He crossed the room, stopping by her side as Barbatos stood up to join them.

"Okay." Her eyes searched Lord Diavolo's before finding the answer that she wanted.

"She's doing much better, my lord. She should be able to use the transportation device by next week," Barbatos said as he broke the tension.

"That's wonderful news. I'm glad to hear that!" Lord Diavolo's eyes moved to Barbatos as he talked.

"How's everything back in the Demon Realm, my lord?" Barbatos placed a hand on his torso, bowing slightly.

"Lucifer did an amazing job taking care of everything while I was away," Lord Diavolo replied.

Ashton looked at Simeon as Lord Diavolo and Barbatos were talking; she noticed Simeon's demeanor was off. Her fingers brushed his as she tried to get his attention; he looked at her with his blue eyes as his fingers intertwined with hers.

"How does everyone feel about playing a game of Monopoly?" She looked around at their expressions, their eyes looking at her as her eyes shone from the idea that she offered. They knew she wouldn't take no for an answer. They followed her to the living room.

"I'm going to steal everyone's property this time!" Ashton rubbed her hands together as she took a spot next to Simeon on the floor.

The game went on for hours, and Ashton became bankrupt first as she landed on Simeon's largest hotel. Her head turned away from him as she handed him all her property. Light pressure perched on her shoulder; gentle nudging tickled her neck, causing her to meet his eyes. "Don't be mad," he said, his breath hitting her lips as he mumbled into them.

"Hey, no! Your turn, take your turn," she said, pointing to the game with flushed cheeks.

He went back to the game, and she noticed everyone watching them. Cold, clammy hands wrapped around his waist; warmth flooded his back as hot breath hit his neck. Her cheeks radiated embarrassment, his shoulders supplying shelter to hide behind. His glances kept her heart pounding, stealing kisses on occasion.

Simeon claimed the last property in the game, and everyone congratulated him. Lord Diavolo and Lucifer leaned back against the sectional as Ashton helped Barbatos put the game away. "That was fun," Lord Diavolo told everyone as he let out a contented sigh. They nodded in agreement. "We should get going back to the Demon Realm," Lord Diavolo said, continuing after a moment.

"What? Why? I thought you were going to stay for a bit." Ashton dropped the game from her hand as she was putting it back under the table; it sprang open, and the pieces fell out.

"I can't leave the Demon Realm unattended. I do have duties that I have to fulfill as the prince. I'm sorry, but we must return. We'll also prepare things for when you're able to come back as well," Lord Diavolo said, trying to reason with her.

She kept her eyes on the floor as she picked up the pieces that fell out of the game. Her hands shook with anxiety, as the bedroom door close behind them. She couldn't watch them leave a second time. Her body froze as a hand covered hers; looking up, she met Simeon's eyes, her own welling up with salty water. "It's okay," he said, his quiet voice resonating in her soul as caring arms embraced her.

Ashton closed her eyes, brushing away the tears that escaped; her voice cracked as she said, "I'm going to finish picking this up, take some meds, and then head to bed."

"Without dinner?" Simeon asked as he kissed the top of her head.

"I'm not hungry," she replied as she went to pick up the rest of the pieces on the floor.

"Let me finish this. Barbatos has your meds already on the counter," he said, cupping her face in his gentle hands. "Okay?"

Her eyes were hollow as she looked back in his eyes, nodding her head. He gave her a soft kiss on her lips, helping her up. She made her way over to the kitchen bar, taking her meds as she went to her bedroom.

Her bed was soft, welcoming as she lay down on it. She looked up at the ceiling. *I wonder if Barbatos and Simeon will take me to get a new tea set tomorrow? If I asked, they would. I tried so hard to forget what tomorrow is, but in the end, the memory always comes back. The day I walked out of the underground with what I thought to be my freedom.* She closed her eyes, drifting off to sleep as her thoughts settled.

Ashton bolted straight up in bed, shaking, clutching her knees close to her. "Simeon," she said with a croak, trying to gain her voice. "Simeon." She tried again, to no avail. Her hand raked her hair violently, and she stood up wrapping her arms around herself tightly, quickly making her way to Simeon's door.

Her knuckles rapped lightly on his door; she did not wait for a reply as she opened it, peeking in. "Simeon," she whispered fearfully into the darkness. "Simeon." Her voice gained a small amount of volume.

Simeon stirred in his sleep; opening his eyes, he blinked as he let out a heavy breath. "Hmm? Ashton?" He noticed a dark figure standing in the doorway.

"It's me," Ashton replied.

"Are you all right? Come here," he sat up, lifting the blanket to welcome her. She wasted no time crawling into his bed, wrapping her arms securely around him. "Did you have another nightmare?"

"Yes," she said as she buried her face into his chest, grasping his shoulder.

He secured the blanket around her, rubbing her back with his hands. *Is this what it was like for her all those years? This is the fourth time she's come to my room with nightmares,* he thought as he told her it would be all right. The slow, repeated movement of fingers in her hair accompanied by humming had her eyes closing.

Simeon's eyes fluttered open as the sun shone through the curtains. He yawned as he looked down at Ashton, still asleep; he wished she could stay in that peaceful state. Ashton stirred in his arms as the sun hit her eyelids; her hand flew to her eyes, covering them. "Mmm no." Simeon moved slightly trying to block the sun from her eyes without waking her, but he failed.

She blinked several times before the room became clear. Her hair went flat as Simeon gingerly stroked it. "Good morning, snowflake. Are you feeling better?" he asked.

"Mmm . . . mmhmm." She snuggled into his side as he chuckled and vibrated his chest.

They lay there in each other's arms as they heard a "grrr" sound. Their heads turned to Simeon's stomach. "I guess it's time to move?" Ashton asked.

"You don't have to, it can wait," Simeon said, trying to suppress his stomach's growling again.

"No, I think your stomach will be happier with both of us if you feed it," she said as she sat up.

Simeon's arms wrapped around her waist as he buried his face into her neck. "I don't want you to move."

She leaned back in his embrace. "I don't want to, either, but I'm sure Barbatos is already out there cooking breakfast for us."

"You wear the necklace he got you a lot. Is there a reason?" he asked, jealousy getting the better of him at the mention of Barbatos's name.

"Have you ever looked at the colors? Hazel and sapphire, like our eyes. Barbatos may have gotten it for me, and I like him for that, but it keeps me close to you when you aren't close by," she whispered.

His hands fell to the bed as she got up, slowly making his way to the door behind her. "Good morning, my lady," Barbatos said, greeting her with a raised eyebrow. "Simeon, good morning."

"Good morning, Barbatos." She bit her bottom lip nervously.

"You don't need to be nervous, my lady. I know this isn't the first time that you've gone to his room because you couldn't sleep," Barbatos said, speaking words of comfort to her. "Now, if you would please go change, breakfast will be on the table shortly."

She scurried off to her room to change before she made her way to the dining-room table. Barbatos and Simeon were waiting patiently, chatting idly to pass the time. She filled her plate with food, about to take a bite as Simeon leaned across the table, brushing her bangs behind her ear. "Would it be all right if I got a moment of your time after breakfast? I have something that I would like to give you," Simeon asked.

"You're finally going to show me what's in that box from yesterday?" Ashton asked between bites.

"Yes." Simeon flushed red.

"Yes, you can have a moment of my time. Since I'm so busy doing all these things that I have to do," she said, her voice dripping with sarcasm.

"You'll be able to do more soon, just be patient," Barbatos told her as he laughed.

"I know, it's just hard. I'm not the kind to sit back and do nothing for long," she replied.

After breakfast, Barbatos cleaned up while Simeon retrieved the box from his room, leading her downstairs. Her confusion grew with each step they took, until he stopped her in front of the glass case.

"Do you remember when we went to the tea shop and out to dinner?" Simeon started saying as he turned to face her. "You told me that each year, you got a new tea set. That they had a significant meaning to you on this day. And you couldn't take your eyes off the blue one, with the pink flowers." Simeon placed the box gently on the floor, helping her sit down. He sat opposite of her with the box between them.

"Yeah, I remember that. It's the first time I shared anything personal about myself with someone else."

His warm hand enclosed hers, taking the uneasiness in her stomach away, bringing life back to her discolored face.

"I know that it's difficult for you, and I genuinely thank you for sharing it with me. Today isn't easy, but I know that getting a tea set on this date is important to you." He gestured to the box for her to open it. As she did, he continued, saying, "I went back the next day and picked it up. You were mesmerized by its color, and it was as if it belonged to you. I had to get it for you."

Her fingers slowly grazed over the porcelain. She could feel her eyes sting with tears as they flowed freely down her cheeks. Simeon reached over, wiping them away with his thumb.

"Today makes eleven years. From the day that I escaped," she said with a strained voice, looking down at the tea set before continuing. "I never wanted to kill. I didn't have a choice. Kill or be killed. I just wanted to get out of there. Out of the torment. So, one day, I walked in and demanded he let me leave. He gave me an impossible task that should have killed me, and he was shocked when I walked back in there. I was barely hanging on, but I made it. That's when we signed our contract. He couldn't have any contact with me at all. Like a restraining order. And I, in turn, would give up all my rights to kill him." Her voice broke.

"It was always supposed to end up that way. With me killing him. It's how it works in the underground." Her eyes lifted to meet Simeon's; he held no judgment, just love. She scooted the box aside, clambering onto his lap. Her arms wound around his neck, nuzzling into him. Supportive arms caressed her back, filling her with encouragement.

"I started collecting tea sets the day after I left. One for each year I was out. Because of how fragile they are, but tough as well."

Her breath was heavy as she tried to regain control of her emotions, looking over at the glass case. "This is the first time in my life that I haven't had to face everything alone." She paused for a moment. "Thank you for the tea set. I had meant to ask if all of us could go out and find one today. Now I don't have to."

"You're welcome, I'm glad you like it. Would you like me to help you find a spot for it?" he asked her once her grip loosened.

"Please," she whispered.

"Of course." He helped her up, leading her to the glass case and finding a spot for the tea set.

They took the recycling upstairs to the correct bins on the way to the kitchen. She wanted to check on Barbatos, since they spent quite some time downstairs, when the alarm sounded.

BEEP BEEP BEEP

"Intruder on premises," Kaname said, its voice ringing through the entire house. Ashton froze as the alarm continued.

BEEP BEEP BEEP

"Intruder on premises!"

Ashton's breathing became heavy as she looked at the ceiling, her eyes darting everywhere. "Kaname, put the house on lockdown, NOW," she said. "No one is to get in or out without my permission." Her voice shook with fear.

"Commencing lockdown." Kaname's voice rang through the house.

BEEP BEEP BEEP

CLICK

"House is now on lockdown. No one may enter or leave."

Ashton raced up the stairs to the library, clutching her side from the pain as she made her way to the corner bookshelf. Simeon and Barbatos were on her tail. "What's going on?" they asked in unison.

She didn't hear them as she counted the spaces on the bookshelf. She pulled a book out as a door slid open, and she placed her eye in front of the iris scanner. The system read her iris, opening the door into her security room.

"What's going on? What did the system mean?" Barbatos and Simeon asked in unison again as they entered the security room behind her. There were screens everywhere, showing her entire property.

"It means that there's someone here on the property who shouldn't be. Someone other than us," she said, making eye contact with them, her voice raised with alarm. "Kaname, show me where the intruder alert came from. Bring it up on the computer screen," she said, speaking to the air as she kept their gazes.

"Yes, Ashton." Kaname brought up the isolated incident on the far-right computer screen.

"Thank you," she said, swirling her chair around and wheeling over to the screen.

Barbatos and Simeon moved behind her, watching the screen with her. She pressed buttons on the computer, making the screen move backward, until she pressed play. They watched as the scene played out. "There!" She pointed to a corner of the screen. "The shadow right there on the ground."

Ashton's fingers flew over the keys on the computer, zooming in on the corner. "Sangchul." Her jaw dropped as she leaned back in the chair, her eyes wide.

"Who?" Barbatos asked.

"He was one of Franko's top men. He trained him just as hard as he trained me. Except without all the punishment and abuse," she replied as she watched the screen.

"Why's he here?" Simeon's teeth ground together; his hand rested on her shoulder for support.

"That." She pointed on the screen. "He placed something on the ground."

"He did?" Barbatos asked.

"Yeah." She rewound the camera feed, showing Barbatos where the intruder placed something on the ground.

"How did you spot that so easily?" Barbatos asked incredulously.

"That's what I was trained to do, spot every detail," she said, her voice becoming strained as she answered. "Kaname, is the intruder still on the property?"

"Scanning property for signs of an intruder . . . no intruder detected . . . foreign object found." Kaname's voice echoed in the room.

"Kaname, take us off lockdown," she told the computer system.

"Exiting lockdown," Kaname said.

BEEP BEEP BEEP

CLICK

"Lockdown has been lifted," Kaname said.

"Let's go see what Sangchul left us," she said, standing up and making her way to the door.

"You can't go out there, what if he's still here? Your ribs are fractured," Simeon said, his face creased with worry lines as he pleaded with her to stay somewhere safe.

"Simeon, I had Kaname scan the property for intruders, and he's not here anymore," she said as she crossed the room to him. She placed her hand on his cheek, and he closed his eyes, tilting his head into her hand. "I'm safe, okay? I've done this my entire life on my own—it's nothing new to me," she said, failing at her attempt to reassure him.

His eyes flew open, looking into hers with deep hurt. "But you aren't alone anymore," Simeon said. "I'm here with you." His voice broke with anxiety and fear.

"Then come with me to retrieve what he left, both of you," she said, looking into his eyes before meeting Barbatos's, whose reply was a singular, curt nod.

She turned on her heels, making her way outside to where Sangchul had been. She found an envelope underneath a rock in plain sight. She moved to pick the envelope up with confidence, in case Sangchul was watching her. Inside was a single threat.

You will die for killing him!

Her hazel eyes grew fierce as she slowly scanned the property around her, making her way back into the house. She closed the blinds once all of them were inside. Constricting pressure caused a burst of pain to fly through her body; her hand banged on Simeon's rigid shoulder, making him realize she could not breathe.

"You can't stay here, not with the threat. We need to get you back to the Demon Realm," Barbatos said, speaking quickly, and taking out his phone, he dialed Lord Diavolo's number.

"If she goes back now, the transportation device will do more damage," Simeon said, trying to warn Barbatos but failing as Barbatos walked away from them on the phone.

"Lord Diavolo and Lucifer are going to the portal now. They'll be there shortly, and we'll leave to go back to the

Demon Realm. They won't be able to get to her there, and the threat may pass in due time. You should pack your things in the meantime," Barbatos explained when he walked back over.

She couldn't get a word in as they spoke quickly, urgently, with fear of her safety prominent in their voices. She didn't want to stop them, though—what she wanted was to go back to the Demon Realm.

"We will do whatever it takes to protect you," Barbatos said, turning to her and placing his hand on her shoulder despite the menacing scowl from Simeon.

Simeon followed her to her room, helping her pack her things, even though he had his own to pack. Uneasiness, fear, and dread filled the air, his protectiveness growing tenfold. She knew he wouldn't leave her side any time soon.

Barbatos, Simeon, and Ashton stood in the center of the bedroom, ready to leave. She could feel the sweaty palm of Simeon's hand on her back as he stood close to her side, his hot breath moving her hair.

"AAAAHHHHH." She let out a bloodcurdling scream as she clutched her side, landing in the transportation device at the Demon Realm.

26

HOSPITAL STAY

Ashton lay unconscious on the cold operating table, hooked up to blood drips, IV drips, and anesthetics. The demon doctors worked quickly to repair her punctured stomach before placing the ribs back in their proper location.

The air in the waiting room was heavy as everyone was on edge. Simeon paced, his hands shaking violently as his thoughts raced: *I knew it was a bad idea for her to go through the transportation device this early. One of her fractured ribs refractured, puncturing her stomach when she went through the transportation device. I did my best to perform a healing charm, but I don't know if it worked with how nervous and shaky I was. Is she going to be okay? What if she isn't? The moon is bright tonight—I never got to take her on a moonlit walk.*

Seth walked over to Simeon; the eyes of the demons lifted at the action. Leviathan stepped over, stopping Seth in his tracks. "I can't get past this level. Could you help me?"

Seth looked at Leviathan, hurt clear in his eyes. "Okay," he replied in defeat.

Barbatos turned back to his lord. "This is the note that was placed on her property." He handed Lord Diavolo the single threat, allowing him to read:

You will die for killing him!

"What do we do?" Lord Diavolo spoke his thoughts aloud.

"I'm not sure. Is she safe here in the Demon Realm, my lord?" Barbatos asked.

"I believe so, I think. I never agreed with my father's methods, but there is one thing that he did. He made it difficult for angels, demons, and humans to roam freely among the three realms. Angels need permission to come to the Demon Realm, and humans don't know that the Demon Realm and Celestial Realm even exist," Lord Diavolo said as his fingers played with his lips nervously. "This Sangchul guy that you mentioned, he shouldn't even know that this realm exists."

"That's a good point, my lord. But what if she chooses to go back to the Human Realm at the end of the year?" Barbatos questioned while he stood properly beside his master.

"Even if they were able to get into the Demon Realm, we are the strongest demons. We could easily kill them if we had to. But we can't force her to stay here against her will, but we should try to get through to her. Show her how important it is that she stay here," Lord Diavolo said as worry creased his expression.

Barbatos was about to speak; his mouth was open as a doctor came in. "I'm looking for the family of Ashton Lure."

Simeon's body spun around to face the doctor, his heart picking up speed. "That's all of us." Lord Diavolo got up from his seat, walking over to place a hand on Simeon's shoulder.

The doctor looked around at the crowded room to find all seven of the demon brothers; Lord Diavolo, Barbatos, Adrian, Seth and Simeon were watching her. "Um . . . yes, right, all of you are here for Ashton Lure." She looked down at her notes before continuing. "Her surgery was successful. Whoever performed the healing charm on her did an excellent job. That stopped her internal bleeding before she bled out before she could get here. We repaired her punctured stomach and placed her ribs in their proper location. She's in the recovery room now," the doctor said, giving them the update.

"When can we see her?" everyone asked in unison with anxious voices.

"She's still tired, coming in and out from the anesthetics. It may be overwhelming for all of you to go in at once, but you can go in two at a time to see her." The doctor told them the room number, letting them decide who would go in first.

"Simeon will go in and—" Lord Diavolo started to say.

"I'm not leaving her!" Simeon exclaimed, cutting Lord Diavolo off, his voice stern.

"Simeon will go in, and the rest of us will go in one by one." Lord Diavolo's eyes moved to Simeon, giving him a knowing look.

Simeon entered the room, Belphegor right behind him, as they decided to go youngest to oldest. Simeon crossed the room, sitting in a chair beside the bed, his hand taking hold of her cold one. Belphegor kissed her hand before he exited the room, allowing his other brothers to see her for themselves.

One by one, each of the brothers came in, caressing her arm, letting her know they were there for her before leaving. Simeon's eyes remained fixed on her sleeping body. A hand touched his shoulder, startling him. He looked up as Barbatos whispered, "We're going to be going back to the castle. Let us know if something changes, and don't forget to take care of your own health as well. You did an amazing job with the healing charm—it saved her life."

"Okay." Simeon's reply was weak as he turned back to Ashton, kissing her hand. A soft click sounded as Barbatos exited the room.

Ashton moaned as she groggily woke up from the anesthetics. She looked to her side, finding Simeon resting his head on his arms, asleep. Her smile was weak, and she reached over, ruffling his hair with as much strength as she could muster. He stirred, lifting his head. He blinked several times before realizing Ashton's hazel eyes were staring at him. "Hey," she said with a croak, trying to smile.

"Hey." He bit his bottom lip to keep him from crying. *She's awake!*

"Come here." She used all her strength to scoot her body over in bed, patting the spot beside her. "Come here," she repeated, her tired eyes looked to Simeon.

The bed dipped from Simeon's weight as he climbed in beside her. She lifted her head off the pillow as Simeon put his arm around her. She laid her head back against his biceps, eyes closing as the anesthetic put her back to sleep. He placed a loving kiss on her forehead, caressing her cheek as he hummed to her. *I'm so happy I found you,* he thought.

The demon doctor assigned to her case decided to keep Ashton in the hospital for several weeks while she healed. Each day that passed, her strength began to grow.

Simeon sat in the chair beside her bed while they talked, interrupted when Beelzebub, Belphegor, and Leviathan knocked on the door. "You wouldn't believe this game. It's the latest one that just came out, and I'm already halfway through it," Leviathan said. He held his gaming system up and showed her the part he was stuck on.

"I know that you'll be able to beat it, and what about that, um"—her eyes closed, and she took in a breath before continuing—"the anime you were excited about, has that come out yet?"

"Hey, don't hog all the attention, I want to give her some cookies I made," Beelzebub said, huffily.

She took a nibble of the cookie. "It's good. Thank you."

"You have to eat more than that, you didn't even get to the good part," Beelzebub said as he ate six cookies at once.

"She isn't able to eat a lot of solid foods yet. If she were, then she would." Simeon winked at her, and she handed him the cookie.

"I brought you a fluffy pillow. I know the hospital has some, but this one is a special one because it's extra comfy," Belphegor said while he yawned.

"I'll have to switch them out later," she said while her eyes dipped closed.

Simeon stroked her hair, and the three brothers left. She woke up later that night and saw Simeon reading in the corner. He looked up from his book and smiled at her. "Hey, snowflake." She patted the bed, and he lay beside her. She looked into his eyes. "Kiss me."

His lips brushed hers in a tender kiss, and her hand came to his cheek, deepening the kiss. She pushed into him, and he let her have dominance over his lips before they pulled away, panting. She moaned and leaned into him as sleep took her over unwillingly.

Simeon was reading her their angel-studies homework when Satan came into the room. "The last batch that I gave you was for when we were away in the Human Realm, but these are for the few weeks that you two have missed." His hands were full of notes and papers from their teachers, and he placed them on the rolling tray.

"That looks like a lot—we missed about a month, if not more," she said, sighing, and eyed the stack of papers.

"Don't worry, I'm going to be helping the two of you with it, so don't get overwhelmed already," Satan said with a chuckle. *I must do this; I have to repay them for how I acted in the Human Realm. This is my chance to redeem myself.*

"But Simeon and I have only one class together," she pointed out.

"Well, technically, Simeon is taking demon history as well, just at a different time. The only two classes that are different are demon and angel physiology," Satan said as he opened the demon-studies textbook.

Each of them opened to the page Satan told them, and he used the nurses' white board to write things down if he needed. They worked on demon history first before moving to angel studies, starting where they left off before going to the Human Realm.

She stifled a yawn, and her eyes closed for a second. Simeon and Satan burst out laughing at her reaction. "Is it that boring?" Satan asked.

"No, I'm just still tired a lot," she said, looking at Simeon. "Right?"

"Mmhmm . . . sure." He grinned at her, and she weakly hit his arm.

A knock came from the door, and Mammon, Asmo, and Lucifer entered. Simeon marked the page where they left off and put the books away. *That's enough studying for right now. We've been at it for a few hours.*

"Thank you, Satan, for helping us," Ashton said, smiling brightly at him as he went to leave for the evening.

"You're welcome. I'll be by tomorrow to help further," Satan replied as he left.

Asmo pounced and sat on the bed beside her. His hands flew as he told her about a new skin product that helps with scarring. "We can totally try it on these scars."

She bit her lip and looked at Simeon. *Why can't hospital gowns have long sleeves!*

"Asmo, that's enough. I told you to behave yourself," Lucifer said, snapping at his brother. A scowl shaded his face, and he crossed his arms.

"But I'm behaving myself," Asmo said in protest while pouting.

"Yo, move over, I want to spend time with her as well," Mammon said as he pushed Asmo off the bed. Asmo and Mammon fought, and Lucifer grabbed them by their collars, excusing him and the others. She drifted to sleep by the time they came back in.

Later that week, Adrian, Seth, and Barbatos stopped by with some brownies for her. "We brought you some brownies, and you don't have to worry—I made them. Adrian didn't help at all because we wanted you to be able to eat them."

Seth spoke excitedly as he held out the container of brownies for her.

"Thank you, I'll enjoy them later." Her voice was soft as she spoke to Seth. She handed the container to Simeon, and he placed it on the stand beside her bed.

"Okay, you have to let me know how they taste." Seth fisted his hands to ground his excitement.

"I can do that." She smiled at him.

"Why don't we head back? We have a lot of homework to do, and I'm sure Ashton could use some rest?" Adrian asked Seth, letting him know it was time for them to leave.

"Okay . . . C-could I give you a hug?" Seth asked.

"Of course." She opened her arms as Seth gave her a gentle hug.

They left, and she scooted over, patting the bed for Simeon. He climbed onto the bed as she cupped his face, bringing his lips to hers. They pulled back, gasping for air before Simeon closed the gap again. He kissed her with passion as his hand caressed her arm.

A few days later, Lord Diavolo came to visit her. "Simeon, you need to go shower and change."

"It's all right, Simeon, you go and take care of yourself." Ashton reassured him with a smile.

He looked into her shining eyes, sighing in defeat. "I'll be back soon." He leaned down to kiss her before he exited the room.

Lord Diavolo watched Simeon leave, closing the door as he did. "You look like you're doing a lot better." Lord Diavolo's voice was low.

"I feel a lot better—the doctors have been a tremendous help. I appreciate everything that everyone has done for me." Ashton bit her bottom lip in reply.

"We care deeply about you, feeling the need to protect you in whatever way you'll allow," he told her, pausing for a moment before continuing. "Have you given any more thought to being a full-time resident here in the Demon Realm?"

"I have." She moved her eyes to the window, looking out at the moon as she released a deep breath.

"And?" His voice gave away his impatience, wanting her thoughts on the subject.

"I can't take up full residency here in the—" she started to say.

"I would highly recommend that you reconsider. I don't want you going back to the Human World," Lord Diavolo said. "Especially alone, not with that threat lingering in the air. They could be waiting until you're alone and attack you. Like he did." Lord Diavolo's anxiety raced out in his words as he sat on the bed beside her.

Her eyes met his, and she saw the worry, concern, and fear that filled his honeydew eyes. She reached her hand to his cheek, caressing it with her thumb. "If you let me continue, I can explain. I can't take up full residency here in the Demon Realm because I made a promise to you when I first got here. A promise that I would help you reunite the realms," she said.

His eyes widened as he tried to grasp what he heard. "If I take up full residency, then I'll no longer be a citizen of the Human Realm. I wouldn't be able to help you reunite the realms, so I'm going to give you a new proposal. Instead of having me become a full resident, let me stay on as an ambassador of the Human Realm." She stared at him as he took in what she had just told him.

"I never even considered that. It never crossed my mind. I was too blinded by you getting hurt, and then the threat . . . I couldn't think straight, but what you say makes perfect sense. Of course, you're more than welcome to stay on as a human ambassador!" he said, his words tumbling out with excitement.

She and Lord Diavolo talked more about her plan as an ambassador as they waited for Simeon to return. The door opened, and Simeon entered, smiling. Lord Diavolo winked, taking his leave. Simeon walked over to her and gave her a kiss.

They ate the brownies Seth had brought them and worked on the homework that was growing less and less each day. The doctor came in and smiled at her. "You've been doing an exceptional job, and you should be able to leave tomorrow."

"Thank you." She smiled back. The doctor exited the room, and she turned to Simeon. "Did you hear that? Tomorrow is my release date—I can go home."

"Are you excited?" He knew the answer already, but he still asked, knowing she wanted him to.

"Yes, I'm very excited to leave." Her grin spread across her face as she looked at the ceiling.

"I heard that there's going to be a feast for you," Simeon mentioned as he rested his arm across her stomach.

"The feast will be nice, but I'm worried about it." Her face fell slightly.

"Why are you worried about the feast?" Simeon's hand came up to caress her cheek as he lay beside her propped on his elbow, looking at her.

"Even though my eating has improved, it's still difficult for me to handle solid foods," she replied.

"I'm sure Barbatos will keep in mind that your stomach's still fragile," Simeon said, comforting her with his words.

"You're right. He's a well-rounded butler, of course he'd do that." She leaned up and kissed him and his hands strolled her body, landing on her thigh. She moaned, and his kisses became sloppier, trailing down her neck. She tilted her head and gave him access. Her hands came to his side and dug into him. "Mmm, Ashton," he said, moaning into her skin and biting her neck.

He looked into her eyes, filled with worry of going too far and not being able to control himself. He placed a tender kiss on her lips and laid his head on her shoulder while he moved his hand off her thigh and to her side.

Her hands folded around him, and her fingers twirled with the tips of his hair as she placed a kiss on the top of his head.

27

BOYFRIEND

The next day, Asmodeus came to the hospital before the hospital released Ashton. He held the same yellow dress she wore to her first feast. "I'll be back when you're released," Simeon told her, leaning down to kiss her before leaving.

"So, I started thinking, and it'd be fabulous if you wore the same dress you did for your very first feast! Since the dress looked so stunning on you." Asmodeus's hands flew through the air as he spoke rapidly.

He held the dress out to her, encouraging her to change into it. She stepped out of the bathroom twirling slowly in the dress. "Ooo, you look fabulous, just like I knew you would. I have impeccable fashion skills!" he said. "Sit down on the bed, and I'll put your hair up before doing the makeup." Asmodeus's voice commanded her to obey him.

She sat there perfectly still as Asmodeus brushed her hair, putting it up in a magnificent yet simple hairstyle. He skipped to his bag, pulling out his makeup kit before returning to the bed. "Close your eyes," he told her as he began to work.

A knock sounded on the door as Asmodeus finished applying her lip gloss. They turned as Simeon entered the room. She blinked several times as she wrapped her mind around how handsome Simeon looked in his white tuxedo that sported a yellow tie to match her dress.

Giggles erupted beside Ashton, but she ignored them. Asmodeus stood up, picking up his makeup supplies, putting them in his bag as he turned to leave. "You have good timing, I just finished," he said. "I'll just leave the two of you alone now." Asmodeus's voice was chipper and filled with glee.

"You look stunningly gorgeous," Simeon said, his breath hitching as he spoke. His eyes sparkled as his stomach made a tingling sensation with each step he took toward her.

"Thank you. You look . . . wow." She bit her bottom lip nervously as her heart raced.

Simeon stopped in front of her, holding out a box and opening it. Her eyes grew wide as she looked down at the gold bracelet that had alternating red and yellow roses all around it.

"The red roses are to show you how much I love you. And the yellow roses are to show how much you can trust me. They normally mean friendship, but I don't want to be your friend. I've been trying to find the right time, and when I did, my nerves got the better of me. I'm sorry it took me so long to ask, but Ashton, would you be my girlfriend?" His cheeks flushed as red as the roses on the bracelet. He anxiously waited for her reply, confirming what he knew was already between them.

"Yes, yes, I'll be your girlfriend!" Her hand came to her lips as she tried to not spill happy tears down her cheeks, ruining the makeup Asmodeus had so lovingly put on her face.

He let out an audible breath as he placed the bracelet around her wrist. Warm hands cupped his cheek, tugging him into a rough kiss. He placed his hands beside her on the bed, bracing himself from the force she used to pull him into the kiss.

"Everyone's waiting for us at the feast," Simeon said breathily into her lips as they parted for air.

She forcefully kissed his lips again before she rested her forehead on his. "Shall we?"

He held his hand out to her, escorting her to the feast that awaited them. *I'm still worried about the threat that was on the note. When you receive something like that from the underground, it isn't something to take lightly . . . But for now, I'll enjoy the feast with all my new friends and my boyfriend. I have the demon brothers, a demon prince and butler, angels, and even a sorcerer on my side. I feel safer here than I have in my entire life,* she thought as they made their way into the dining room. She looked around at all her new friends, grinning as they watched Simeon escort her in on his arm. *I'm no longer alone, for the first time in my entire life. I've gained an entire family.*

Simeon pulled her chair out and leaned down in her ear to say, "I love you." Her face went red, and she looked at him. "I love you, too."

AUTHOR'S NOTE

I would like to thank you for reading my novel and I hope you will stay tuned for the next book in the Reuniting the Realms series: Underground: Revenge From The Past.

Will Simeon make it out alive?

Don't forget to follow on:

Facebook: Reuniting the Realms

Twitter: @tinker806

Instagram: reuniting_the_realms

TikTok: @reunitingtherealms

Website: www.reunitingtherealms.com